URGENT HANGMAN

The Slim Callaghan series
by Peter Cheyney

Urgent Hangman (*1933*)
Dangerous Curves (*1939*)
You Can't Keep the Change (*1940*)
Sorry You've Been Troubled (*1942*)
It Couldn't Matter Less (*1943*)
They Never Say When (*1945*)
Uneasy Terms (*1947*)

The Lemmy Caution series
by Peter Cheyney

This Man Is Dangerous (*1936*)
Poison Ivy (*1937*)
Dames Don't Care (*1937*)
Can Ladies Kill (*1938*)
Don't Get Me Wrong (*1939*)
You'd Be Surprised (*1940*)
You Deal My Lovely (*1941*)
Never a Dull Moment (*1942*)
You Can Always Duck (*1943*)
I'll Say She Does (*1946*)
G-Man at the Yard (*1953*)

Peter Cheyney

URGENT HANGMAN

A Slim Callaghan Mystery

COLLIER BOOKS
Macmillan Publishing Company
New York

First published in 1938

Collier Books
Macmillan Publishing Company
866 Third Avenue, New York, NY 10022

This is a work of fiction. Names, characters, places, and incidents either are the product of the author's imagination or are used fictitiously. Any resemblance to actual events or persons, living or dead, is entirely coincidental.

Library of Congress Cataloging-in-Publication Data
Cheyney, Peter, d. 1951.
Urgent hangman / Peter Cheyney.
p. cm.
ISBN 0-02-031060-9
I. Title.
RR6005.H48U78 1989 89-478 CIP
823'.912—dc19

First Collier Books Edition 1989

10 9 8 7 6 5 4 3 2 1

PRINTED IN THE UNITED STATES OF AMERICA

CONTENTS

'See how she twists and turns in parlous straits.
"Finger your neck, sweet, the urgent hangman waits."'

At the tender age of fourteen, **Peter Cheyney** (1896–1951) persuaded his parents to let him drop out of school so that he could become a writer. His first published story followed within the year. Between that auspicious beginning and his untimely death, Cheyney went on to publish 150 more short stories, thirty-five novels, and a host of radio dramas. His series characters included Lemmy Caution, an American G-man stationed in Europe during World War II; Sean Aloysius O'Mara, a smooth-talking secret agent; Alonzo McTavish, gentleman jewel thief; and Slim Callaghan, the wise-cracking Sam Spade of London's criminally laden East End. Slim is the only British private eye, from the hard-boiled school of hard knocks, still surviving in print from the golden age of detective writing. Cheyney was an inveterate storyteller, which is suggested by his favorite working method: He preferred to *tell* his books, rather than write them—dictating to his faithful secretary, Miss Sprague. Devoted readers of Peter Cheyney will be long in her debt as they relish the spontaneous, tough quality of her boss's delicious prose.

CHAPTER ONE

Presenting Mr Callaghan

Callaghan turned the corner into Chancery Lane. A gust of cold wind met him, blowing back the flaps of his not-so-clean raincoat, sending the rain through his threadbare trouser legs.

He was five feet ten and thin. He had sevenpence halfpenny and a heavy smoker's cough. His arms were a little too long for his height and his face was surprising.

It was the sort of face that you looked at twice in case you'd been mistaken the first time. The eyes were set wide apart over a long, rather thin nose. They were a light turquoise in colour and seldom blinked. His face was long and his chin pointed. He was clean shaven and women liked the shape of his mouth for reasons best known to themselves.

Except for the face he looked like anybody else looks in London. His clothes were ordinary and decently kept. His shoes were bad and one of them needed mending. Callaghan was not inclined to consider such trifles. At the moment he was concerned with the matter of the office rent.

The rain had already soaked the brim of his soft black hat and made a damp ridge round his forehead. His thick black tousled hair under the hat was wet.

As he turned the corner a bus, rounding from Holborn, shot a stream of watery mud over his shoes.

He walked along quickly under the lee of the Safe Deposit on the left-hand side of Chancery Lane. He felt in his raincoat pocket for the packet of Player's, produced it, found it empty, threw it away. He began to curse, quietly, fluently and methodically. He cursed as if he meant it, getting the full value from each word, finding some satisfaction in thinking of a word that he had not used before.

Half-way down Chancery Lane he turned into Cursitor Street, walked down it for twenty yards, turned into a passage, then into a doorway. He kicked the street door open and began to climb the stairs past the second and third floors up to the fourth.

There he halted outside a rather dirty door with a frosted glass top, on which was painted 'Callaghan. Private Investigations.' He stopped cursing when he saw that there was a light in the office.

He put the key back into his left-hand raincoat pocket and kicked the door open. He stepped into a medium-sized outer office.

Standing in front of the typist's table against the window on the left-hand side was Effie Perkins. She had her back to him and she was patting her red hair into place with long, white, well-kept fingers. As she turned round Callaghan gave her one of those top-to-bottom looks which took in everything from the four-inch heels to the trim, tight-fitting skirt, then upwards to her green eyes as they met his.

He looked at his wrist-watch.

'Why the hell haven't you gone home?' he said. 'I told you not to wait. You'll get your money on Saturday. Get out. I want to do some thinking.'

She smiled. She managed to convey a certain definite animosity in that smile. It seemed as if Miss Perkins didn't like Callaghan rather because she liked him a little bit too much.

'I thought you'd like me to stay on, Slim,' she said, 'at any rate until you got back. I got on to Mellins this evening. He says that if the rent isn't paid by Saturday you get out. He says that if you try any fast stuff about moving out the furniture he'll get damned nasty with you. Mellins means business.'

He hung his raincoat on the rack in the outer office and walked over to the door leading to his own room. His shoes squelched.

'To hell with Mellins,' he said. His voice was hard and had a peculiar brittle quality, not unpleasant. 'An' did you have to stay around to tell me that – or are you gettin' a kick out of it? You're like every other damn skirt. You get an idea into your head, an' if it looks as if it's comin' off you get pleased with yourself, even if it isn't goin' to do you any good. Get out of here, will you, an' if you want a reference I'll say that you're a first-class typist when you've got anything to type, that you've got one hundred per cent sex appeal an' nothin' to use it on, which is rather gettin' you down, an' that you're tickled silly because you think that Callaghan Private Investigations is goin' up the spout. Well, you're damn wrong. Now go home.'

He went through the door and over to his desk which stood in the centre of the room facing the doorway. He threw his wet hat into the corner, sat down and put his feet up on the desk. He examined the sole of his left shoe, which was in danger of parting from the upper, with a close attention.

She followed him into the room, stood watching him.

'Why don't you get some sense, Spike?' she asked softly. 'You're finished here and you know it. You're a fool. You've got brains and drive and you get around. Why don't you take that job with the Grindell Agency? You'd get a pay envelope every week, anyway.'

'Like hell I would,' he said. 'An' what's the big idea of you tryin' to get me workin' for that lousy Grindell, eh? Shall I tell you what the idea is? You're goin' to work there, aren't you? You knew the balloon was goin' up here weeks ago, an' you think it 'ud be clever to have me workin' around there. An' what's the big idea, Perkins? You tell me that. What's the big idea?'

He sat there with his feet on the desk looking at her waiting. He looked her over carefully. She flushed.

Callaghan grinned.

'I thought so,' he said. 'Still lookin' for a soul-mate, eh, Effie, with the accent on the soul?'

'I'd like to hit you,' she said, 'you cheap runt. I hate the sight of you. I always have.'

'Rot,' said Callaghan. 'The trouble with you is that you need a little fun an' games, an' the boss has always been too busy.'

He took his feet off the desk.

'Now do some talkin',' he said. 'You didn't wait here to tell me about Mellins. I knew all that yesterday. Something's been happenin' around here. What is it? Stop thinkin' about yourself an' what you'd like to do to me if you had me tied up, an' say what's on your mind. After which you can get out an' stay out. Do I make myself clear?'

She smiled. She had a nice set of teeth and knew it. Her mouth would have been good, too, except that there was a discontented droop at the corners. But her eyes weren't smiling. They were resting on Callaghan, and they were as cold as ice.

She looked at her wrist.

'It's eleven-thirty,' she said primly, 'and at eleven-fifteen we were supposed to have some business. We were supposed to have a client round here, a woman. Somebody's been ringing up for you the whole evening, and by the sound of 'em anybody would think you were really important for once.'

Callaghan put his feet back on the desk and looked at her carefully.

'So that's why you've been hangin' around,' he said. 'I suppose you wanted to have a look at her. Curiosity's a shockin' thing, isn't it?'

His voice changed.

'Well,' he said, 'who was it and what did they want?'

She went into the outer office and came back with a telephone pad in her hand.

'A Mr Willie Meraulton came through at seven-thirty,' she said. 'He came through at eight, eight-thirty, eight-fifty and again at eight fifty-nine. He rang again at ten o'clock and again at ten forty-five. I said that I thought you'd be back before eleven. I said that he could sort of leave a message with me.

'He seemed very angry and sort of upset. He said that a lady was coming round here to see you. He seemed sort of careful to say that it was a lady.' She paused for a split second and looked at him with a smile that was definitely nasty. 'Her name's Miss Meraulton. He said she'd tell you all about it when she got here.'

He tcok his feet off the desk.

'Who put him on to me?' he asked.

She tore up the telephone message. The nasty smile was still evident.

'Fingal put him on to you,' she said. 'He said Mr Fingal had mentioned your name to him. So it looks like one of *those* sort of cases, doesn't it?'

Callaghan's nose twitched.

'An' supposin' it is one of *those* sort of cases, you fool,' he mimicked. 'Supposin' it is? Well, what the hell's it got to do with you? All right, well, you've said your piece, now go home. I'm gettin' tired of lookin' at you.'

She turned on her heel, went to the door and opened it. As she did so the outer office door, immediately opposite, opened. A woman stood in the doorway.

Callaghan, standing upright, looking over Effie Perkins' shoulder, pursed his lips into a silent whistle.

'Good-night, Miss Perkins,' he said. 'I'll write you on Saturday.'

He walked past her and out into the outer office, stood looking at the client.

'You're Miss Meraulton, aren't you?' he said. 'Come in an' sit down.'

He went back into his own office and put a chair in front of his desk. Then he went behind it and sat down. As the woman came into the office Effie Perkins closed the communicating door.

The girl stood in front of the desk. Callaghan looked at her almost as if she was too good to be believed.

She was tall, slim and supple, but curved in all the right places. She had an air. Her face was dead white and there was a suggestion of blue about the eyes, of tiredness or strain. She wore an expensive, supremely cut black frock of heavy silk marocain – an evening frock, caught over the shoulders with crossed straps of the same material, each of which bore a diamond fleur de lys.

Her hair was dead black and her eyes, which regarded Callaghan with a certain steady disinterest, were violet. Her high-heeled black shoes peeped attractively from beneath the edge of her frock.

Callaghan continued to look. He looked her over from top to toe as if he were entering for a memory test. He went on looking, even although her finely-cut nostrils twitched disdainfully and she moved slightly as if to show disapproval of being looked at like a prize cow.

He grinned up at her.

'Well ...' he said.

She moved an arm out from the shelter of the short cloak of fox furs that was draped across her left shoulder. There was a handbag in her hand. She opened it, took out an envelope and put it on the desk. Callaghan looked at it, but remained quite still.

Then she sat down and crossed her knees. Every movement was slow, graceful, yet somehow quite definite. The idea flashed through Callaghan's mind that here was a skirt who wasn't going to stand any damn nonsense from any one. She was in some jam or other, but she wasn't frightened, or if she were she wasn't showing it. She had to be in a jam, a certain sort of jam, a not-so-good jam, or else she wouldn't be sitting in front of *his* desk looking at him like he was two-penn'orth of dirt.

His grin, which suited his peculiar face, deepened.

He wondered when she was going to begin to talk and just what her voice would be like. It always took them some time to get started, because the cases that Fingal sent women to see Slim Callaghan about were usually peculiar cases concerned with young gentlemen who couldn't be got rid of, who were making themselves a nuisance after they'd served their purpose and who wanted to try a little blackmailing.

There flashed through his mind swift pictures of half a dozen women who had stood or sat in front of that desk and told the old, old tale:

'I thought I was fond of him. I trusted him, and now he says he wants two thousand pounds to go to South America and another five hundred to stop the man who saw us at the wherever-it-was hotel from writing an anonymous letter to my husband.'

Callaghan had heard that tale so often that he thought it ought to be set to music.

But this wasn't one of those things. It couldn't be. She wasn't old enough. They had to be between forty-five and fifty for that sort of thing. This one was about twenty-six, maybe twenty-eight, possibly younger.

What the hell! Maybe he shouldn't have sacked Perkins. Effie was good. She'd been with him for five years. She knew his technique. Supposing here was a good case, one in the bag, and he needed an assistant who was at least as sharp as Effie Perkins.

He smiled at her. The smile – which was as much a part of the business as the telephone – illuminated his face. It said: 'Madame, Callaghan Investigations are an honest firm. We may be a bit smart occasionally, but we are a very good firm, and our clients are always safe with us. We never talk. So let go and get it off your chest.'

She said:

'Do you mind if I smoke?'

He nodded. He knew she would have a voice like that – low and the words very clearly enunciated. She took a thin case out of her handbag and his mouth watered when he saw that they were Player's. He wondered if she would offer him one. When he lit a match for her and walked round the desk to light the cigarette she laid the opened case on the desk, indicated that it was at his disposal. Callaghan took one and was glad of it. He hadn't smoked for seven hours.

'Mr Callaghan,' she said. 'I will be as brief as possible, because it is more than likely that I am wasting both your time and mine. I have come here only because Willie Meraulton, to whom I am engaged, insists on it. He believes that I am in some sort of danger. It seems that a Mr Fingal has recommended you as a person who might be of assistance under certain circumstances.'

Callaghan nodded. This was going to be good!

'I should tell you,' she went on, 'that August Meraulton is my stepfather. Possibly you have heard of him. Most people who know him think that he ought to be in a madhouse. I feel that way occasionally myself. He is an extremely rich man and can afford to indulge in certain idiosyncrasies such as making the life of everyone around him a misery and generally creating hell upon earth for such people as are unable to see eye to eye with him.

'His brother was Charles Meraulton, who died five years ago. He, too, was rich, and he left his money to his five sons – I suppose you would call them my half-cousins. They are Willie Meraulton – a grand person, whom I am going to marry – Bellamy, Paul, Percival and Jeremy. If you read the papers you will probably know about them. They've spent their money, and they have little interest beyond chasing odd women and drinking too much.

'Briefly the position is this: My stepfather – who has become even more peculiar since the death of my mother three years ago – does not expect to live very much longer. He has *angina pectoris*, an illness which does not go well with his sort of temper. He knows that Bellamy, Paul, Percival and Jeremy are just waiting for him to die, and die quickly, so that they may have some more money to waste. He knows, too, that they are aware that under his will his estate is to be equally divided between his five nephews and myself.

'Two days ago he gave a dinner-party. There were present the five of them, myself and my stepfather. He told them that he had made a new will, that it was typed on a thin piece of copy paper and that he was carrying it round with him in his watch case. He said that when he died and it was read most of them would hate him more than they did now, but that if, by some chance, he felt better disposed towards them he'd tear it up and they'd still get their money. Do you understand?'

Callaghan nodded.

'I suppose that most of 'em have already pawned or mortgaged their expectation under the original will?' he asked.

'Exactly,' she continued. 'He has therefore created the situation under which the four of them – I do not include Willie, who is nice and who works hard and still has his original legacy from his father – do not know whether his death will make them rich or bankrupt. If he revokes the new will – the one in his watch-case – or destroys it, then they may be able to get through. If not, each one of them will face ruin, and, if I know anything of them, possibly something worse.'

Callaghan blew a smoke ring carefully. He was looking out of the window, thinking.

'Willie is terribly worried,' she went on. 'He believes that if any of the four could get August out of the way quickly and quietly they'd do it. But more importantly he knows that they are aware of my own quarrels with my stepfather. Today he told me that all sorts of weird things are going on, that he was afraid for me.'

Callaghan looked up.

'Afraid for *you*?' he repeated. 'Why?'

She shrugged her shoulders.

'Willie says that they're all half crazy. He says that he has a fearful idea that one of them will do something to August to get that new will and destroy it – or employ someone else to do it for them. He says that if they do they'll somehow try to hang it on to me.'

Callaghan grinned.

'Isn't that bein' rather a bit far-fetched?' he asked. 'D'you mean that your young man Willie honestly believes that one of this precious quartet is goin' to do in the old boy an' then somehow frame you for the murder?'

She nodded.

'That is what he means,' she said.

Callaghan looked at her. He looked at her for a long time.

'What do *you* think?' he asked.

She shrugged again.

'I don't know what I think,' she said in the same cool tone. 'I'm rather worried and very bored with it all. Today Willie telephoned me that I was to get into touch with you. Mr Fingal said that you were the sort of man who could "keep up" – those were his words – with Bellamy, Paul, Percival and Jeremy.'

She smiled a little grimly.

'Willie said that Mr Fingal tells him that they'd have to be very smart to be smarter than Mr Callaghan.'

She looked at him with a sudden gleam of interest in her eyes.

'That was damn nice of Mr Fingal,' he said. 'Maybe he said some other things as well?'

She raised her eyebrows.

'I believe he said some other things,' she continued. 'I believe he said there were one or two police officers would give half a year's pay to get their hands on you because you've been a little bit more than clever, that you're rather expert in sailing close to the wind.'

Callaghan grinned.

'Very nice of him,' he said.

He got up, stood leaning against the wall behind the desk.

'All right,' he said. 'All right, I'm takin' this case. Maybe you'll tell me who my client is? Is it you or is it your boy friend Willie Meraulton?'

She took another cigarette and lit it with a gold lighter.

'Does it matter?' she said.

He grinned.

'So far as I can see,' he said, 'I'm supposed to be a watchdog. My business is to keep a sort of fatherly eye on your halfcousins – the Meraulton quartet. Well, that's all right with me, but jobs like that cost money.'

She indicated the square manilla envelope on the desk.

'There are four one-hundred-pound notes, eight ten-pound notes and twenty one-pound notes in the envelope,' she said. 'Willie Meraulton said you were to have that on account of your services. Mr Fingal told him that you'd want everything you could get.'

Callaghan grinned.

'Once again Fingal is right,' he said. 'I do – an' don't you?' His tone was still pleasant.

She got up. Callaghan was still leaning against the wall.

'Just one minute, Miss Meraulton,' he said. 'Tell me something. Willie – the boy friend – is worried about you. All right. Well, I reckon that if I was your boy friend I'd worry about you, too. I want to ask you a lot of questions, because even a private detective with a fourth-floor office an' a reputation that makes Scotland Yard sneeze sometimes has to know somethin' about what he's doin'.'

She moved to the door.

'Not tonight, Mr Callaghan,' she said. 'It's late, and I have an appointment.'

'All right,' he said. 'You're the boss. But you might tell me why it was so urgent that you had to see me tonight. Why wouldn't tomorrow mornin' do? Or would you call that a rude question?'

'I might be busy in the morning, and I do not always explain my reasons for seeing people I employ at hours when I want to see them, Mr Callaghan. And may I ask *you* a question? You said that my fiancé was worried about me, and you were good enough to add that if you were my boy friend – as you call it – you would worry about me, too. Why?'

Callaghan smiled slowly. He said nothing. His eyes travelled over her from her hair down to her feet. His glance was as slow as his smile.

She flushed.

Callaghan pulled open a drawer and took out a pad.

'Can I have your address and the telephone number?' he asked.

She gave them.

He threw the pad back in the drawer.

'Good-night, Miss Meraulton,' he said. 'I'll handle this. I s'pose you don't really give a damn if somebody kills August so long as they don't try an' show you did it. By the way, have you always been livin' at this address? Did you ever live in the same house as your stepfather?'

'I left there three days ago,' she said.

She put her hand on the doorknob.

Callaghan walked slowly over to the door and opened it. In the outer office he saw Effie Perkins tidying up her desk, clearing out the drawers. He snarled.

He walked to the outer office door and held it open.

'Good-night, Miss Meraulton,' he said. 'By the way, what's your first name?'

She registered polite astonishment.

'My name is Cynthis,' she said.

She went through the door.

'I think it's a nice name,' said Callaghan. 'I like names with Cyn in 'em. Good-night, madame.'

He closed the door.

Effie Perkins picked up her handbag from her typing table and settled her coat.

'So you're goin',' said Callaghan. 'All right – as you are goin' there's no need for me to tell you that it's damned silly of you to have left your glove lyin' there by my office door where you dropped it when you were listenin' at the keyhole. I hope you enjoyed yourself. Good-night, you red-headed cat!'

He stood there until she slammed the door behind her. Then, muttering a rude word to himself, he went back into his office.

He picked up the envelope from the desk, took out the money and counted the notes. He put them in his hip pocket.

Then he stood in the middle of the office, put up his nose and sniffed like a dog. On the air there was still a vague suggestion of the perfume that Cynthis Meraulton had been wearing.

He walked over to the telephone table and called a Holborn number. He waited, listening to the ringing tone at the other end, drumming on the table with his fingers.

'Listen,' he said, 'is that you, Darkie? All right. Get some of that sleep out of your eyes an' get yourself a piece of paper. Got it? All right, here's what I want: There's an old boy – you've heard of him, he's half nuts – called August Meraulton. I want his address an' anything else you can get. Got that? All right. Well, I want the addresses and telephone numbers of his nephews Willie, Bellamy, Paul, Percival an' Jeremy. Get anything else you can on this bunch an' get it quick. Got that? Well, this August Meraulton has got a stepdaughter Cynthis. Find out why she calls herself Meraulton instead of by her father's name. Now get a move on an' try an' have all that by tomorrow. Send somebody round to the cuttin' people an' get every damned cuttin' on the Meraulton family you can get hold of. I'll call you tomorrow. An' listen, this isn't any cheap business, either. You can make some real money this time. Good-night.'

Callaghan closed the street door behind him, walked along into Chancery Lane, turned left and strolled into Holborn. At the coffee stall he remembered his hunger, bought two cheese-cakes and two cups of coffee. He ate and drank and ordered three packets of Player's cigarettes. He registered a mental note to get some new shoes.

He walked back through Chancery Lane again in the direction of Fleet Street, thinking.

Of course the woman was a damned liar. But she was good. Callaghan was definitely pleased with the memory of her appearance. She had something all right. And what was the hurry about seeing him at that time of night? Why couldn't she have waited until next morning? Still, maybe the boy friend Willie was getting all worked up about her, kidding himself that somebody was going to frame her for a murder. What damned rot! That sort of thing just didn't happen in England, it only happened in America and on the pictures – or did it?

Callaghan remembered one or two odd things that had happened in England all right. Things that never made an inch in a newspaper and that the police never even heard of. He grinned.

He turned down Fleet Street and walked to the office of the

Morning Echo. He sent a slip up for Mr Jengel. Then he sat down and waited.

Five minutes afterwards Jengel came down. Jengel was the *Echo* crime reporter. He was very tall and thin and wore very thick glasses.

He sat down on the seat beside Callaghan.

'Hallo, Spike,' he said. 'What's eating you?'

Callaghan held out a cigarette.

'Looky, Michael,' he said. 'I s'pose you wouldn't have any little tit-bit about the Meraulton family, would you? Something that's never got into the paper, you know – one of them things?'

Jengel lit the cigarette. Then he looked oddly at Callaghan.

'Come outside,' he said.

They went out into the street.

'What's the lay?' asked Jengel with a grin. 'An' who're you working for this time?'

Callaghan grinned.

'So you *do* know somethin'?' he queried, his head on one side. 'Come on, Mike – give – or have you forgotten to remember last June an' the young lady of Peckham?'

Jengel flushed.

'All right,' he said. 'But this is off the ice an' it's sweet.

'I got a flash tonight,' he went on. 'One of those things that break you up. We're not allowed to do a thing about it – well, not till tomorrow, anyhow. I suppose you couldn't tell me why you're so interested in this Meraulton crowd?'

Callaghan shrugged.

'I've got a case,' he said. 'The usual sort of cheap divorce an' blackmail mixed – you know.'

Jengel nodded.

'The policeman on duty in Lincoln's Inn Fields found the old boy August Meraulton lying up against the railings in the rain at eleven-forty-five tonight. He was as dead as a piece of cold mutton.'

Callaghan nodded.

'Too bad,' he said. 'He'd got a bad heart, hadn't he? He was likely to go off like that.'

Jengel grinned.

'Bad heart my fanny,' he said. 'Somebody shot him. He was shot clean through the head. What a story, and we can't break with it? There's a bar until tomorrow. It's just breaking me up.'

Callaghan lit another cigarette from the stub of the last one.

'Look, Mike,' he said. 'This is sort of serious with me. I'm interested, see? It was raining when they found the body, wasn't it? Well, maybe they've parked it in some mortuary not too far away. Maybe it'll be some time before the C.I.D. doctor gets round there. You never know.'

He held the cigarettes out to Jengel.

'Listen, Mike,' he said, 'you're in with the right boys. You find out where they've put the body. Find out if they've had the examination an' search an' photographs all fixed. If they haven't, you find out how many policemen are keepin' an eye on it – an' if there's only the usual one. Find out what the mortuary keeper's name is an' if he's married, an' where he lives an' what his wife's first name is.'

Jengel's mouth opened.

'What the hell is all this?' he exploded. 'I'm a crime reporter, not a blasted inquiry office. How the hell can I do a thing like that?'

Callaghan grinned at him.

'Look, Mike,' he said. 'You never know what you can do till you try. I'll get around to my office an' wait for you to come through. I reckon it ought to take you about an hour to get all that stuff I want.'

He turned up his coat collar.

'An' you get it, Mike,' he said softly, 'because if you don't my memory is liable to go all funny about that young lady of Peckham, an' it wouldn't be so good for you – now would it?'

Jengel threw the cigarette stub away.

'Damn you, Slim,' he said. 'If I didn't like you I'd think you were a louse.'

Callaghan was still grinning.

'Forget about liking me, Mike,' he said. 'Just remember the young lady of Peckham. I'll expect you to call me in an hour – that'll be about one-fifteen. So long, Mike.'

Callaghan went into the call-box outside the Law Courts. He rang a number. At the other end he could hear the ringing tone jangling regularly.

He waited.

'Hallo,' he said eventually. 'Is that Miss Meraulton's flat? Who is it speakin'? Her maid? All right. Well, you get Miss Meraulton out of bed an' get her to the telephone. Tell her it's Mr Callaghan.'

Holding the receiver with one hand, he managed to extract another cigarette. He found a vesta in his waistcoat and struck it against the wall.

Her voice came through.

'Hallo,' said Callaghan softly. 'I'd hate to get you up for nothin', but it seems to me that there has been a nice little murder tonight. Maybe you'd like a minute to think that out.'

He waited. Then:

'All right. Don't argue an' don't start talkin' a lot of rot. I knew all that stuff you told me tonight was just nice honest-to-goodness bunk. See? Now you get some clothes on an' get around to my office about two-thirty. Walk round there. Don't take a cab. *Walk there. Understand?* An' come out quietly so that maid of yours don't hear you goin'.'

He hung up.

Outside the call-box he stood undecided for a moment. Then he examined the sole of his shoe – the bad one. Then he walked back through Chancery Lane to the Holborn coffee stall and bought a cheesecake and a cup of coffee.

It began to rain again.

CHAPTER TWO

It Comes Off Sometimes!

It was one o'clock.

Callaghan sat back in his office chair, his feet on the desk, the inevitable cigarette hanging out of the corner of his mouth. In the ash-tray on the desk were fifteen cigarette stubs.

Only the desk light was turned on. The tilt of the shade threw a beam of light across the desk diagonally, leaving him in the dark, throwing grotesque shadows of the things on the desk on the opposite wall.

Callaghan was thinking about Effie Perkins. He was also thinking about himself, the five hundred pounds - and Cynthis Meraulton.

He wondered about Effie. He wondered if she would be sufficiently nasty to throw a spanner into the machinery. She could - quite easily. Callaghan thought that Effie was probably like that. Somewhere or other he had read something about 'Hell hath no fury like a woman scorned.' Well, Effie had been scorned all right.

Women, he thought, gave him a pain in the neck. You spent half your time trying to make them and the other half trying to ditch them, but life was like that. Life was a matter of women and making ends meet. The devil of it was that no sooner did you make ends meet than some skirt or other moved one of the ends.

He switched his mind over to the Meraulton woman. There was a woman for you! She had everything: looks, grace, a terrific sex-appeal and that peculiar quality which he could not describe even to himself, that quality that goes with breeding. He thought dispassionately that he would give a couple of fingers - but off the left hand, mark you - to make a woman like Cynthis Meraulton.

The idea intrigued him. He grinned when he thought of it, and for a moment looked infinitely more human.

He stubbed out the cigarette, got up, walked into the outer office. He put a piece of notepaper in the typewriter and wrote a note to Effie Perkins:

Dear Effie,

Maybe I've been a bit tough with you now and then, but you know that's just my way. I've been thinking that you're a good typist and I don't dislike you as much as you think. Anyway, I'd be fed-up if you went to work for Grindell.

Drop in and see me some time tomorrow afternoon. There's going to be plenty of work and I'm going to put your wages up to a fiver.

Yours,
S. Callaghan.

He read this effort through, grinned sardonically at the phrasing, sealed it up and addressed it. He put it into his pocket to post. Maybe Effie would fall for that line – and maybe not – but it was worth trying. It only cost the stamp.

He lit another cigarette.

The telephone rang.

It was Jengel.

'Hallo, Slim,' he said. 'One of these fine days I'm going to get back on you for all this. I've had to run my legs off to get this stuff you wanted and I've had to pull a string or two that I was hoping to keep for myself, you louse!'

Callaghan grinned.

'Don't make me cry,' he said. 'What do you know?'

'They took old Meraulton's body in an ambulance to the Ensell Street Mortuary,' said Jengel. 'There wan't any use in photographing it. It was raining like hell and apparently the body was lying up against the railings on the south side of the square – you know, where the cars are usually parked.

'Well, that's where it is. The case is going to be handled by

Gringall – the latest detective-inspector – but neither Gringall nor the medical examiner have been down there yet. Gringall's on some other job, and they reckon he'll get down with the doctor about half-past three. The body hasn't been touched or searched. There's a policeman looking after it at the mortuary.'

Callaghan grunted.

'All right,' he said, 'an' what's the mortuary keeper's name? I suppose he's down there, too?'

'Yes,' said Jengel, 'he is. He's a feller named Tweest, and he's married and he lives with his wife at 16 Tremlet Street, just off King's Cross.'

He gulped.

'Look, Slim,' he said urgently. 'I don't know what you're at, but for the love of Mike go easy and don't get me mixed up in any of your lousy stuff. I can't …'

'Why don't you take it easy?' growled Callaghan. 'Who's hurtin' *you*? You go home and keep your head shut, an' if you get anything else on this business you come through here some time tomorrow. Good-night. I'll be seein' you.'

He hung up.

He stubbed out his cigarette and lit a fresh one. Then he opened the desk drawer and took out a pair of grey fabric gloves and a pocket-knife. He put on his raincoat, put the gloves and knife in the pocket, picked up his hat and went downstairs.

He walked up Chancery Lane along Holborn into New Oxford Street. He cut through by the post office and came out at the end of Ensell Street. There was a telephone call-box on the corner.

He went into the call-box and stood inside with the door open, checking up on being able to see the doorway in the wall of the mortuary yard, half-way down the street.

Then he stepped back into the call-box and looked in the directory. He got the number and dialled the mortuary. A gruff voice answered.

'Hallo,' said Callaghan, talking in a very deep voice. 'Who is that speakin'? Is that Tweest, the attendant?'

'Yers,' said the voice. 'It's me – Tweest. Wot is it?'

'This is Scotland Yard speaking for Detective-Inspector Gringall. Call the constable to the phone, will you?'

'O.K.,' said Tweest. 'Hold on.'

Callaghan waited. Then:

'Is that the constable? Centre speaking. You're the officer who found the body, aren't you? Right. Will you please report immediately to Mr Gringall here? I'm sending a relief to take over there. And get along as quickly as you can.'

He hung up. Then he stood half-way in the box watching the mortuary door. Two minutes afterwards he saw the constable come out, walk across the street and take the short cut that would bring him out into Seven Dials. Callaghan got back into the box and waited while he smoked another cigarette.

When the cigarette was finished Callaghan tore two pages out of the Directory. He rolled each page up into a ball and put each ball of paper inside his mouth, pushing it up under the jawbone above the teeth. The process materially altered the shape of the top of his face, and would also affect his voice. He turned up his coat collar, put his hat on dead straight and walked down Ensell Street to the mortuary. He rang the bell and waited.

Three minutes afterwards Tweest opened the door of the mortuary yard.

'Are you Tweest?' asked Callaghan. 'I'm Detective-Constable Harris from Centre – Scotland Yard to you – I've come as relief for the officer who had to go, and I'm sorry to say I've got a bit of bad news for you.'

Tweest stood holding the yard door open. He was an elderly man. He began to look scared.

'Bad noos,' he said. 'Why – wot's 'appened?'

'It's your missus,' said Callaghan. 'You live at 16 Tremlet Street, King's Cross, don't you?'

Tweest nodded.

'She got herself knocked down by a car tonight,' said Callaghan. 'She's not badly hurt. They've got her home an' the doctor's round there now. You'd better get along. I'll stay around here until you come back.'

Tweest said nothing, but turned and walked quickly across the yard. Callaghan followed him.

Luckily for Callaghan the mortuary office was not too well lit. The paper balls, becoming wet with saliva, were beginning to taste. Tweest struggled into his overcoat, grumbling and cursing to himself. Then, with a muttered word that he would be back in an hour, he went off.

Directly the yard door closed behind the departing Tweest, Callaghan got busy. He walked through the mortuary office along the passage and down the stairs. At the bottom of the short flight of stairs was a door. It was unlocked. He put his head in and switched on the light. There were two or three hand ambulances standing about in the cold stone room, and on the mortuary table was something covered over with a sheet.

Callaghan walked over and turned the sheet back. It was August Meraulton all right.

The bullet had smashed through the frontal forehead bone above the nose to the right. It wasn't a particularly pleasant sight. Callaghan switched the sheet right down and felt in his pocket for his gloves. He put them on, undid the top and underneath coats on the corpse, noted with satisfaction the gold chain ending in each waistcoat pocket. He pulled the chain and the watch came out.

He looked at the watch. It was still going. It said one forty-five. Callaghan reflected with a grin that the late August had not realized when last he wound up that watch that he wouldn't wind it up again.

He took out the penknife, opened it, opened the back of the watch-case and saw, lying between the outer case and the cover, a folded piece of old gold-coloured copy paper. He put it in his waistcoat pocket.

Then he put the sheet back over the face of the corpse, took a look round, closed the door behind him, walked up the stairs, through the office, out and across the yard. He opened the yard door carefully, looking up and down the street before he stepped out.

He walked quickly into High Holborn and turned down towards Chancery Lane. He halted on the corner and stood for a moment thinking, then he crossed the road and cut down the Gray's Inn Road.

He walked down to the end of Guildford Street, turned left and into Hunter Street. He stopped at one of the houses towards the end, rapped on the door. He continued rapping for five minutes, after which a head appeared at the window above and began to curse.

'Shut up,' said Callaghan. 'Put your trousers on an' come down here an' don't make so much damn noise.'

Two minutes afterwards the door opened. There was a gas jet in the dingy hall behind, and silhouetted against it Callaghan saw the ponderous figure of Darkie.

Darkie stood with his mouth open. The top half of him was clothed in a virulent blue and red pyjama jacket, the bottom in a pair of striped trousers.

He was fat. His belly hung over the tight waistband of his trousers and his round face and thick lips gave him the appearance of a surprised goldfish.

'Crumbs!' he muttered. 'Slim! Where's the blinkin' fire?'

Callaghan closed the door behind him and followed Darkie into the sitting-room. He sat down in a rickety chair, produced a packet of Player's and offered one. Darkie took it and struck a match. Recovered from his first surprise, he now took the nocturnal visit as a matter of course.

Callaghan drew the smoke down into his lungs and sent it out artistically through one nostril.

'Look, Darkie,' he said. 'Have you done anythin' yet?'

'Give us a chance,' said Darkie. 'You only come through after twelve. But I 'ave. I gotta idea. I gotta idea I read something or other about these blinkin' Meraulton boys in the paper four months ago. A bust-up in some night club or bottle party or something like that. Vine Street raided the place an' Bellamy an' Paul Meraulton was down there an' took a swipe at a copper just for luck.

'So after you rung I called through to Sizer at the old Jay Bird Club, an' does 'e know 'em! Sizer says that these fellers are a lot of first-class you-know-whats. They got class an' all that, but they're as barmy as a lot of bleedin' monkeys. Wine, women an' song, says Sizer, that's their lay. I told 'im to get around an' see some more of our frien's around the 'ouses we take an interest in an' let me know wot 'e can. That's wot I done, but I don't reckon to start proper until tomorrow, an' then I'm gettin' 'old of Fred an' 'Arry an' that blinkin' Wilpins wot only come out five days ago. That boy's a fair knock-out at gettin' the lowdown on anybody, an' 'e's got a way with servant maids that's worth a lot.'

Callaghan nodded. He felt in his breast pocket. He brought out the letter he had typed to Effie Perkins and the bundle of banknotes.

He peeled off two ten-pound notes and handed them over.

'Listen, Darkie,' he said. 'There's plenty more where that came from. Now tomorrow you get busy – damn busy see? All right, an' there's somethin' you can do now.

'I want you to get out to Willesden right away an' deliver this letter to Effie Perkins. You've been there before. I missed the post tonight, an' I want her to get it first thing in the mornin'. All right. You get some clothes on an' take a cab out there an' see you put it through the right letter-box. It's important, see?'

'I gotcha, Slim,' said Darkie. 'Things is movin', eh?'

Callaghan grinned. His teeth, which were big and white, gleamed for an instant.

'Yes,' he said, 'things are movin' all right.'

He put on his hat.

'I'll call you tomorrow,' he said, and went out, closing the front door quietly behind him.

Callaghan walked into the Gray's Inn Road, picked up a crawling cab and told the man to drive to the top of Chancery Lane. From there he walked to the office.

Arrived, he closed the street door behind him, locked it, and began to walk up the stairs. He stopped once or twice on the way up because his cough troubled him – a cough the result of a hundred cigarettes a day.

Inside his own room he switched on the desk light and slumped into his chair behind the desk. He threw his hat in the corner, lit a fresh cigarette, opened the bottom drawer and drained the last remnants from the rye bottle.

Then he sat back in his chair and began to laugh. And he had no queries as to what he was laughing about or who he was laughing at. This time, if he slipped up, he'd be for it. This time he was going to make the other little jobs look like so much chicken feed.

If it came off there'd be some money – some real money. Callaghan didn't think about anything else. He thought he would stop thinking right at that moment just in case he began to think of what might happen if it *didn't* come off.

At twenty past two he went downstairs and opened the street door. Then he returned to the office, arranged the light shade on his desk, cleaned out the cigarette tray and straightened his tie.

He was sitting with his feet on the desk when she came in. He didn't even bother to remove them for quite ten seconds after she stood in the room, before the desk.

Then he got up.

'Sit down,' he said. 'We've got to do a little talkin'.'

She sat down. She was wearing a black suit with a full Persian lamb coat over it, and a small tailor-made Persian lamb hat. There was a suggestion of lace at her throat. Callaghan hoped that she'd cross her legs so that he could see, from behind the desk, what sort of shoes she'd got on. He was rather pleased when she did so, and he could see that they were black suede court shoes. He liked neat shoes and he liked the shape and smallness of her feet. Also the soles were wet. She had walked.

He took out a fresh packet of Player's and pushed them over towards her. He let her light her own cigarette. He wasn't moving. The scene had got to be played just the way it was.

She was nervous. He was rather glad about that. The idea of Cynthis Meraulton being nervous pleased him. She'd be a damn sight more nervous before he was through with her!

But when she spoke her voice was as cool as ever.

'You seem to work at very late hours,' she said. 'Is this necessary? Even if ...'

He interrupted.

'Supposin' you let me do the talkin',' he said. 'Maybe it's goin' to be better if I do the talkin' an' you do the listenin'. An' let me tell you somethin': You got me into this - mark you I don't say that I'm not playin' along in it because I want to, but you've got to understand one thing, madame, an' that is from now on you're goin' to do what I tell you to, otherwise we're both goin' to be in the cart. See?'

She moved.

'I don't ...'

'I know,' said Callaghan. 'You don't understand. That's what you were goin' to say, isn't it? Well, I think that you understand damn well, but just for the sake of argument, supposin' you tell me what it is that you *don't* understand?'

She was breathing faster, he noticed. She wasn't being quite so cool.

'There was only one thing I *could* understand from your rather cryptic message on the telephone,' she said. 'And that was that something had happened to my stepfather. I understood that. But I didn't understand why I should walk round here, why I should not take a cab, or why I should sneak out of my flat without my maid knowing anything about it. Also, I didn't understand why it was necessary for me to come round here at all - at two-thirty in the morning.'

He stubbed out the cigarette, lit another.

'So you didn't understand all that, eh?' he said, giving an

imitation of the tempo of her voice, of her precise enunciation. When he did this he looked strange, almost reptilian. The light on the desk brought out the shape of a scar down by the side of his left temple – a knife scar.

'Women are funny,' he went on. 'Are they funny? You don't understand any of that, do you? You don't understand why I asked you to come round here? Well, you're here, aren't you, and you walked. What did you think I wanted you here for? Did you think I wanted to seduce you or what? – because if you did, I can tell you that Callaghan Investigations never seduces its clients – well, not often!'

She got up. She could move quickly when she wanted to.

'You fearful little *tough*!' She almost hissed. '*How dare you?* Willie will kill you for this.'

Callaghan grinned.

'Like hell he will,' he said coolly. 'Why don't you relax an' sit down? You'll find that all that emotional stuff is just a waste of energy. An' another thing: I'll bet you any money you like that the boy friend Willie will have to spend too much time wonderin' how the blazes he's goin' to keep himself from gettin' pinched for bein' accessory before, an' probably after, the act to worry about whether he's goin' to punch me on the nose for suggestin' that one of these fine days somebody might want to seduce you.' He concluded thoughtfully: 'It's a nice word an' it sounds so much more interestin' than talkin' about gettin' married.'

He got up from the chair and stood in his usual position behind it, with his back to the wall and his hands in his coat pockets, the cigarette hanging from the left-hand corner of his mouth.

She found herself wondering why she looked at his mouth. It was an extraordinary mouth. A sensitive mouth, too well-shaped to be part of the physical make-up of a cad who was a particularly nasty private detective.

She wanted to go, to get out of this grubby fourth-floor office, but she sat down. When she looked at him again he was smiling. Strangely enough she felt more comfortable when he smiled.

'Since you want to understand such a lot of things, I'll do my best to explain 'em,' he said. 'I'm probably wastin' words because I'm pretty certain that you know what I'm goin' to say. I told you to walk round here an' not take a cab because, just in case you don't know, cab-drivers are a damn useful crowd of people – to the police, I mean. Haven't you ever wondered what it is that makes cab-drivers so damn bad-tempered? Well, it's bein' asked questions – an' a lot of those questions are asked by smart alecs at Scotland Yard, smart alecs like Detective-Inspector Gringall, who's handlin' this case. D'you think I want some cab-driver to go rushin' up to Scotland Yard tomorrow an' start yellin' his head off that he brought you around here tonight? The same thing goes for your maid. What people don't know can't worry 'em. You understand that?'

'Yes,' she said slowly. 'I understand *that*.'

'All right,' he said. 'Well, here it is in a nutshell. To-night somewhere in the region of about eleven-ten to eleven thirty-five, somebody decides to shoot your stepfather clean through the head. They decide to do it in Lincoln's Inn Fields.'

He lit another cigarette from the last stub.

'That's one for the bag, eh?' he said, smiling slowly. 'That's one for the bag all right, isn't it? Here's you comin' round here at eleven forty-five with some cock-an'-bull story about your boy friend Willie bein' frightened for you an' thinkin' that the wicked Meraulton boys – Bellamy, Paul, Percival and Jeremy – they sound like a first turn on the music halls to me – 'Bellamy, Paul, Percival an' Jerry in their well-known act: Fun on the Trapeze' – are goin' to get rough with the old man an' try something really rough with him an' then hang it on to you, an' sure as a gun while you are talkin' about it it's already been done, which is what is commonly known as an extraordinary coincidence.'

He watched her, drew the smoke down into his lungs, sent it out through his nostrils and then began to cough. She waited.

'These cigarettes will be the end of me if I'm not careful,' he said apropos of nothing. He took another drag.

'Everything is goin' to be all right,' he said. '*Possibly*, that is. I never believe in findin' any trouble until it comes to find me, an' so I'm goin' to take it that way, an' wait until tomorrow when we shall know *all* about it.'

She moved again.

'Know all about what?' she asked.

She could not keep the tremor of excitement out of her voice.

He grinned. He looked rather like a wicked schoolboy.

'About Effie,' he said quietly. 'If Effie keeps her mouth shut, we're OK. If she doesn't there's goin' to be the hell to pay. Effie doesn't like me very much at the moment. I'd sacked her today. I had two reasons for sackin' her: the first one was that she was beginnin' to think I was the answer to a maiden's prayer, an' the second one was that she gives me a pain in the neck.

'All right. While you were in here talkin' tonight she was listenin' at the door. She'll read the papers tomorrow, an' if she wants to be really nasty she'll buy herself a cab an' go around to Scotland Yard to dear Mr Gringall an' start shoutin' her head off, in which case I shall have to do some heavy thinkin'.

'Maybe I've headed her off. Maybe the little billet-doux I sent her three-quarters of an hour ago will stall her off; but you never know with Effie.'

He paused. He was looking at her. There was a half-smile playing about that extraordinarily active mouth of his which kept her silent. She knew that he knew exactly what she was going to say before she said it. She realized hopelessly the futility of argument. She said nothing.

'All right,' he continued mischievously. 'Take it that I've heard it all. Take it that I'm a lousy son of a she-dog for suggestin' that you shot your stepfather in Lincoln's Inn Fields tonight. Take it that I make every fibre of your high-grade chassis quiver with indignation at the insult. Right – an' when we've taken all that as read let's get ahead with it.'

He sat down at the desk suddenly. The movement was

amazingly quick for a man who moved as slowly as he usually did. He pointed a long forefinger at her.

'You tell me somethin',' he said, still smiling. 'Just what were you doin' between eleven an' eleven-thirty tonight? An' don't pause before you answer. Come on, now, out with it!'

She hesitated. His smile became suddenly very mischievous. He might have been playing a game.

'I thought so,' he said. 'Well, I'll tell you what you were doin' an' where you were. You left home three days ago because you were havin' a first-class row with your stepfather, an' you decide in the meantime that quarrellin' with your stepfather is a silly thing to do, so you make a date to meet him, an' for some reason best known to yourself you get the late lamented old geezer into Lincoln's Inn Fields an' you let him have it, an' I'll bet they find the gun you did it with over behind the railin's in the shrubbery tomorrow.

'Probably two or three days ago you have put the idea into the boy friend's – Willie Meraulton – head that one of the trapeze act Bellamy, Paul, Percival or Jeremy will take a sock at the old man an' you tell him they'll try an' hang it on to you.

'Maybe you're pretty hard-up yourself, that's why Willie stakes you to the five hundred to come around here an' get me to keep an eye on the half-cousins, but you don't worry to do that – not until your hand's been forced – an' it was forced tonight, wasn't it?

'For some reasons best known to our little Cynthis you have to make a quick job of the old man – an' you've got the nerve to do it. I've met women like you before. You're high, wide an' handsome an' full of breedin' an' what not, you're so full of quality that you've even got enough guts to kill.

'I can sympathize. I've often felt like killin' fellers myself.

'But you'd heard about me. Maybe you knew the sort of reputation I've got. I'm supposed to be a fairly tough *hombre*, an' you realized that you'd got to have an alibi.

'Well, *I'm the alibi*. I'm fallin'. I need that five hundred and whatever else we can take the poor mug Willie for, so unless Effie does the dirty on us everythin' is goin' to be perfectly all right an' lovely.'

He lit another cigarette.

'In other words, little Cynthis,' he said, '*the time you came into this office tonight to tell me that you suspected your half-cousins of havin' designs on the old boy was eleven o'clock, an' you didn't leave here until five minutes to twelve, an' I think it's damn cheap at five hundred on account, anyway.*'

There was a complete silence. She could hear a clock ticking somewhere. She looked at him. He was still smiling.

Her head fell forward on the desk. She began to sob bitterly.

Callaghan grinned and took another cigarette.

CHAPTER THREE

There's One Born Every Minute

Callaghan awoke and gazed at the ceiling. He threw back the bedclothes, put his feet on the floor and rumpled his thick black hair with long fingers.

Then he began to dress.

This done, he walked over to the table in the corner of the room and took the cover off a dilapidated portable typewriter. He inserted a sheet of plain paper and wrote a note to the landlady.

'*Dear Mrs Lake,*

I'm going away for quite a bit. Keep my room for me. I'm leaving everything. If anybody wants to know where I am, tell the truth – you don't know. I enclose twenty pounds – ten weeks' rent. Maybe I'll be back before then.

Yours truly,

S. CALLAGHAN.'

He went over to the window, ran a ruminative finger over his unshaven chin. Then he felt in his waistcoat pocket and produced the thin, folded sheet of gold copy-paper that he had taken from the dead man's watch-case. He opened it carefully and read the indifferently typed last will and testament of August Meraulton:

'*January* 10, 1938

'*This is the last will and testament of me, August Meraulton, of Clesalla House, Knightsbridge, London. I am of sound mind and I revoke all previous testamentary dispositions. I leave everything I possess in any shape or form to my stepdaughter Cynthis Marion Trevinnon, who changed her surname at the request of her mother (my late wife) and myself to that of Meraulton. Witnesses to this will are unnecessary inasmuch as its existence is known (although its contents are not) to my lawyer, Herbert Arthur Ferdinand Gazeling, of 467 Lincoln's Inn Place, and to my five nephews, William, Bellamy, Paul, Percival and Jeremy Meraulton, who were beneficiaries under my previous will now nullified.'*

The signature 'August Meraulton' was scrawled at the bottom.

Callaghan read this through twice, then put the paper back in his pocket and stood looking out of the window.

He walked back to the table, pulled the telephone towards him and dialled Darkie's number. He got a sleepy hallo.

'Darkie,' he said, 'did you deliver that letter to Effie Perkins? Right. Now listen to this an' don't make any mistakes. You tell Fred to go to my office in Chancery Lane – he'll find a key under the doormat. Tell him he's to stay there an' answer telephone calls. He's to tell everybody who comes through that Mr Callaghan has gone to Edinburgh on business, that he'll be back next month. Got that?

'Next thing. You get all the stuff you can on that Meraulton crowd, like I told you. Use your intelligence an' get me information that matters. Here's the sort of stuff I want to know: I want to know how these fellers live – because all of 'em seem to be good an' broke – find out where they're gettin' their money from, an' check on the woman angles. I want to know about their girl friends, see, where *they* live, what they're like an' whether they're of the gold-diggin' type. You got that? All right – an' another thing: if you do get a line on any of the lady friends, find out if any of 'em are married.

'Now here's the most important thing: Maybe one of these fellers, either Bellamy, Paul, Percival or Jeremy may be a specially bad hat, see? Well, if one of 'em's really bad, you check up hard on him. Find out anything interestin', find out if he's ever threatened anybody or knocked anybody about. I want the sort of stuff that might make him look like as if he could murder somebody if he felt that way. See? Then you meet me at Lyons in Shaftesbury Avenue at three this afternoon an' let me know what you've done. I'll be seein' you.'

He hung up, lit a cigarette, walked up and down the room for a few minutes, then went back to the telephone. He rang up Cynthis Meraulton.

The maid answered. Callaghan said who he was. A minute passed and she came on the line.

'Good-mornin', madame,' said Callaghan. 'An' how're you this mornin'? It's nice to see a bit of sun in January, isn't it? Will you listen to me carefully now? This is what you have to do, an' if you take my advice you're goin' to do it without any argument. Just pack one or two bags – just as if you were goin' away for a fortnight, see? All right. Then you tell your maid that you're going away for a week or so, an' you tell her to get a taxi an' take 'em to the cloakroom at Euston Station an' bring you the cloakroom ticket back.

'Right. When she gets back she finds you dressed for a train journey. She gives you the cloakroom ticket. All that is goin' to take about half an hour, so that you're all ready to leave your flat at ten-thirty.

'At ten-thirty you leave. You go downstairs an' you walk along Victoria Street till you come to the Times Furnishing Company. Outside there will be a feller about five feet six, wearin' a bowler hat an' smokin' a meerschaum pipe. That'll be a man named Henry Kells. You give him the cloakroom ticket. You don't have to talk to him.

'Then you take a cab an' you go to the Delvine Court apartments in South Kensington. You take one of their furnished apartments for a fortnight, see? I'll see that your bags are delivered there this afternoon. That's easy enough, isn't it?'

'It doesn't sound particularly difficult,' she said. Her voice was tired. 'But it does sound rather melodramatic. Is it really necessary?'

'You'll do it, or I'll lay you six to four that you'll be in Brixton Prison tonight,' said Callaghan cheerfully.

There was a pause for a moment. Then:

'Have you been in communication with Willie Meraulton?' she asked. 'Does *he* know what you propose doing – about all this mysterious business of moving so secretly? Does he approve of it?'

Callaghan grinned into the mouthpiece.

'Absolutely,' he lied easily. 'Mr Meraulton said that you were to do what I said.'

'Very well,' she said. 'I'll do what you say.'

He sensed the antagonism in her voice. She didn't like him very much. Callaghan found the thought rather amusing.

'All right, madame,' said Callaghan. 'I'll be along some time today or this evening to see you. I wouldn't go out if I were you. Just stay around in the apartment an' listen to the wireless. They have built-in gramophones, too! So long, Miss Meraulton.'

He hung up, waited and dialled another number. He spoke to Kells, instructed him to wait outside the Times Furnishing Company for her, to collect the bags at Euston and deliver them at the Delvine Court Apartments.

Then he put on his hat, lit another cigarette, took out his wad and inserted two ten-pound notes in the letter to the landlady, addressed the envelope, stuck it up against the clock on the mantelpiece where she would see it, walked quietly down the stairs and out into the street.

He walked to Holborn, went into a barber's shop. Had a shave, a face massage and a hair trim. Whilst this was going on he lay back in the barber's chair at ease and thought very deeply.

Shaved and massaged, he walked along to an outfitters and emerged, twenty minutes later, in a new suit, new shoes, new overcoat, new everything. Now he had an air. His new things seemed to produce a certain peculiar quality of personality not noticeable previously.

He bought a copy of the *Daily Sketch* and went into Slaters, ordered a cup of coffee and twenty Player's and sat down. He looked at the pictures in the paper before turning to the news pages and the Meraulton murder story:

'AUGUST MERAULTON MURDERED

Late last night a police officer found the dead body of August Meraulton, one of the richest men of the decade, whose eccentricities have made headlines for the press of several countries during the last five years.

He had been shot through the head at close range and had been dead for some little time. He was wearing no hat or overcoat. Early this morning detectives working on the case found a .22 Colt automatic pistol with one cartridge fired on one of the flowerbeds near the south railings of the Square.

Detective-Inspector Gringall – one of the Yard's youngest and most brilliant officers – who is in charge of the case, is desirous of contacting anyone who saw last night in the vicinity of the Ensell Street mortuary a man answering to the following description:

About five feet eight. Slim appearance. Round face with cheeks inclined to bulge. Speaks thickly, and wears soft hat well over forehead. Wearing a drab, rather stained raincoat.

If you think you saw this man either in Ensell Street, or in the vicinity of the call-box at the junction between Ensell Street and Greene's Passage, please telephone 999. You will be helping the police.

Callaghan grinned. He thought that there was very little chance of any one recognizing him from the description that Tweest had given. Turning up his coat-collar had made him look shorter and the two pages from the telephone directory had supplied the 'bulge' in the cheeks. Besides, Gringall could think what he liked. Suspecting was one thing, but proving was another.

He finished his coffee, paid his bill and left. Outside he called a taxi and told the driver to take him to the Meraulton Estates and

Trust Company in Lower Regent Street. Ten minutes afterwards he was sitting in Willie Meraulton's office.

He liked the look of Willie. Willie was a man all right. Broad-shouldered, fair-haired, with eyes set wide apart beneath an intelligent forehead, he represented a class for which Callaghan had more than a sneaking admiration.

When he entered the office Willie had shot him a look – a quick, searching look. Callaghan, smiling to himself, knew exactly what was going on in the other's mind.

Willie indicated a chair and Callaghan sat down. He took a cigarette out of the box that the other offered, examined it, saw it was Turkish and put it back. He brought out the packet of Player's and lit one.

Callaghan began to talk. He talked softly. He managed to convey something of subserviency in his method of speech, in the tone of his voice. He did this deliberately. His technique with a man of Willie Meraulton's cut had to be different.

'Mr Meraulton,' he said, 'I think that we both know we're in a tough spot. At any rate you know *you* are, and when I'm done talkin' you'll know that I am.

'All right. Well, I'm goin' to tell you what I think, an' then I'm goin' to tell you what I propose to do about things. I haven't got a lot of time, because if I'm not very much mistaken things are goin' to start happenin' very quickly, an' I always like to be just a little bit in front of 'em.'

Willie Meraulton nodded. His eyes rested steadily on Callaghan, assessing him, summing him up.

'Cynthis Meraulton, who tells me that she's engaged to you, came to my office last night. When she came in I noticed that her shoes were wet. I gathered that she'd been walkin' an' I wondered why. She told me that Fingal had put you on to me, that you'd suggested that she came round an' saw me because she was expectin' a little bit of trouble of some sort from one or all of your brothers.

'I thought it was a damn funny time to come an' see me. I'd

been told that you'd been ringin' my office all the evenin', but I thought that you'd be wantin' to make an appointment for today. Is that right?'

Willie nodded.

'That's right,' he said.

Callaghan went on:

'Late last night I got a bit of advance news. I heard that August Meraulton had been found shot in Lincoln's Inn Fields. When I heard it I remembered that Miss Meraulton's shoes were wet.

'I ought to tell you about her shoes. I noticed that they were wet, but not too wet, so I got the idea that she hadn't been walking very far, that maybe she'd been driving a car that she'd left somewhere an' finished the journey on foot. I got the idea that her shoes were just wet enough to have walked from somewhere in the vicinity to my office – from a place as near as, say, Lincoln's Inn Fields. It sort of hit me that *she'd* shot the old geezer, that she'd had a date with him in Lincoln's Inn Fields and shot him. I telephoned to her an' got her to come back again an' see me at three-thirty. I told her that I knew she'd shot August an' she didn't deny it.

'Well, I reckon I can get her out of this business. All I've got to do is to switch the time that she was in my office, that's all. I reckon that a court has got to take my word just as well as anybody else's.' He smiled frankly. 'You see, Mr Meraulton, I'm puttin' all my cards on the table.'

Willie Meraulton said nothing. His eyes were troubled.

'Just now I'm trying to put myself in the position of Gringall – the man at the Yard in charge of this job,' Callaghan went on. 'Gringall's a fast worker. He's not goin' to let any grass grow under his feet. Just let's save a lot of talkin' an' you answer a few questions for me, Mr Meraulton.'

Meraulton looked out of the window.

'I'll tell you anything I can,' he said soberly, 'anything that will help Cynthis.'

'Well,' said Callaghan quietly, 'I take it that the first suggestion that Miss Meraulton made to you that she was in some sort of danger from your brothers was made a few days ago. I take it that you gave her that money – that five hundred pounds – then, just as soon as you'd made inquiries about me from Fingal an' he had told you that he thought I was the man for the job?'

Meraulton nodded again.

'That's right,' he said. 'But why ...?'

Callaghan smiled at him.

'Listen, Mr Meraulton,' he said. 'You were head over heels in love with Cynthis, an' I'm not surprised. I reckon you still are. Well, try an' understand my position. I don't want to go askin' her a lot of questions as to what has happened between you people. I'd much rather ask you. When I've had your answers it won't be necessary to discuss these things again with her. All right. Well, you didn't see her last night at all, did you?'

'No,' said Meraulton. 'And I think that you're right to ask me every sort of question that you want to, so that you don't have to trouble her too much. Sometimes she's inclined to be a little temperamental, not to remember things too well.

'I *was* to have seen her, though. I telephoned her yesterday morning and asked her to go to the theatre with me. She said she would. But at seven o'clock she telephoned through and said that she would rather not. She said she had a headache. I didn't see her after that, and it's no use saying that I did, because I went and dined at my club, and I was there playing billiards until one o'clock this morning.

'Another thing,' Meraulton continued, 'when she discussed this business with me, which was soon after the dinner-party that August gave all of us, she did not say that she alone was threatened. She told me that August had told her, in confidence, that *he* expected trouble from one or all of the four, and that very likely she might be included in it.'

He got up, walked about the office. Callaghan saw the nerves at his temples twitching. He stopped his pacing in front of the private detective.

'You're certain she did it?' he asked. 'Absolutely certain?'

Callaghan looked at him.

'No, sir,' he said easily with a wry smile, a knowing smile (one that said quite plainly: 'You and I understand each other, MerauIton. I'm going to tell you a packet of lies, because that's what you want to hear, so here goes'). 'Not *now* I'm not. Not since you've just told me that August Merauiton told her that he was expecting some trouble from your brothers and that she might be included.'

Willie Merauiton sat down at his desk. His face was drawn.

Callaghan got up. He walked over the few feet between his chair and the desk, and stood, one hand resting on the polished top. He was dominating the situation and the knowledge pleased him.

'My idea is this,' he said, looking at Merauiton with the same wry smile. 'It looks to me that your uncle knew that he had some danger to fear from your brothers, either individually or collectively. He knew as well that for some reason which he doesn't seem to have disclosed he expected that his stepdaughter Cynthis might be in some sort of danger, too. She comes to you and tells you all this, and you make inquiries an' find out about me an' you think I ought to be employed as a sort of watch-dog. So you give her five hundred to cover my expenses. For some reason or other she doesn't come an' see me then as she should have. Fortunately, or unfortunately, she waits till last night an' then does it on impulse after she's been on the telephone to you, an' you've told her you'll ring me up an' fix a time for her to see me today. For some reason - some impulsive reason - after she's broken her appointment with you, she comes an' sees me last night, an' luckily for her I can *say* she was with me at the time that August Merauiton was killed.'

Callaghan stopped for a moment. His eyes were still smiling as they rested on Willie.

'Of course,' he continued, 'you an' I know that that isn't *exactly* right. *We* know that she arrived at my place just after the murder. We know, in fact, that the old boy was killed just about long enough before she got to my office to allow her to walk up the east side of Lincoln's Inn Fields, through the passage into Holborn, down Chancery Lane to my office *after* he was shot, but we don't *have* to tell anybody that, Mr Meraulton.'

He lit another cigarette.

'I asked her what she'd been doin' since eleven o'clock,' he went on, 'an' she couldn't tell me. She just began to cry. I came to my own conclusions an' I told her that I'd stand for that fake alibi, that she had been in my office durin' the important time.'

Willie picked up a paper-knife.

'It's damned sporting of you, Callaghan,' he said. 'But it won't work. The police will get it out of her. Police questioning can be difficult, you know.'

'Like hell it can,' said Callaghan. 'But the police won't be questioning her for some time. I've taken care of that. They don't even know where they can find her.'

He sat down on the edge of the desk.

'You tell *me* something, Mr Meraulton,' he said. 'What sort of lads are these brothers of yours?'

Willie frowned.

'They're pretty rotten,' he said. 'They'd stop at nothing for money. They're all up against it. Bellamy's desperate. He's just got to have money. He'd do anything to get money.'

'Ah,' said Callaghan. 'What's he do with his money?'

'Women,' said Willie tersely.

Callaghan pondered.

'Who's the one at the moment?' he asked.

Willie stabbed the blotter with the paper-knife.

'A particularly beautiful and peculiarly nasty Frenchwoman – an actress called Gallicot,' he said. 'Why?'

Callaghan did not answer. He was thinking. Then:

'What do you know about August Meraulton's hats?' he asked.

Willie raised his eyebrows.

'Hats!' he said. 'Why hats?'

'You tell me an' I'll tell you,' said Callaghan.

Merаulton pondered for a moment.

'I don't think anyone's ever seen him wearing anything except one particular hat,' he said. 'It was a sort of joke with us. He used to wear a slate-grey homburg – you know, the conventional thing with a bound edge to match. He used to get them at Greene's in Dover Street. He used to buy a seven and one-eighth hat – which was a little too big for him – and put a piece of white blotting paper inside the sweatband. He said that gave him a perfect fit.'

'I see,' said Callaghan. 'Go on.'

'We were chaffing him about that hat last week,' Merаulton went on, 'and he said he'd buy a new one somewhere, but it would have to be a cheaper one than Greene's sold. He thought they were too expensive.'

'That's fine,' said Callaghan. 'That's very good.'

He stubbed out his cigarette and began to cough. Then:

'Mr Merаulton,' he asked, 'supposin' this business hadn't happened last night. Supposin' the old geezer was still alive, well, if you were asked, who would *you* think would be the person who'd want to do him in the most?'

Willie did not hesitate.

'Bellamy,' he said. 'I'd put nothing above Bellamy. He hated the old man, loathed him – even more than Cynthis did!'

'I shouldn't tell anyone else that,' grinned Callaghan. 'But just why did Cynthis loathe the old man?'

'She had every reason to. August was a fearful person – bad-tempered, cynical, and at times positively devilish. He gave Cynthis' mother hell. He made her life an absolute misery. He treated her like a fiend. Not that he treated anybody too well. Bellamy hated him like the devil. He is the one who, I should have thought, would have killed him. Unfortunately,' he went on, 'there can't be any suggestion of that. At ten o'clock last night the whole four of them came to me at my club and tried to get a guarantee out of me for a further loan against their interest under August's will. They said they could get the money if the Merаulton Estates Company – which I control – would certify the original will and guarantee the loan against the estate. Needless to say, I refused.

'Well, Paul, Percival and Jeremy went off to one of their night haunts, and Bellamy, I am given to understand, went off to his lady-love.'

'An' where does she live?' asked Callaghan.

'She has a flat, I believe, a maisonnette in Gordon Square.'

Callaghan nodded.

'So they've all got alibis,' he said. 'The whole damn boilin' of 'em have got alibis.'

He lit another cigarette.

Meraulton got up. He looked out of the window. His shoulders were sagging a little, Callaghan thought. He looked thoroughly beaten.

Pretty tough, thought Callaghan. Pretty tough being in love, and the girl friend facing what the Americans would describe as a murder rap. He was taking it pretty well, too, but then his sort always took everything pretty well.

Meraulton turned round.

'What are we going to do, Callaghan?' he asked. 'What are *you* going to do?'

Callaghan got off the desk. He put his hands in his pockets.

'You've got to realize that my business is a pretty expensive sort of business, Mr Meraulton,' he said. 'It costs money. Of course, you've been very generous; but operations even up to now have been quite expensive ...'

Meraulton's nostril twitched.

'How much more do you want?' he asked.

'I think I'll be needin' another three hundred, at least,' said Callaghan. 'With another three hundred I could almost see my way fairly clear, I think.'

He brought out the packet of Player's again.

Meraulton went to a drawer, opened it, took out a packet of banknotes. He counted out thirty ten-pound notes. He pushed them over the desk.

Callaghan picked them up and put them in his pocket. Then he sat down.

'Now listen, Mr Merauiton,' he said very softly. 'Let you an' me get this thing straightened out between us. I know how you're feelin', and I'm one hundred per cent for you. I've been in love myself' – he smiled inwardly at that one – 'I know how it feels.

'Now quite a lot depends on that hat, that slate-grey hat that August used to wear – that one an' only hat of his. Now I reckon that they're goin' to find that hat at his place. He hadn't got one on last night. But we've got fate workin' for us here, because no less a person than Mr Willie Merauiton can prove that some time last week the old boy said that he was goin' to buy himself a new hat an' that he wasn't goin' to Greene's in Dover Street for it, because they were too expensive. All right, then, if that's so he might have bought one anywhere else in London – nobody knows where, just casually at any shop where he'd seen one.

'Now that,' Callaghan went on, 'is what I call a very pretty situation. It's a situation that we might be able to do a lot with.'

He picked up his hat.

'You sit tight, Mr Merauiton,' he said, 'an' don't worry. I'll be seein' you in a day or so an' maybe I'll have somethin' to report to you. In the meantime maybe you'd like to tell me two things: First of all, just where does Bellamy live?'

'He has a flat in Pointer Mews, Chelsea, on the Embankment side,' said Merauiton. 'Number twelve.'

'I think I'll go an' have a word with him this afternoon,' said Callaghan. 'Just a friendly sort of talk. In the meantime this conversation between you and me is just goin' to be forgotten.

'The other thing I wanted to know was, when did you an' Miss Merauiton think of gettin' married?'

Merauiton looked up.

'Does that come into it?' he said. 'If you must know, we were keeping our ideas on the subject fairly quiet. August Merauiton objected very strongly to the idea of Cynthis marrying anybody. That was what half the trouble was about. He expected her to stay on and run the house, act as an unpaid housekeeper and listen to his fatuous conversation all day.'

He got up.

'I feel I want to marry her right away,' he said. 'I want her to feel that she has at least one friend. God knows she's going to need friends.'

Callaghan looked sorrowful.

'You're right there, Mr Merаulton,' he said. 'But just at the moment I don't think that any sort of marriage is indicated at all. Let's clear this job up an' then you can get married in a church with flowers an' organs an' all the rest of it. It's a damn shame to marry a woman like Cynthis in a registry office. It would be doin' the illustrated papers out of some very good pictures. No, when she gets married it'll have to be in white satin an' orange blossoms. Well, I'll be gettin' along.'

Meraulton put out his hand.

'There's just one thing, Callaghan,' he said. 'I'm not a poor man, and I'll give every penny I've got to help Cynthis. But this business has cost me eight hundred pounds inside twenty-four hours. I should hate to think that the three hundred I've just given you was a payment to you merely to keep quiet about what you know about Cynthis.'

Callaghan looked unutterably shocked.

'Mr Meraulton,' he said stiffly, 'Callaghan Investigations never blackmails its clients.'

He walked to the door. When he turned and faced Meraulton he was grinning.

'Maybe I'll want to get at you almost any time,' he said. 'Where can I get you?'

Meraulton gave him the address and the telephone number. Callaghan repeated them, memorizing both. He put his hand on the doorknob.

'There's one other thing,' he said. 'I've got an idea you'd better not try to get into touch with Miss Meraulton. If she comes through to you, don't take the call. Tell somebody to tell her you're out of town.

'I've got a good reason for that. Before long, if not now, the police will be listenin' in to every telephone conversation they can muscle in on. I'm even keepin' out of my own office for the same reason. Gringall is a very consistent feller. Good-day, Mr Meraulton.'

He closed the door behind him softly.

At three o'clock Callaghan went into Lyons in Shaftesbury Avenue. Darkie was sitting drinking tea at a table in the corner of the first-floor room. He wore an air of practised detachment.

Callaghan went over to him and sat down. Darkie fumbled in the inside pocket of a voluminous overcoat and produced two or three folded sheets of paper. He pushed them over the table.

'There's plenty there to be goin' on with, Slim,' he said. 'I've worked fast. Maybe there'll be some more tonight.'

Callaghan grinned.

'I hope I'll be around tonight to get 'em,' he said.

There was a certain grimness in his tone.

He ordered a cup of coffee and sat looking at the table mechanically. He was thinking hard.

'It's damned funny, Darkie,' he said. 'You go out to find somethin' and you know you're goin' to find a certain thing an' you don't. You find somethin' else. Somethin' quite different.

'Darkie,' he said. 'There's two things for you to do, an' don't make any mistake about either of 'em. I'm goin' off in a minute. Directly I've gone you do some telephonin' an' try an' get that feller we used in the Garse case – you remember that fake Marquis chap – on the telephone. Find out if he wants to earn a little money. Tell him to stay put at wherever he's to be found, an' maybe I'll get in touch with him. His name was Ribbinholt, or Rivenholt or somethin', wasn't it?'

Darkie nodded.

'The second thing is this,' Callaghan went on. 'I'm goin' to see a feller this afternoon at four o'clock out Chelsea way. A feller named Bellamy Meraulton. I reckon I'll get there at four. Well, at four-fifteen I want you to telephone through to his place – get the number out of the book in the meantime. When he comes to the telephone you keep him there talkin' about somethin' or other. Say you're the Telephone Company testin' or the Sanitary Inspector askin' about the drains – say anythin' you like, but keep him at the telephone for four or five minutes. You got that?'

'I got it,' said Darkie.

He looked down at the table.

'Slim,' he said uncomfortably, 'you wouldn't get yourself into something you couldn't get out of, would you? I know you. If there's a woman in a case you can be as bleedin' barmy as a blinkin' schoolboy.'

Callaghan looked at him.

'Gettin' sentimental?' he asked. 'You'll be makin' me cry in a minute. Well, so long, don't forget Ribbenhall – or whatever his name is – an' don't forget that telephone call at four-fifteen sharp. I'll be seein' you.'

He drank the coffee, got up and walked out. He walked down Shaftesbury Avenue to Long Acre, then cut down into the Strand.

In the Strand he found a hat shop. He tried several hats of different colours. Eventually he bought a seven and one-eighth size slate-grey homburg with a bound edge to match.

He began to walk towards Charing Cross. On the way he entered a chemist shop and bought one safety razor blade and a piece of adhesive plaster.

He continued on his way. At Charing Cross he went into a tea-shop and drank two cups of tea. He was thinking hard, concentrating on small points, on essential facts.

On his way out he went down into the Men's room. There was no one there. He took the new grey homburg out of its wrapping and threw the bag into the refuse box. Then he wet his hand and rubbed the sweatband of the hat until it looked as if it had been worn. Then he unwrapped the razor blade and cut the top of the index finger of his left hand deeply. When the blood was running freely he allowed it to run over the under side of the front of the hat brim, to stain the front of the leather sweatband.

This done to his satisfaction, he washed his cut finger, bound it up with the adhesive tape, pushed the new hat into the inside pocket of his overcoat and went out.

Outside he took a cab and told the driver to take him to the Embankment end of the street leading to Pointers Mews, Chelsea.

He leaned back in the seat and relaxed. Then he began to grin.

Callaghan was beginning to enjoy himself.

CHAPTER FOUR

Portrait of an Expert Liar

Callaghan stood before the front door of No 12 Pointers Mews ('luxurious and artistic self-contained flats for gentlefolk') with his finger on the doorbell and the grey homburg hat securely held under his overcoat between his left arm and his body.

When the door opened its space disclosed the figure of a manservant who regarded the caller with open hostility.

'Mr Meraulton is not at home,' he said shortly. 'In any event he would not wish to see any one!'

Callaghan smiled. There was a world of pity in that smile.

'Don't you believe it,' he said quietly. 'An' don't try and look insolent, or else I might put my fist on the end of that silly-lookin' beak of yours. Just you run inside an' tell Mr Bellamy Meraulton that Mr Slim Callaghan of Callaghan Investigations would like to see him for a few minutes, and you can tell him as well that if he doesn't like the idea the loss will be his an' not mine. Now get goin'!'

The man hesitated for a second, then turned away. Uninvited, Callaghan followed him into the hallway.

He waited for a moment while the man went across the hall into a room on the other side. When the servant returned he indicated that the visitor was to follow.

Callaghan stepped across the hall and into the room. Facing him, sitting almost in the shadow, ensconced in an arm-chair in front of the fire, sat a corpulent figure.

Bellamy looked about forty-seven years of age. He was entirely bald. His eyes were light blue in colour and moved restlessly about. The end of his nose - the underneath part around the nostrils - was tinged with a bluish tint.

Callaghan noticed it. So Bellamy was a dope-taker as well as the rest of it. That bluish tinge spelt cocaine!

When Bellamy spoke it was in a hard, cynical and abrupt voice. His words, carefully spoken, exploded like pistol shots.

'What do you want?' he said. 'Who, may I ask, is Slim Callaghan, and by the same token what do I want with Callaghan Investigations, whatever and wherever that organization may be?'

He shifted in his seat and the folds of his blue-and-oyster shot-silk lounging gown caught the reflection from the fire.

Callaghan was unperturbed. He put his hat down on an occasional table, and sat down in the arm-chair facing Bellamy. He put his right hand into his coat pocket and brought out the packet of Player's. He lit the cigarette nonchalantly, and all the while his eyes, hard and unmoving, looked straight at Bellamy.

'Listen, Mr Bellamy,' he said. 'I know that you won't mind my calling you Mr Bellamy. I'm doin' it in order to distinguish you from the rest of the quartet. I don't want to get mixed up in my own mind ... see?'

He inhaled deeply. On the other side of the fireplace Bellamy was breathing quickly.

'The fact of the matter is,' Callaghan went on, the smoke trickling from his nostrils, 'that I find myself in a little bit of a mess. And whenever I find myself in a mess I always try to do the right thing - the straight thing.'

Callaghan paused. There was a certain cooing note in his voice, a sibilance that suggested a complete honesty of purpose, a supreme straightness of moral character. When he lied, his whole being was concentrated on getting the particular lie of the moment over. Both the stage and the world of films had lost a great actor in Mr Callaghan.

In spite of himself Bellamy was interested. He wriggled forward in the chair, pushing his fat stomach in front of him with an effort.

'Maybe what I'm goin' to tell you won't interest you very much,' continued Callaghan, 'an' maybe it will. I'm goin' to take the chance. But if you think that I've come here to do you a good turn just for the sake of standin' for a lot of damn rudeness from you or anybody else, you think again.'

Bellamy's face broke into an unwilling smile. For some reason Callaghan found himself thinking of that type of American watersnake called the moccasin, that fearful thing with the wide mouth that brings a horrible death slowly.

'I'm sorry if I seemed rude, Mr Callaghan,' said Bellamy. 'I'm upset, worried. It's understandable, you know.'

He got up, walked over to the sideboard and poured himself a drink. He looked towards Callaghan and nodded towards the whisky decanter. Callaghan shook his head.

'No, thank you,' he said. 'I just want to keep my mind on what I'm doin''.

'The fact is, Mr Bellamy,' he went on, 'I've got the idea in my head that you're in some sort of trouble or some sort of danger. I don't quite know which. I've been worryin' all day about what my duty is, an' I've come to the conclusion that the right thing for me to do was to come to you an' put all my cards on the table.'

Bellamy went back to his chair. He said nothing. Callaghan continued:

'Last night, as you know, August Meraulton was murdered. Somebody shot him in Lincoln's Inn Fields. Well I happen to know a thing or two about that business, an' I happen to have some ideas of my own on the subject. When I'm consulted in a case, whatever my client says to me is under the seal – Callaghan Investigations never lets its clients down – but at the same time I'm not the sort of man to stand by an' see an innocent man get mixed up with a murder that he never committed.'

He stubbed out the cigarette, although there were a dozen more puffs left in it, and coolly proceeded to extract another. Out of the corner of his eye he could see the plump white little finger of Bellamy's right hand beating a tattoo on the arm of the chair.

Callaghan lit the cigarette. He did not speak.

Bellamy smiled again – a knowing smile. It made his plump,

vicious face seem even more distorted, the light blue eyes even more bulging.

'I presume, Mr Callaghan, that this has to do with me?'

Callaghan grinned.

'An' how!' he said knowingly. 'Like hell it has!'

Bellamy folded his hands across his stomach.

'I'm beginning to be almost interested,' he said. 'Please continue.'

Callaghan smiled. He knew he had Bellamy where he wanted him.

'Mr Bellamy,' he lied. 'When I was brought into this Meraulton business – which was some days ago – in a very confidential capacity, which had of course nothin' to do with this murder, because the murder hadn't happened then, I obtained certain information. At the time that information didn't mean a great deal. Havin' regard to the fact that August Meraulton has been killed it means a lot, and, believe it or not, it means a hell of a lot to you!'

He paused for effect. And, pausing, permitted himself a quick sensation of self-admiration for the lovely lies that were tripping so easily off his tongue. Then he went on:

'If you've read your papers,' he said, 'an' I don't doubt that you have, you'll see that the police are tryin' to get their hands on some man who was seen in Ensell Street last night. You've probably wondered why or maybe you've guessed. That man is the man who stole the thing that the police think will show the motive for the murder of your uncle. The will that he told you all about last week, that he was carryin' around in his watch-case.

'Well, Mr Bellamy, I'm not here to answer any questions. I'm here to tell you a few things, an' then, when you've heard what I've got to say, to ask you whether you'll care to retain my services as ...'

The telephone shrilled. Its jangling broke through the soft cadences of Callaghan's voice. He made no attempt to continue talking.

The man-servant came to the door.

'There's someone on the telephone,' he said. 'He says he's speaking from the Silver Pirate Club. He wants you personally.'

Callaghan grinned to himself. Darkie was pulling a really good one with his Silver Pirate Club stuff.

Bellamy got up and walked out of the room. As his footsteps faded across the hallway Callaghan took a quick look round the room. In the opposite corner was an antique clock on a wooden pedestal. Moving as quickly and silently as a cat, he crossed the room, grabbed out the grey homburg hat from beneath his overcoat and stuffed it down behind the clock in the angle between the walls, pushed it down as far as it would go. Then, as quickly, he returned to his seat.

He was smoking and looking at the ceiling when Meraulton came back.

Bellamy went back to his chair, sat down.

'You were saying, Mr Callaghan,' he said, 'that I might like to retain your services. Why?'

Callaghan shrugged.

'I said I wasn't answerin' any questions,' he said, 'an' I'm not. If you've got any sense – an' I should think you were pretty quick in the uptake – you're goin' to want lookin' after.'

He leaned forward.

'Listen, Mr Bellamy,' he said urgently. 'I've got an idea in my head that the police theory is that August Meraulton wasn't killed in Lincoln's Inn Fields at all, that he was killed somewhere else an' his body chucked there just to throw suspicion on somebody – somebody who didn't do it, but somebody who might not have liked the late lamented August very much.'

He paused for effect once more. When he began to speak again his voice was slow and deliberate.

'Whoever it was got into the mortuary went after that will,' he said, pointing with his finger. 'Whoever it was went to the mortuary knew, when he did it, all about that murder. He took that will because takin' that will was goin' to throw suspicion on the man who would have lost most if the will had been found an' proved, an' who would that have been? If I'm not very mistaken it would have been a gentleman named Bellamy Meraulton - *you*!'

Bellamy Meraulton gripped the arms of his chair. His face was white. A little bead of sweat stood out on his forehead.

'If that will comes to light, you an' the rest of the quartette will have nothin'. If it doesn't come to light the man who took it knows that its disappearance is goin' to throw suspicion on one of you four - that's why he took it. Now, Mr Bellamy, don't you think that it would be worth your while to have me lookin' after your interests?'

He paused, smiling benevolently across the fireplace. He noticed that the shot-silk sleeve of Bellamy's lounging gown was pushed back and he could see on the forearm the puncture marks made by the hypodermic syringe. So Bellamy took it both ways. Cocaine by the nose and morphia in the arm. A nice little fellow to get around with.

Bellamy sat back in his chair. His eyes were wide, the pupils dilated. Bellamy was frightened.

'What is it you want?' he said thickly. 'How much do you want, supposing I wanted you to keep an eye on things for me, to look after my interests generally?'

'I'd want a couple of hundred,' said Callaghan. 'It's an expensive job lookin' after people.'

Bellamy wriggled.

'It's a lot of money,' he said. 'And I haven't got it. But I'll tell you what I'll do. I can give you a hundred tonight. I can get it by then, and I'll find the other hundred within a day or so. But I want to know all about it. I want to know who's trying to pull me in on this thing. I want to know . . .'

Callaghan put up his hand. Bellamy's voice was almost on the note of hysteria.

'You'll know all right, Mr Bellamy,' he said. 'You'll know when you pay over that first hundred an' not before. Maybe I'll be able to tell you tonight.'

He got up, stood looking at the other. His smile was friendly.

Bellamy's hands were trembling. His eyes moved restlessly about the room, evaded Callaghan.

'If you can meet me tonight,' he said, 'I'll have that money. I'll have that first hundred, and I want to hear the whole thing. I want to know what's going on. I shall be at the Green Signal – a bottle-party place – at half-past twelve or one o'clock. I shall have to go there to get the money. The place is just off Pallard's Place near Lisle Street. I'll tell them to expect you, to let you in. You'll be there?'

Callaghan grinned.

'Don't worry, Mr Bellamy,' he said, 'I'll be there, an' I'll look after you. Good-day to you, Mr Bellamy.'

He walked across the room. At the door he turned and looked at Bellamy, who had gone back to his seat, who was staring into the fire.

'Don't you worry,' grinned Callaghan. 'Callaghan Investigations never lets its clients down!'

If there was a hint of mockery in the words it did not convey itself to Bellamy. He looked up, nodded, managed a smile.

Callaghan went out.

Callaghan looked at his watch. It was five-thirty. He walked down the road towards Chelsea and stopped at a tea-shop – one of those genteel places usually kept by two maiden ladies and a cat. He went in and ordered a pot of tea and twenty Player's.

He sat in a seat near the fire, inhaling deeply, exhaling slowly, allowing the smoke to trickle out of his nostrils.

After some minutes of rumination he felt in his pocket and produced the sheets of paper that Darkie had given to him. He spread them out and began to read Darkie's neat, precise writing, memorizing the details.

Darkie had got a move on. Callaghan's eyes took on a new interest as he read:

Report. 11.1.38.

Dear Slim,

Here's what I got to date. I'm still working. I can't do nothing with Kells today because you're using him, and you've got Mazin stuck in your office. Mazin says that somebody's been ringing since ten o'clock this morning. They won't leave any name. They just ask if you're in, and if not when you're likely to come back. They've been told that you're in Edinboro', but the same voice keeps on coming through, so it looks like they think that you're a blasted liar, don't it? I got Wilpins working. Wilpins has already put some very nice work in on the under-housemaid at the late August's place in Knightsbridge. She seems to think that the butler could tell a thing or two if he wanted to. She may know something or she may just be trying to be mysterious. You know what women are like after a murder, always blinking wise after the event, as Napoleon said.

The main fact is that old August Meraulton had an office on the west side of Lincoln's Inn Fields. No 696B. It was a top room where he used to go and work sometimes. He used to keep this place very quiet. And he was pretty careful not to let any of the nephews except Willie know about it. The butler told this skivvy that he overheard August telling Willie about it and making Willie promise that he wouldn't tell any of the others. Not that Willie was likely to – he's got it in for the other four good and proper.

Now about Willie. They say that Willie is a good fellow. Everybody likes Willie. He is the fellow who runs the Meraulton Estates and Trust Company, which is the company that looks after the August Meraulton Estates. Old August had got a lot of use for Willie first of all because it looks as if Willie is the one decent bloke in the family, and secondly because he's a good business man. Old August told the butler one day when he was canned that Willie had practically doubled the money that he'd inherited from his father Charles Meraulton, and that he had a nose for finance. Willie lives at Cressley Court, just off Park Lane. His bills are always paid right on the minute and everybody speaks very high of him. That's all about Willie.

Bellamy is the boy. Bellamy is a real perisher, and no mistake. How he's managed to keep out of quod beats me. He takes dope and spends most of his days in bed or hanging around, and most of his nights at a couple of rorty bottle parties – The Silver Pirate and The Green Signal – both of 'em belong to the same fellow, a man named Arnault Beldoces, a tough bloke with about six aliases, who's been in stir four or five times and has got a record as long as Regent Street – where he drinks like the devil and gets up to anything else that's going. Wilpins says that he gets his dope at one or the other or both of these places, and that he reckons the proprietor makes a bit extra by working the black on Bellamy when he feels like it . . . Bellamy is running a skirt named Eulalie Gallicot. This skirt is French and says that she used to be a star actress. Naturally she's a liar. Wilpins has got the idea in his head that this Gallicot woman is Beldoces' sister and that she helps in putting the screw on Bellamy when necessary.

Bellamy hated the old boy August like the devil. He's made a lot of scenes when he's been drunk at the night clubs, shoutin' his head off about what he'd like to do to August if he got half a chance. I don't know what you're at in this business, but if you're lookin' for a first-class red-herring, I reckon that Bellamy is as good a suspect for this job as anybody. Nobody knows where he gets his money from. He lives well and always has dough on him, although everybody knows that he's spent, mortgaged and pawned everything he's got, and that he owes a packet. Bellamy has got to get some money from somewhere soon.

Paul is a funny sort of cuss. He's forty-four and has got a job with the Walker-Fleet Company as a commission man. He makes himself about six pounds a week and spends sixty. He don't drink as much as the others and spends a lot of time at Somerset House and the Transfer Registry looking up things. I don't know why he does this, but there's some idea that he reckons he ought to have got more than he did from his father. He seems to think that Bellamy pulled a fast one there too and got more than he ought to. Paul isn't married and he doesn't seem to have any one particular woman hanging around. He just goes for the whole damn lot – the night club sweetie type – you know.

Percival is another perisher, too. He ought to be stuffed and put in a case. He's never sober at all. If somebody sees him and he isn't drunk they think he must be ill. He gets around with Bellamy. He's a sort of yes man for Bellamy who pays for his drinks and takes it out of him when he's in a bad temper.

Jeremy is a different sort of cuss. Jeremy has got a house called the Show Down half-way between High Wycombe and Oxford. This Show Down place is a show down all right. Jeremy has got some girl called Mayola Ferrival down there. She's a Spanish American and they throw parties – card, liquor and women parties – nearly every night of the week. Wilpins says that if you get out of the place with your shirt still on you're doing fine. There have been plenty of complaints about this place but they never come to nothing. People who've been down there and got taken for their cash prefer to lose it and shut up. Jeremy is tough, and he don't like Ballamy or Paul or Percival. They don't like him neither.

Most of this information comes from Sizer of the Blue Jay. I can't vouch for all of it, but Sizer has never let us down yet, and it looks as if it's OK. Sizer says that there have been two or three police cases going to break against one of these four at different times, but they always get the prosecutors straightened out somehow. Sizer says it's marvellous how they get away with it. He says he could understand if they had a bundle of money to pay off would-be prosecutors with, but as they haven't he reckons they must be hypnotists, or something blinking funny like that.

Since I started writing this report I've got a bit more from Wilpins on the telephone. He says that this French girl of Bellamy's – Eulalie Gallicot – is a real hot momma. She lives at Clarendon House near Gordon Square, Bloomsbury (Telephone Hol. 56435). She does herself pretty well, too, but Wilpins says he doesn't know where the money comes from, unless Beldoces hands it out. I don't think this is right, because Beldoces isn't doing so well himself and is very tight with the dough.

Now here's a bit of news, too. On the night that old August was done in the whole lot of 'em met and had dinner together at the Blue

Jay. Sizer says he's never seen such a family gathering. And they didn't get drunk, either – which was a thing that surprised everybody. They went off about ten o'clock, and by the conversation that the waiter heard while he was serving their dinner, they all reckoned to go along to see Willie Meraulton. The waiter told Sizer that by the conversation they were going to try and get some dough or some guarantee out of Willie.

Sizer says that Jeremy came back to the Blue Jay at eleven o'clock and had a couple of drinks and did some telephoning. Then he cleared off. Later Paul and Percival came back there – they arrived about one-thirty and had a drink and then went round to the Silver Pirate. Bellamy didn't come back, Sizer has got an idea that he went round to see Eulalie.

That's all up to date.

So-long, guv. Look after yourself.

Darkie.

Callaghan sipped his tea slowly. It was good tea, and he liked tea. Sitting by the fire, he looked like any other man who was just on the right side of forty, who kept himself in good condition. His new clothes had already settled into his well-knit figure.

Miss Dapple, one of the ladies who kept the tearoom, gave him a quick glance as she passed with a tray. She rather liked the way his thick black hair fell in uneven natural waves over the back of his head.

In the kitchen she said:

'I like that customer by the fire, Polly. He looks nice. You could trust a man like that, I feel sure.'

Callaghan finished his tea. He produced a little black notebook – the sort of thing you buy at Woolworth's for threepence – and began to make notes. He went on writing for some little time.

Then he got up and went to the counter. He asked if he could telephone. Miss Dapple pointed to the call-box in the corner, gave him a look which was as near arch as she could make one.

Callaghan dialled Holborn 56435. When he heard the ringing tone he took his new handkerchief out of his breast pocket and stretched it over the telephone transmitter mouthpiece. He put his mouth close up against the handkerchief and spoke distinctly.

'I want to speak to Miss Gallicot,' he said in answer to the 'hallo.'

The voice and accent were French.

'Who ees zis?' said the voice.

'Never you mind, sweetie,' said Callaghan. 'You get Miss Gallicot to the telephone, an' you tell her to get there quickly – that is if she's got any sense.'

'Mademoiselle vill not come unless she know who speaks,' said the voice just as definitely.

'Oh, she won't, won't she?' demanded Callaghan. 'All right; well, you tell her that maybe this is a friend of Arnie Beldoces speakin'. Remember I said maybe. You tell Eulalie that if she knows what's good for her she'll get a move on.'

He heard the receiver being put down. Then after a minute another voice came on, a high-pitched, slithery voice reminiscent of the first row of the chorus in any of the strip-tease French revues.

'What ees eet?' demanded the voice. 'Thees ees Eulalie Gallicot.'

'Fine,' said Callaghan. He removed the handkerchief. 'Now listen, Eulalie, an' listen carefully. I'm comin' around to see you some time this evenin', so you be in. You be in, even if you do telephone Beldoces an' he says he don't even know who I am. The reason that I'm askin' you to be in is that you're likely to fall into plenty of trouble over this Meraulton murder. Don't pretend that you haven't read all about it, and don't pretend that you're not dyin' to ask Bellamy for all the details.

'But I don't think that you're goin' to see very much of Bellamy in the future unless you do what I tell you, an' when I tell you that maybe he's going to come into a lot of money, well, then, perhaps you'd like to know just how you can play him for a slice of it. I'm the boy that can tell you.

'Keep your head shut and don't talk about this telephone call to anybody at all. And there's another little thing. If I were you I wouldn't get myself too mixed up with Bellamy these days. Understand? Maybe he's going to be in a rather bad spot in a minute, and when a man finds he's mixed up in a murder charge he's liable to say anything to save his skin, such as the fact that he was around at your place last night some time between eleven and one o'clock. Well, maybe he was and maybe he wasn't, but if you take my tip you'll just say he wasn't, otherwise you'll be gettin' some sweet publicity that'll do you and Beldoces a bit of no good besides gettin' you sent back to France as an undesirable alien – an' you wouldn't like that, would you?'

There was a pause.

'When shall you be 'ere?' said Eulalie.

Callaghan grinned.

'I'll be with you about eleven o'clock,' he said. 'My name's Callaghan. I'm a private detective. If I were you I'd just stay in until you see me. Say you're ill and don't see anybody, especially Bellamy. An' take the telephone receiver off the hook. See?'

'I see,' said Eulalie. 'M'sieu ... I am ver' frightened, mos' frightened. I have fear. What happens?'

'That's all right,' said Callaghan. 'You don't have to have fear if you do what I tell you. Well, bye-bye, I'll be seein' you.'

He hung up. Went out of the box, paid his bill and left.

Callaghan walked up the road towards Chelsea. He saw the black car out of the corner of his eye as it swerved round the corner behind him. He lit another cigarette.

The car accelerated quickly. Shot across the road. Crept along the kerb beside him.

Callaghan stopped. He turned and faced the car. His hat was slightly on one side and the cigarette hung out of his mouth at a jaunty angle.

'You can always tell a Squad car by the drivin',' said Callaghan cheerfully.

The Flying Squad sergeant smiled pleasantly as he got out of the car.

'Mr Callaghan - Mr Slim Callaghan, I believe. Detective-Inspector Gringall sends his compliments, and says he'd be very grateful if you could spare a few minutes to get along to Scotland Yard with us. It's about the Meraulton murder. Mr Gringall says he would very much like to see you for a few minutes if it's not very inconvenient.'

Callaghan's face broke into a sunny smile.

'I'd do anything for Mr Gringall,' he said.

He stepped into the back of the car as the sergeant opened the door and sank back in the seat with a sigh.

Callaghan drew on his cigarette with pleasure.

The car shot off.

'The Meraulton murder, hey?' he said cheerfully to the police officers in front. 'Just fancy that, now. Why, I was only readin' about that case this mornin'.'

CHAPTER FIVE

Meet Mr Gringall

George Henry Gringall – commonly known as 'The Jigger' – was the youngest detective-inspector at Scotland Yard. He was forty-one, weighed twelve stones, had a small bristling moustache, a direct and spontaneous manner. He was no fool.

Gringall, if you remember, brought in Layell Jonas for a double murder, solved the Merreth case, caught Dromio Fenanzet – who had the best vice organization that has ever existed in this country – and wiped out the 'Marseilles' gang, a process which got him his last step.

Gringall believed in direct methods when possible. He could also be clever if necessary. He neither chewed gum, smoked curved pipes, had an income of his own, solved cases over a chessboard, asked crime reporters to give him a hand in solving cases, or looked under the edges of carpets for clues. Nobody had ever heard Gringall talk about 'a clue,' and he once said that if he met one he probably wouldn't know what it was.

He was (and is) characteristic of the policemen who succeed in keeping England a very orderly place. If he was inclined towards routine it was because the greater part of police work in this country *is* routine.

Finally, like several other people, he had no wish to underrate Mr Callaghan. Only fools underrated Mr Callaghan, and it has already been said the Jigger was no fool.

Callaghan was humming softly to himself as he walked along the passage to Gringall's room. Gringall was sitting at his desk drawing fruit on the blotter. His detective-sergeant, Louis ('Lucy') Fields, who disguised an agile mentality under a front of almost childish credulity, was examining his fingernails with a polite attention.

Gringall got up and smiled happily. He said:

'It's nice of you to come along like this, Slim. I thought you might be busy and I told the boys that if you were busy you were to make your own time. Sit down.'

Callaghan sat down. He put his hat on the desk and produced his packet of cigarettes. He offered one to Gringall, who took it, and another one to Fields, who refused it with a grin.

'Nice work gettin' hold of me like that,' said Callaghan. 'Just when I'm havin' a quiet walk along the Embankment and around the houses I'm bein' chased by Squad cars. Did you have a general wireless out for me?'

Gringall smiled cheerfully.

'Well, I wanted to get you as soon as I could,' he said. 'That is if it was all right with you, and so we gave out a general description. One of the beat men saw you.'

'Nice work,' said Callaghan again. 'The man on the Chelsea an' Embankment beat, I suppose?'

Gringall nodded. Callaghan nodded, too. He knew Gringall was lying and he knew that Gringall knew it, too, but it told him something.

Gringall blew a smoke ring and watched it sail across the room.

'Look, Slim,' he said, 'I'm in a bit of a fix, and you can do a lot to help. I'm not asking you to make a statement, and I'm not even taking a note of what you say. This is just a little talk between you and me. Now I want to talk straight with you for a minute before we begin. You know as well as I do that there are half a dozen officers up here who don't like you very much. Faxley, for instance. Now Faxley doesn't like you. He thinks you did him out of a nice pinch in that case down at Mobberley. He says you swung it on him properly. Then there's Branting. Branting don't like you either. But I'm not like that. I've always reckoned that the life of a private detective in this country is always a matter of ups and downs. Possibly I'm a bit broader-minded than most people here, and I want you to know right away that so far as I'm concerned everything between us two is absolutely friendly. Understand?'

Callaghan looked touched.

'You'll make me burst into tears in a minute, Gringall,' he said. 'But I think you're a nice feller. You're polite - sometimes anyhow.' He exhaled a cloud of smoke. 'What's on your mind?' he asked.

Gringall began to draw some more fruit. He drew a banana and then an orange.

'It's this Meraulton case,' he said. 'They've given it to me and I don't like it much. You know how it is - policemen can't afford to make a mistake, and there are one or two people round here who think I got my promotion too quickly. That's why I don't want to make one.'

He smiled disarmingly.

'All right. Well, we were just going through the usual routine this morning when some girl rings up. Effie Perkins is the name. She's got an awful cock-and-bull story, Slim, but we've got to check everything. To cut a long story short, this girl says that last night Cynthis Meraulton - the stepdaughter of the dead man - was up in your office. She says that she's got some idea that you're trying to fake an alibi for this girl.'

He pushed the cigarette-box over to Callaghan.

'Well, I tell you straight, I don't believe her,' he said smilingly. 'Directly I heard this I said rubbish. First of all I didn't see any reason why anybody should want to try and alibi Miss Meraulton, and secondly, as I said to Fields here, I'm certain that you wouldn't try one like that. Fields said - and I've got to admit it - that you would. I disagreed with him. I said no, Callaghan wouldn't try a hard one like that. I reminded him that Justice Fairwood warned you in that Mere case - you remember you were the star witness - that he thought you'd fabricated that alibi. That was the word - "fabricated". Then again there was that case with that girl in the Walnut job. Branting always said that he could have driven two cars and two horses through that evidence you supplied about the appointment at Brighton on the Tuesday – you remember? Well, that got her off, didn't it? Branting's never forgot that.

'I said to Fields, "Here, Callaghan is too clever to try anything like that, because if it didn't come off it would be the end of him. It's compounding a felony, making himself an accessory after, and all sorts of things ..."'

Callaghan interrupted.

'Makin' himself an accessory after *what*?' he asked. 'Are you suggestin' that my client Miss Meraulton is suspected of a crime?'

Gringall bit his lip. Then he laughed.

'No, don't get all het up, Slim,' he said. 'I was just talking, you know that.'

Callaghan smiled amiably. He lit another cigarette.

'Look, Gringall,' he said, 'all this is easy. Miss Meraulton's a client of mine. She came round to the office last night a minute before eleven or so to see me about a job that a woman friend of hers wanted me to do. She stayed round there until five to twelve. I remember the time, because I wanted her to go. I'd got an appointment myself, and I didn't want to be late for it.'

Gringall nodded.

'I see,' he said. 'Well, that's that. But this Effie Perkins says that Miss Meraulton didn't get to your place until eleven-thirty or just after. I suppose she's got the time wrong.'

Callaghan nodded.

'Maybe,' he said. 'But I don't think it's like that. She's just doin' it deliberately. You see,' he allowed the smoke to trickle out of his nostrils, 'I sacked her yesterday, an' I've got an idea that she's not very fond of me.'

He grinned at Gringall.

Gringall grinned back sympathetically.

'Women are the devil, aren't they?' he said. 'The things they say just because they're annoyed with a man.'

He helped himself to a cigarette and thought for a moment.

Then he looked at Fields, who was twiddling his thumbs, wondering when the Jigger would get down to hard tacks.

Gringall said:

'Fields, we shall have to do something about that Effie Perkins woman. She's got to be taught a lesson.'

He turned to Callaghan.

'You see, Callaghan,' he said, his voice hardening a little, 'this Perkins woman is definite about what she says. She's a damn' sight too definite for me. We asked her to come down here and talk about it, but she wasn't just content to talk. She's made a statement – a very definite statement – and she says that she's prepared to go into the witness-box on it if necessary.'

He pushed the ash-tray over to Callaghan, and offered another cigarette. Callaghan took it, lit it and began his slow trick of inhaling and exhaling. His eyes were on Gringall. Gringall, looking back, thought that they were like eagle's eyes – steady, relentless and very bright.

The detective-inspector leaned his forearms on the desk; then he brought his hands together and folded the fingers. Callaghan began to grin. He said to himself:

'Here he goes. This is where he starts in.'

'I'm going to do a thing I don't often do,' Gringall continued. 'I'm going to tell you just what's in my mind and why I'm prepared to disbelieve this Effie Perkins woman. That is, if I get the support from you that I'm hoping to get. Fields here will tell you that one of the first things I said to him when this Effie Perkins was gone was this:

'"I'm not prepared to accept this story just because it's one against Slim Callaghan," I told Fields. "A lot of officers here would jump at the chance of getting a story like that on Callaghan, especially if they could make it stick. But I'm not so foolish. What good would it do me? After all" – and Fields agreed with me here – "the thing I've got to do is to bring in the murderer of August Meraulton, not to go running around trying to wipe up some private detective, just because he's been a trifle over-smart once or twice."

'You see, Slim, I had a damn' good reason for not accepting that story right away, and here it is: You may be this and you may be that, but I'll be shot if you're such a fool as to throw a definite suspicion on a woman who's a client of yours merely by faking an alibi for her if she didn't need one.

'I said to Fields, "I'm going to talk straight to Slim Callaghan about this job, because if what this woman Perkins says is true, then it looks as if we don't have to look very much farther for the person to pinch in this job. It stands to reason that if Callaghan is deliberately and definitely faking an alibi for this Meraulton woman, then he's doing it for a good reason, and that reason can only be one thing: he knows that she needed that alibi because she was with August Meraulton in Lincoln's Inn Fields when he was killed – or alternatively that she killed him."'

Gringall's face broke into a kindly smile.

'You see, Slim,' he said, 'I'm telling you why I didn't believe her story. I'm showing you that I'm on your side of the fence before we start, and now I'm asking you to clean this matter up so that we can teach this Effie Perkins a lesson, so that we can teach her that this department of Scotland Yard is not here just to have its time wasted by young women who want to work off a grudge.'

Callaghan looked at the ceiling. His expression was mildly benevolent.

'Oh, I don't know, Gringall,' he said. 'I wouldn't like to see you bein' too hard on Effie. She's a nice girl, really, she's just a bit worked up, that's all.'

A mild note of sarcasm came into his voice.

'Besides,' he went on, 'you'll be wantin' to save all your time an' energies for solvin' this case, won't you? You won't want to spend a lot of time tryin' to show young women like Effie Perkins that they're just bein' foolish.'

Gringall's fingers began to tap on the desk top. His voice was a little more incisive when he spoke.

'Look, Callaghan,' he said, 'I've asked you to come down here and play ball with us over this thing. I've put myself in your hands. It looks to me as if you're not going to even try to give us a hand. Do you think you're being wise?'

Callaghan smiled at him blandly.

'Oh, I see,' he said. 'I was supposed to say somethin', was I? An' I didn't say it. Well ... what?'

Gringall got up and walked over to the window. He looked out.

'This girl Effie Perkins has got a definite story,' he said. 'Her story practically amounts to an accusation against you. Also, she sticks to it. She even preferred to stick to that story and come down here and make a statement of it, rather than accept the proposition that you put up to her ...'

'Just a minute,' said Callaghan. 'What proposition?'

'You sent her along a letter,' said Gringall. 'You had that letter delivered some time pretty good and early. You wanted her to get that letter before she read the newspapers and saw the story of the Merault on murder.'

Callaghan looked blank, then amazed; then a smile of understanding spread over his face.

'I've got it,' he said. 'You mean when I wrote that note to her and said that she could start work again. That, because there was a lot of work floatin' about, I'd put her money up to a fiver. Well ... that's a pretty normal thing for an employer to do, isn't it?' he asked. 'When he's sacked a girl who's been with him for five years an' suddenly discovers that some big business may be comin' along an' that he's goin' to need her services?'

He paused for a minute in order to allow his next words to be more effective.

'An' you call that a *proposition*, do you?' he said. 'That's a nice way of puttin' it, isn't it, *Mr* Gringall? You send out a wireless to pick me up an' get me along down here, all ... "Mr Callaghan, do you mind this," and "Mr Callaghan, do you mind that" ... an' when I get down here a bunch of nasty suggestions, all cloaked in sweet language, are chucked at me.'

He stubbed out his cigarette with an angry gesture.

'Before I've been in this damn office ten minutes I'm told that I'm fakin' alibis an' making myself an accessory after some crime or other that somebody or other may have committed some time. It's then politely suggested to me that my actions have thrown suspicion on a client who happened to be in my office at a time when I've just sacked a damn silly typist. I'm told that Chief Detective-Inspector Faxley don't like me very much – as if I care two hoots whether he likes me or not. I'm told that Detective-Inspector Branting don't like me, neither – which I take as a great compliment, because Detective-Inspector Branting is just a fat fool who hasn't got enough brains to bring in a crook even if the feller was already handcuffed to a couple of cannon balls an' the evidence chained around his neck!

'I'm reminded that Mr Justice Fairwood "warned me" in the Mere case that he thought I'd "fabricated" an alibi. Well, that's a damn lie, and you know it, because if Fairwood had known that he'd have had me pinched for perjury before I left the court – which he didn't do – an' the reason he didn't do it was because, although he may have *thought* things, he couldn't definitely bring himself to believe what was against the evidence.'

He paused to take out another cigarette.

'Don't try any of your smart stuff with me, Gringall,' he said. 'It won't wash. Mind you, I'm damn sorry for you fellers. If this was America maybe you could take me downstairs an' get to work on me with a piece of rubber tubing or something like that so that I could take the chance of talkin' or not, just as I liked. But you can't do that. We don't have third degree in this country, an' so far as I'm concerned you're just another copper tryin' to be smart!'

Callaghan struck a match on the underside of the desk and applied it to his cigarette. The gesture was not lost on Fields, who looked at Gringall with an apprehensive eye.

Gringall was breathing a little heavily. His ears had reddened a trifle – a sure sign of temper with him.

He went back to his desk and sat down.

'Very well, *Mr* Callaghan,' he said tersely. 'Well, if we can't handle this interview one way, possibly we can handle it another way. I'm putting you in possession of certain information which we have here in the Criminal Investigation Department which concerns yourself. As an investigating officer in the Meraulton case, I'm asking you whether you care to make any statement to me. If you don't want to, you'll probably say so, and I shall have to deal with the matter from another angle ...'

He stopped as Callaghan's fist smashed down on the top of the desk.

'*No you don't*,' said Callaghan. 'That's just another threat!'

His voice was low and brittle. The words were cold and incisive. They took on a vibrant quality, the more effective because they were quietly spoken.

'No, you don't, Gringall. I've had enough of your damn threats, an' you know what you can do with 'em. Maybe I'm just a second-rate private detective to you, but by heck I know the law of this country, an' I'm tellin' you that if I have one more threat, open or concealed, out of you, I'm going to walk out of here an' go to my lawyers an' swear an affidavit on the sort of thing that's been goin' on at this so-called "interview", an' we'll send a copy to the Commissioner of Police.'

He stopped, allowed the usual stream of smoke to trickle from his nostrils.

'Now, listen to me, Gringall,' he went on. 'Let *me* give *you* a tip, an' I'm not threatenin' you an' tellin' *you* what I'll do an' what I won't do while I'm givin' it to you. You want to ask me some questions. All right. Ask 'em. Go right ahead an' ask 'em. I'll answer 'em. An' I'll answer 'em just how I damn well please, see? Perhaps I'll tell the truth and perhaps I won't, but you can't do anything about it, because I'm not on oath, an' if I like to tell another, a different story tomorrow, I reserve the right to do it. I'm askin' you to remember that so far as I'm concerned *you're* just another policeman tryin' to find out where to start, an' I'm a free citizen of Great Britain, with all the power of the law behind me to protect me against cocky police officers who try an' get too clever an' blackmail me into talkin' the way they want me to talk. Understand?'

Gringall snorted. He was licked and he knew it. He went off on another tack.

'I've got to take my hat off to you, Slim,' he said. 'There aren't any flies on you, and I can see that it's no use trying to do it any way except the way that's right for you. Now I'll put it to you this way: I want your opinion on two or three aspects of this case, and I'm going to ask Fields here to leave the office while you and I talk it over ...'

'Don't worry about Fields leavin' the office,' said Callaghan. 'I bet you've got a dictaphone rigged up an' he'd probably be listenin' on the other end.'

He began to grin.

'I say, Gringall,' he said, 'wouldn't it be damned funny if you *had* got a dictaphone rigged up an' they've taken down all that stuff I was just sayin' to you!'

He began to laugh. Gringall laughed, too, and Fields joined in. To Callaghan their laughter sounded forced. So they *had* got a dictaphone working!

Callaghan began to think quickly. He was in a jam, and he knew it. Sitting there, drawing on his cigarette, he knew that he had reached a high-spot in a career not entirely uneventful.

Suddenly, for no reason at all, there flashed across his mind a picture of Cynthis Meraulton. He saw her sitting on the other side of his desk in the Chancery Lane office, remembered the clear outline of her face, the flash of her eyes, the vague suggestion of perfume that remained after she had gone.

There was a skirt for you, thought Callaghan. A one-hundred-per-cent woman, and even if she was a killer she had something that a lot of women would like to have.

Well ... here we go ... he said to himself.

* * *

Gringall was still drawing fruit on the blotter.

Fields was still looking at his fingernails.

Callaghan altered his face. He put on an expression of extreme smartness, of ill-concealed cleverness. He saw Gringall's eyes flicker.

'Look, Gringall,' he said, 'what's the use of arguin' and yelpin' at each other? It's not goin' to do either of us any good. I'll do what I can to help you – if I'm treated properly, that is – an' the best way we can begin is for you to tell me just what's worryin' you. If you suspect Cynthis Meraulton of havin' done this job, well, say so. I may be clever an' I may be smart, as you say, but I'll see myself thrown off the end of a pier before I'm goin' to try an' shield a murderess.'

Gringall nodded.

'I'm not making any accusations at all, Slim,' he said. 'I don't want to make 'em. They don't help. What I want is evidence, and you know that as well as I do.'

He leaned across the desk. Fields, watching him, thought to himself: Here's a clever pair of so-and-so's. I wonder which of 'em is best. I'm backing the Jigger to win, but only because he's a policeman with all that means behind him. This Callaghan is as smart as paint.

'I don't have to tell you,' Gringall went on, 'that the first thing that a policeman looks for in a murder job is motive. Motive is the thing. When a good officer dies they ought to find the word "motive" written across his heart.

'All right. Well, let's stop worrying about Miss Meraulton and where she was and why she was there. Let's go down to the question of motive.

'Here's my guess: Gazeling, August Meraulton's solicitor, says that some days ago the old boy made a new will. He typed it out himself on a piece of gold-coloured copy paper that he got from Gazeling. He told Gazeling that he was carrying it round with him inside his watch-case. Gazeling didn't know what this new will was, but he did know that it wasn't going to be so good for any of the Meraultons – except possibly Cynthis Meraulton and Willie Meraulton.

'It's my guess that somebody killed the old boy to get that will, that they killed him on sudden impulse and then got frightened and cleared off without getting the will, either because they thought somebody was coming or else because they hadn't got the nerve to get at the dead man's watch.

'If it was a woman did it, you can understand the last angle.

'But *somebody* got that will. Late last night – or rather early this morning – some clever bird went into the call-box at the end of Ensell Street and put a fake message purporting to come from me and got the officer who was down at the morgue around here on some cock-and-bull story. This bird then goes along to the morgue with his coat collar turned up and tells another fake story to Tweest, the attendant, about his wife being knocked down. He gets rid of Tweest. Then he goes down in the mortuary and prises August's watch-case open with a penknife – you can just see the marks. He was wearing gloves, too, because his gloved fingers had wiped *all* the fingerprints off the watch-case – August Meraulton's prints, I mean – that ought to have been there.

'This bird is either the murderer or he's a bird who is completing the job that the murderer hadn't got the time or the nerve to finish. If I could find that man, half my job would be done.'

Callaghan nodded.

'I read your appeal in the paper,' he said.

He smiled at Gringall.

'You know,' he went on, 'it's funny, but except for the two inches off the height and the bulging cheeks the description might even have fitted me!'

Gringall attempted to look surprised.

'You don't say so,' he said. 'Well, of course, turning up the coat collar would have made this bird look a bit shorter, and as for the cheeks – well, I found two pages torn out of the telephone directory in the call-box and somebody had rolled 'em up and pushed 'em up under his cheekbones to alter the shape of his face. He spat 'em out on the mortuary office floor – after Tweest had gone, I suppose. A clever bird, that.'

He lit another cigarette and thought for a moment. Then he looked at Callaghan with his usual cheerful smile.

'I want your help, Slim,' he said. 'Just any ideas you've got on this job. I know that you've got some connection with the MerauIton family because you'll admit that I'm entitled to believe that Cynthis Merauiton didn't come round to your place to ask you what the time was, did she? And I don't expect you to help me for nothing at all.

'Look here, Slim, possibly you've heard that there's some talk about having a registration for private detective agencies in this country – more or less on the American system – licences, and all that sort of stuff. Well, if it comes in there'll be two or three people up here will move heaven and earth to stop you getting on that register. If you give me a hand over this job by talking straight to me – and I know you could talk if you wanted to – then I'm going to see that you get your licence when the time comes. I can't say fairer than that, can I?'

Callaghan nodded. His face took on the look of perfect frankness that he used when telling blatant lies.

'Gringall,' he said, 'you're a sport. I like you, an' I'm goin' to talk. I'm not goin' to talk about Miss Meraulton. I can't. She's my client, an' the business I'm handlin' for her – an' it's got nothin' to do with this murder case – is both delicate and concerns the reputation of another woman. Therefore I'm not goin' to even mention her name.

'But I tell you straight that I'm interested in this murder, an' I believe I can give you a pointer on the motive question. I believe I can give you a pointer about the feller who pulled that business at the morgue, too.

'I believe that you're right off the rails. I believe that you're startin' off by believin' that August Meraulton was murdered in Lincoln's Inn Fields, up against the railin's. Well, I don't believe he was. He hadn't got a hat on, had he? All right. Well, you've probably checked on that an' you've found that the one an' only hat that he used is safe at his house, an' so you've come to the conclusion that he went to Lincoln's Inn in a cab, got out an' was walkin' along by the railings – probably to meet somebody – when he was shot. But I don't believe that. I believe he was killed somewhere else and taken along there in a car an' put down there by the railin's.

'An' I'll tell you why I think that. August Meraulton told his nephew Willie last week that he was goin' to buy himself a new hat. He said that he wasn't goin' to his usual place for it, either, that they were too expensive. I reckon that the man who killed August Meraulton knew that he'd bought himself that new hat that afternoon, an' so he grabbed it an' took it away. This killer was smart. He knew that the fact that you found the old hat at Meraulton's home would lead you to believe that August had just walked out of his place without his hat, intendin' to take a cab to Lincoln's Inn Fields for the purpose of meetin' somebody.'

Callaghan looked at Gringall and then at Fields. He was watching to see how it was going over, but their faces said nothing.

'Look, Gringall,' Callaghan went on, 'you tell me that somebody went down to the morgue to steal that new will that Meraulton had made. Well, who would want to steal it? Gazeling told you that the new will probably didn't affect Willie or Cynthis Meraulton, so it wouldn't be either of them. Who was the person that it would affect most?'

He paused for effect. Then, pointing his finger, went on:

'The person whom it would affect most would be the person who had most to lose if he didn't get his share under the original will. The person who's spent every bean he's got, who's up to his neck in debt, who's desperate for money. A man who's got to have money because he's got to have drugs.

'When a man takes cocaine it's bad enough. A sniff now an' again don't make a man a murderer. But when that feller is such a cocaine fiend that he has to go on to morphia to get over the cocaine hangovers, you'll admit that he's in a pretty bad way. You'll admit that he'll stop at nothin', you'll admit that his brain an' nerves are in such a state that, under certain conditions, murder wouldn't mean a thing.

'That's the sort of killer who, when he'd done the job, would have a nervous an' mental reaction an' wouldn't be able to touch the dead body.

'You find that feller an' you've got the man you're lookin' for.'

Gringall looked up from the blotter. There was a new light in his eyes. Callaghan grinned to himself. Gringall was falling for it!

'I see,' said Gringall. 'I see.'

He began to smile.

'Tell me something, Slim,' he said. 'What were you doing at Bellamy Meraulton's place this afternoon? Are you handling some business for him, too?'

'No,' said Callaghan. 'I went to see Bellamy because I wanted to ask him a few questions about the job that Cynthis Meraulton came to see me about – the family matter I told you about.'

He stopped talking, and a wise smile appeared on his thin face.

'Mark you, Gringall,' he said, 'I'm not going to say that while I was there I didn't take a quick look around to see if I could see something. I was interested, just as anybody would be. I looked around when Bellamy was lookin' in his appointment book to see when he could meet me tonight. Just before he told me it would have to be between twelve-thirty and one-thirty I was lookin' around to see if I could see any sign of it. But Bellamy's no fool. I saw nothin' at all.'

'You mean,' said Gringall, 'you mean you were lookin' to see if there was any sign of the late August Meraulton's new hat, and at the same time you're telling me that Bellamy will be out tonight between twelve-thirty and one-thirty?'

'Right in both places,' said Callaghan.

He got up.

'I must be toddling along,' he said.

Gringall got up and walked round the desk. He stood in front of Callaghan.

'Slim,' he said, 'you've been very helpful. I suppose you wouldn't be a bit more helpful and tell me where I can find Cynthis Meraulton. I want to talk to all of 'em, you know.'

'Sorry,' said Callaghan, 'I can't. I don't know. Well ... so long, Gringall.'

He walked over to the door.

'You find that hat, an' you've got your man,' he said as he went out.

CHAPTER SIX

Soft Pedal for Callaghan

It was twenty minutes to seven when Callaghan left Scotland Yard. He hailed a taxi by the Cenotaph and told the man to drive to Piccadilly Circus. He went downstairs into the subway and telephoned Darkie.

'Listen, Darkie,' he said. 'Directly I've done talkin' to you I'm goin' over to the post office an' I'm puttin' one hundred pounds – ten tenners – in an envelope and registerin' it to you. Got that? All right. Did you get in touch with that feller Ribbenhall, or whatever his name is?'

'Yes, guv,' said Darkie. 'His name's Revenholt. He's at home now standin' by in case you want to talk to him. His number's Mayfair 55463.'

'All right.' Callaghan made a note of the number on the edge of the telephone directory. 'Well, I'm goin' to ring him up in a minute. I'm goin' to get him to do a little searchin' for me. I want him to find out somethin' about Paul Meraulton – the one you say works for the Walker-Fleet Company, the one who earns six pounds a week and spends sixty. I'm puttin' Revenholt on this job, because I may be needin' you for somethin' else. You see Revenholt in the mornin' an' give him twenty pounds of the hundred. Tell him the other eighty's waitin' for him when he's cashed in with the information that I want. Show him the money so he'll know you've got it. Got that?'

'I got it,' said Darkie. 'How's it goin' along, Slim?'

'Not too badly,' Callaghan replied vaguely. 'So long, Darkie. I'll be seein' you.'

He hung up. Waited a minute, then called Revenholt.

Roderick Eustace Maninway Revenholt slid off the settee on which his slim figure was stretched, and lounged over to the telephone.

He was thirty-one, five feet eleven inches high, and possessed a superb figure, wavy brown hair, large and attractive blue eyes, no money.

In spite of the fact that he had no money of his own, he was always to be found in good restaurants, wore the best clothes, had a nice taste in silk shirts. He had, too, a very large circle of lady friends, most of whom were much older than he was. When things were good he did no work. When they were not he condescended to act in an informative capacity for any private detective agency that would pay him.

He was not immoral. He had no morals whatsoever, and the fact did not perturb him. He never thought in terms of morals.

At the moment he was broke. He was glad of a chance to make an honest penny. He would have been glad of the chance to make a dishonest one if the process had been necessary.

He stubbed out the cigarette end into the Lalique glass ashtray and listened to Callaghan.

Callaghan's voice was cool and quiet.

'Hallo, Revenholt,' he said. 'Darkie's been on to you already, hasn't he? Good. Tomorrow mornin' he'll see you an' give you twenty quid. When you've done the job there's another eighty. Now listen:

'I'm very interested in a feller named Paul Meraulton. He's a man of forty-four, an' works for the Walker-Fleet Company on commission. He earns six or seven pounds a week an' spends a lot more than that. This Paul Meraulton seems to spend a lot of time down at Somerset House. I want to know why. That's the first thing.

'The second thing is, I want you to take an interest in all these four Meraultons - Bellamy, Paul, Percival and Jeremy. There's another one - a fifth - Willie; but I'm not interested in him.

'I want you to find out for me if all or any of these four are interested in any registered companies, public or private, joint-stock or otherwise. If they are, I want you to make me out a list showing just what companies they're interested in an' the extent of their holdin's. You got that? All right. Just repeat it, will you?'

He listened. Then:

'All right, Revenholt, I'll be seein' you. Work fast, now!'

He hung up. He walked across the Circus to the Shaftesbury Avenue Post Office and dispatched the money to Darkie.

Callaghan realized that he was tired. He disliked the feeling, not because he minded being physically tired, but because there was a great deal of quick thinking to be done.

He lit a cigarette and hurried back across the Circus to a Regent Street outfitters. He bought a dinner suit, evening overcoat, shoes and accessories, and changed into them.

He descended to the barber's shop. He was shaved, took a face massage and a cold shampoo. He lay back in the seat during the barber's ministrations and relaxed. He was beginning to see a spot of daylight – only a spot, but daylight, nevertheless. He wondered if his luck would hold. Whilst he was being manicured he ordered a cup of black coffee to be brought, and smoked two cigarettes.

Then he went upstairs again, bought a large suitcase, had his other clothes with some additional purchases packed into it, paid the bill, gave orders for it to be sent to the Axford Private Hotel in Orchard Street to await his arrival that night.

When he went out into Regent Street he looked almost distinguished. Evening kit suited him. His lean face underneath the black soft hat, above the white silk muffler, looked keen and refined.

He picked up a cab and drove to the Delvine Court Apartments in South Kensington.

She opened the door when he rang. She looked at him strangely for a moment, and he sensed that she had taken a second or two to recognize him. He was pleased about that.

She stepped back and held the door for him. He entered and shut the door. She was already leading the way to the sitting-room.

The room was cosy. There was an excellent coal fire burning, and in the corner a first-class radio sent out the soft chords of a foxtrot. She walked across to the instrument and turned it off.

Callaghan watched her, caught his breath a little as she moved. His eyes followed her hungrily.

She was wearing a black velvet coat and skirt. The golden-beige silk stockings and the small crepe-de-chine court shoes with tiny diamante buckles set off her slim ankles and exquisite feet.

At her throat was a ruffle of beige lace. Here was a woman who could pick clothes and who knew how to wear them, Callaghan thought.

When she turned and faced him he saw that her eyes were tired, but that under the tiredness there was a certain hostility - a cold antagonism. He realized that he must be careful. One false move and she would go right off the handle. If she did, she could ditch the whole business - and him.

'Won't you sit down?' she said. 'You'll find some Player's cigarettes in that box on the table.'

She sat down in the big chair by the side of the fire, watching him - waiting for him to speak.

Callaghan took a cigarette, offered her one and, when she shook her head, lit his own cigarette with his new lighter. He began to speak quietly.

'You don't like me very much, do you, Miss Meraulton?' he said. 'Well, I'm not very surprised at that. Lots of people don't like me very much. But the thing is that when you saw me for the first time - last night I mean - you didn't like the *idea* of me even before you met me. I can understand that, too. When people come to see men like me, they come usually because they are in some sort of jam - a nasty jam more often than not - an' they sort of associate me with it, an' so they begin by not likin' me at all. I'm tellin' you this so that you'll understand me when I say that as often as not I'm prepared to dislike *them* for the same sort of reasons. I'm prepared to believe the worst of them. D'you see what I mean?'

She hesitated for a moment. Then:

'I think I understand what you mean,' she said. 'But you don't *have* to be a private detective, do you? There are lots of other, more interesting businesses for a man – jobs that aren't quite so ...' She paused, seeking the right word.

'Sordid is the word you're lookin' for, isn't it?' he said. 'Well, Miss Meraulton, somebody has to be a private detective, you know. They're necessary evils – an' some of 'em even do a bit of good now an' again.'

He inhaled deeply.

'What I was tryin' to get into your mind was this,' he went on. 'When you came to see me last night the whole set-up of events seemed to me to indicate certain things. I came to some quick conclusions. I'm used to makin' up my mind quickly, an' quite often I'm right. But I realize that I can be *wrong*, too. I was wrong last night – dead wrong.'

Her lip curled a little.

'You mean you've altered your opinion about one or two things?' she asked.

'I mean that I thought you killed August Meraulton,' he said. 'I know now that I was wrong to blazes, but I'm not sayin' that I wasn't justified in comin' to the conclusion that I did last night on the facts that I had before me. You know it wouldn't be the first time that somebody had come to Callaghan Investigations in order to get themselves a first-class fake alibi.'

'I think it's very nice of you to be so open about it, Mr Callaghan,' she said coldly. 'I'm fearfully obliged to you for not thinking that I'm a murderess!'

He grinned. In spite of her anger she could not help thinking that he looked like a mischievous schoolboy.

'That's quite all right,' he said. 'I think that with a bit of luck you and I will get along fine from now on.'

He stubbed out the cigarette, lit another.

'I suppose you telephoned through to Willie Meraulton after I rang you this mornin' an' told him just what you thought about me. I suppose you told him that you never wanted to see my face again?'

She looked squarely at him. She was beginning to think that this rather peculiar man was more than ordinarily intelligent – something of a psychologist. Looking at him, she found herself thinking that there was something oddly interesting about him, something vague and elusive.

'I intended to do just that,' she said. 'But, strangely enough, I've been unable to get him either at his office or anywhere else. I suppose you wouldn't know anything about that?'

Her eyes were suspicious. He decided to tell the truth.

'I'm responsible,' he said. 'Detective-Inspector Gringall's handling this case. I've a great respect for his mentality. Gringall's no fool, an' he's got a rotten case. You know you've got to *prove* murder in this country. The accused can just shut up an' say nothin'. Even if he won't go into the witness-box at the trial the prosecution have got to prove their case right up to the hilt, an' even if they do it on circumstantial evidence, the evidence has got to be damn good circumstantial evidence.

'I knew that Gringall would be castin' about for anything to start off with – tryin' to find a kickin' off ground, if you know what I mean. I knew that the first thing he'd do would be to have the telephone lines of all the Meraultons plugged an' have some boys listenin' in. I knew that most of all he would want to know where you were, an' that he'd try an' get a line on that by waitin' for you to telephone Willie. So I arranged that Willie just wouldn't be there. I still think I'm right.'

'I see.' She stretched her hands towards the fire. 'But I still don't see how you thought that would help. Detective-Inspector Gringall will be able to find Willie, won't he? He will ask him all the questions about me that he might have asked me personally.'

Callaghan shook his head.

'No, he won't,' he said, smiling. 'Gringall's goin' to be much too busy with other things to worry about askin' Willie questions about you.' His smile deepened. 'You know, Miss Meraulton,' he said, 'before we're through with this job you're still goin' to thank me for savin' you from bein' questioned and possibly arrested an' generally chivvied about the place. You're still goin' to thank me for keepin' a lot of Meraulton dirty linen out of the newspapers – even if I did think you were a murderess – an' even if you do dislike me so much!'

'That's not quite true,' she said. 'I don't particularly dislike you – well, not as much as I did. But perhaps you'll tell me why Mr Gringall is going to be too busy to talk to Willie about me. Has he found the murderer?'

Callaghan looked modest.

'I found him,' he said. 'I handed him to Gringall on a plate. Don't you know who it is?'

He leaned forward and looked straight into her eyes.

'It's somebody you're a bit sorry for, isn't it?' he said. 'But I think your sorrow is misplaced. I think the feller's a thoroughly bad lot without one redeeming feature in his whole make-up. He's probably played on your sympathy though on such occasions as you've come across him. Bellamy's got brains all right!'

She started.

'Bellamy ... So they know!'

He nodded grimly.

'Miss Meraulton,' he said softly, 'I still want to save you a lot of trouble, a lot of questioning at Scotland Yard, an' all that sort of thing. I think I can do it, too. I think that if I can give Gringall all the leads he wants, suggest them to him, let him check on them for himself an' see they're right, he'll play square with me. I know that your one idea is to keep this rotten business as quiet as possible. I think we can do that without hurting any one much, without obstructing the proper processes of law' – Callaghan grinned inwardly at this last one – 'and without perjuring ourselves.'

He paused for a moment to let his last words sink in.

'I want you to tell me exactly what happened yesterday,' he said. 'Exactly what you did from, say, three o'clock in the afternoon until the time when you set foot in my office last night. Or do you still dislike and distrust me too much?'

'Does that matter now?' she replied. 'I see no reason, if what you tell me is true, to continue hiding here. I feel that I was foolish to listen to you and come here so secretly in the first place. *Now* there is no reason to continue to stay here or to indulge in any more of this running away from nothing – is there?'

Callaghan looked into the fire for some time before answering.

'You're quite right, there isn't,' he said eventually, 'except for one thing – and that one thing is *me*!'

He looked at her again with the same mischievous grin. In spite of herself she smiled. It was almost impossible not to smile at this strange, lean-faced man, who could be so insulting, so consistently interesting, and who regarded murders, faked alibis and any other form of misfeasance purely as a matter of course.

'You see,' said Callaghan, 'I'm not very popular at the Yard. You can understand that. Once or twice I've pulled hot chestnuts out of the fire right under their noses, and there's one or two of 'em don't like me at all.

'Well, I went down there before Gringall had got any ideas at all about Bellamy havin' done this murder an' swore blind that you were with me in my office talkin' over some supposed business that a friend of yours wanted me to handle, from eleven o'clock until midnight.

'Unfortunately for me that typist of mine, Effie Perkins, had read the papers, an' she'd been listenin' to our first conversation. Effie knew I'd alibi you, an' so she tried to get back on me by writin' Gringall a letter an' tellin' him the time you came in an' went out. The right times, too.

'Well, if you come out into the open right away Gringall will take a statement from you just for the sake of appearances, an' I daren't let you tell anything but the truth.'

He paused to light another cigarette.

'Well, I think they'd make it pretty tough for me,' he said. 'They might even stick me in jail.'

He looked at her intently, saw her eyes soften. He breathed a sigh of relief. It had come off all right!

'I don't want you to get into any trouble,' she said. 'I suppose anything you've said or done has been on my account, and I don't see why you should suffer for that - even if you were quite unjustified in thinking what you did.'

She got up and stood in front of the fire. He could see that she'd made up her mind about something.

'I'm going to tell you what happened yesterday,' she said. 'I want to tell someone. I've been feeling so *awful* about it all. If it's going to help you, I don't mind staying here for a day or two more until you've put yourself right with Scotland Yard, and if you want to tell Mr Gringall all about this business you had better do so. I shall, of course, substantiate it afterwards. Will you give me a cigarette?'

Callaghan handed her the box and snapped his lighter into flame. She went back to her chair.

'Willie and I had arranged to go the theatre last night,' she said. 'But in the early evening I had a headache. I telephoned through to his secretary and told her that I thought I should be unable to go.

'Ten minutes afterwards my stepfather - August Meraulton - telephoned. I was amazed at the change in his voice. Usually he was brusque - almost rude - when he spoke on the telephone; but now he seemed like a broken old man. His voice seemed half angry, half pleading.

'He said that it was absolutely necessary that he saw me last night. He said that it was most terribly urgent, that whatever happened I must see him. He said that I was to say nothing to anybody at all, but that I must go to his office in Lincoln's Inn Fields - a top floor office - he gave me the number - at eleven o'clock, and talk to him.

'I asked if Willie might bring me, but he said no. He said that he had already telephoned Willie, and that Willie would probably be doing some very important things for him during the day and until late at night. He said that I must not breathe a word to a soul, not even on the telephone.

'I was fearfully worried about all this, and wondered what had happened. Soon afterwards Willie telephoned me. He asked about my head and whether I minded not going to the theatre. I told him not a bit and that – as he probably knew – I had an appointment at eleven o'clock that night.

'Willie said he understood perfectly. Then he asked me whether I had seen you, as he had asked me to do. He sounded very worried, and I took myself to task for not having been to see you before – which he had wanted me to do days ago, after he saw Mr Fingal about you. He asked if I would go and see you after the eleven o'clock appointment if he could get you on the telephone and arrange for you to be there. I said I would do that, and he told me he would get your office and arrange that you should be there. He asked me to look after myself and to be fearfully careful.'

She threw her cigarette end into the fire.

'Naturally,' she went on, 'I began to worry and rather worked myself into a state of nerves. At a quarter to eleven I telephoned the garage for my car and drove round to Lincoln's Inn. I went by way of Kingsway through Portugal Street and up the west side of the Square. I was not quite certain where August's office was – I had never known previously that he had an office – this apparently, had been kept a great secret – and I stopped the car half-way along the side of the Square and got out and walked, looking for the number.

'It was a beastly night, cold and raining. I looked down the Square and got a great surprise. At the top of the Square is a little passage leading off, I imagine, into High Holborn, and standing there under the lamp on the corner was Bellamy. He had his coat collar turned up and began to walk backwards and forwards nervously. He hadn't seen me. Just as I had made up my mind to call out to him he turned and walked through the passage.

'I found the number of the house. The main door was closed, but when I pushed it, it opened. The place was quite dark inside, there were no lights on. I lit my cigarette lighter and began to walk up the stairs, and eventually, after ages of climbing, I reached the fourth floor landing.

'Opposite me was an oak door with "August Meraulton – Private" painted on it. I knocked, but there was no reply. I could see there was a light on in the room. After a moment I pushed the door open.

'The office was a fairly large room lined with shelves with filing cases and things on them. There was a big desk and all the papers were disarranged. A chair between the door and the desk had been knocked over and was lying in the middle of the floor.

'For some reason I felt terribly frightened. I wanted to run out of the place, but I made myself stay. I told myself that August had been called away and would be back soon. I waited there until about twenty minutes past eleven and then I decided to go.

'I went downstairs, closed the street door behind me, went to the car and drove back down the west side. Then I remembered the appointment with you. This appointment now seemed a matter of importance. Things were happening – extraordinary things – and I remembered that Willie had spoken of my being in some sort of danger.

'I drove round the bottom of the Square, through Carey Street, and stopped at the telephone box. I rang through to Clegella House and asked the butler if he knew where August was. The butler said that he did not even know that my stepfather was out, that his hat – his one and only hat – was hanging in its usual place in the hall.

'Then it occurred to me that perhaps August had decided not to keep the appointment because it was cold and raining – although he was usually impervious to any sort of weather – so I told Meakins that it didn't matter and that I would ring through again – later.

'Then I left the car where it was and walked round to your office and saw you. You know what happened there. After that I went straight home and immediately telephoned Willie. I told him what had happened. He said that there was probably some explanation for it, but seemed terribly worried about it all. He telephoned Bellamy and got no reply, and then tried to speak to Jeremy and Paul, but they weren't in either. He left after arranging to go round first thing in the morning and find out from August what had happened.

'The next thing was when you telephoned and told me that "there had been a nice murder," that I must come to your office at two-thirty. Before I came round to see you I rang Willie again. He was appalled.

'I told Willie about my first interview with you, and he said that the best thing I could do was to go round and hear what you had to say. He said that he would get into touch immediately with Bellamy, if he could find him, and endeavour to find out what had been going on. You know all the rest.'

Callaghan nodded. He said nothing.

She got up.

'Have they arrested Bellamy?' she said. 'Will they arrest him?'

He grinned.

'They won't arrest him for murder,' he said. 'But I'll bet my boots they'll arrest him for *something* so as to hold him. Gringall's got just about all he wants on Bellamy, an' he won't take a chance.'

He got up.

'Miss Merraulton,' he said seriously, 'will you do something for me? I'm askin' you this as a sort of favour, an' I'm afraid that I'm askin' it mainly for my own sake.'

She looked at him. Now she was quite poised again. Her eyes, he thought, were not so hard. Maybe she wasn't feeling quite so bad about him.

'What is it?' she asked.

'Just stay here for three more days,' he said. 'That's the very outside limit. It's quite on the cards that I'll see you or telephone you tomorrow – or Willie will – an' we can all come out into the open. But I want to fix myself with Gringall first. If I get up against him he can ruin me.'

There was a note of quiet entreaty in his voice.

She smiled. Callaghan thought it was like the sun coming out on a rainy day.

'Very well,' she said. 'I'll do that. But understand you've only three days to make your peace with Mr Gringall. In the meantime I shall have a chance to talk things over with Willie.'

Callaghan looked glum.

'I'm afraid you won't be able to do that,' he lied. 'He's in Edinburgh. Something to do with the Meraulton Estates – one of the results of August Meraulton's death. He won't be back until Saturday. But I'll tell you what I'll do. He's going to telephone me tomorrow night. When I speak to him I'll get his address and telephone number and let you know what they are.'

Her face changed again. She was disappointed.

Callaghan walked over to the doorway and out into the hall. He picked up his hat. He turned at the front door as she spoke to him.

'It's all very odd and strange,' she said. 'You're sure you aren't up to any of your usual tricks?' She softened the words with a little smile. 'You're sure you're not keeping me away from Willie or from telephoning him because I'm still suspect?'

Callaghan laughed easily.

'I wouldn't do that,' he said.

He opened the door, turned suddenly.

'I'll tell you somethin', Miss Meraulton,' he said quickly, the words tumbling out. 'I wouldn't let you down. I'd do any damned thing for you.'

He grinned at her again – the schoolboy grin.

'Even if you were a murderess!' he said, and left her there, standing in the doorway, looking after him.

CHAPTER SEVEN

Broken Bottle Party

It was ten o'clock.

Callaghan sat at the table by the window in Lyons Corner House, Shaftesbury Avenue. He looked out and watched people meeting other people, going into the Monico, laughing, talking.

For a few seconds he saw London objectively! Saw it as a place mainly consisting of two parts – a very thin upper crust and a damn thick lower one. The upper crust was the veneer of respectability, 'niceness', cleanliness, which London showed the world; the lower crust – the thick one – all the rottenness, cheap crookery and general lousiness that existed in that Jungle in the heart of the metropolis whose boundaries are known to every intelligent police officer.

He smiled to himself as he thought how little the majority of Londoners knew about London. Some of them vaguely believed that there was 'an underworld', of course – the sort of place that you went to on the 'tube' and found a selected bunch of crooks waiting to show you the tricks of the trade, but most of them would have been surprised and amazed at the really good crime stories – the ones that never got on to the front page – that happened from time to time.

That sort of thing happened in America. It didn't happen in London!

He grinned at the thought. Didn't it!

Everything happened in London. Every damn thing. Every night and every day. Which was why Vine Street had started a Vice Squad under a first-class officer who knew his stuff, knew how to deal with peculiar people who might have been offended if you had suggested that they were crooks, whose viciousness and rottenness probably caused more crime in the long run than was ever started by a professional criminal dealing in what might be called clean, honest-to-goodness crookery.

Wipe out that particular crowd and much potential crime and many potential criminals would never even exist.

Callaghan sipped his coffee and permitted himself a moment's sympathy for the police whose sources of information got less and less in these days when 'stool-pigeons' were beginning to learn that a shut mouth is sometimes a better proposition than a smashed jaw and half a dozen broken ribs.

He smiled even more broadly when he considered what might happen if editors of some of the London 'Dailies' and 'Sundays' were to give half a dozen crime reporters – the boys who really knew their stuff – a free hand for once, and to blazes with the law of libel! He imagined what the front pages would look like on a Sunday morning and just how many really nice people would be packing their bags and getting out quick while the going was good.

He wondered if he would be one of them.

He paid his bill and went downstairs. He walked along to the call-box half-way up Shaftesbury Avenue and rang the *Morning Echo*. Two minutes later he was talking to Jengel.

'Michael,' he said, 'here's somethin' for you if you like to keep it under your hat. It's all the tea in China to a bad egg that Gringall is goin' to move in the Meraulton case tonight. I should think somewhere between twelve-thirty an' one-thirty. My advice to you is to hang about at the corner of Lisle Street an' Pallards Place round about that time. Look out for the Squad car, an' if you see it follow along an' help yourself.'

'Thank you, Slim,' said Jengel. 'How're you goin'? Still bein' a good boy?'

Callaghan hung up.

He crossed the road and picked up a taxi – ordered the man to drive him to Gordon Square. He got out on the corner and walked across the Square towards the Clarendon Apartments.

He waited on the other side of the road and watched the main entrance until he saw the night porter take the lift upwards. Then he crossed swiftly, and, after a quick look at the number indicator in the hall, walked up the stairs. Going up, he began to think about Eulalie Gallicot.

Eulalie Gallicot was thirty-two and looked thirty, stood five feet eight in her very high heels, was dark, well-complexioned and knew how to wear – or not wear – her clothes.

She was French and really had the *chic* which all Frenchwomen are supposed to possess and so seldom show.

Eulalie was very wise. She had started off in the chorus of one of the smaller French strip-revues after the war. She knew quite a lot about life and practically everything that there was to know about men. She had heard England was a good spot to be in, and had schemed to get there, being assisted in the process by a 'financier' in Marseilles who 'financed' people like Eulalie.

She knew just how she was going to handle Callaghan, because she had taken expert advice on that subject.

Callaghan put his black hat down on the table and opened his coat. The over-heated room, too prettily furnished and crowded with occasional tables and ridiculous feminine knick-knacks, backed with red wallpaper and much red velvet, oppressed him.

He took a long look at Eulalie, who was wearing a dark blue watered-silk rest-gown and showing a great deal of leg, with an admiration that was too openly expressed to be real.

'Listen, Miss Gallicot,' he said – 'or is it Mrs Gallicot?'

He waited, and when she smiled and left the question unanswered, went straight on:

'I'm sorry to trouble you like this, but I thought I ought to have a word with you before the police begin to ask you a lot of questions.'

She nodded and smiled prettily. Then she got up gracefully and brought a box of cigarettes to him. He took one, lit it and one for her, stood up until she was seated again. Callaghan knew the type of women who appreciated good manners.

He began to talk, his face relaxed and open, using the quiet frank tone of voice which he had found useful when lying to women like Eulalie.

'I don't want to waste any of your time, Miss Gallicot,' he said, 'so I'll make this as short as possible. I'm a private detective, and I've been retained by the Meraulton lawyers because they have reason to believe that a member of the family may find himself in a little trouble with the police over the murder that you've read about.

'The thing's this: Unfortunately there is evidence that Bellamy Meraulton – a close friend of yours, I believe – was in the vicinity of Lincoln's Inn Fields round about the time of the murder. I believe afterwards he came on to see you. I wonder would you care to tell me what time he got here?'

'I don' mind, m'sieu,' she said. 'Why should I? M'sieu Bellamy arrive 'ere at twelve o'clock – per'aps five or ten minutes after.'

Callaghan smiled charmingly.

'I knew you'd tell the truth,' he said. 'Now the thing I want to tell you is this: We know that if we're left alone we can get Bellamy out of this thing as easily as snapping our fingers. The only thing we're afraid of is that he may try to give himself a false alibi an' say that he was here much earlier – say eleven-thirty or eleven forty-five. If he does that he'll be silly. The thing for him to do is to tell the truth. When I spoke to you earlier today I thought that it might be a good thing for you to say that he didn't come here at all, but after thinking it over I came to the conclusion that it would be better for you to tell the truth.'

'I mus' tell the trut',' she said. 'Eet is mos' necessary. I shall tell only the trut'!'

'Good,' said Callaghan. 'That's fine!' He tried a shot in the dark. 'I suppose you rang your husband, Arnault Beldoces, after I telephoned you today?'

It came off.

'Yes,' she said, 'I spoke to 'eem. 'E said I mus' tell the trut', that I mus' not get into some troubles wiz ze police.'

Callaghan got up.

'Thank you, Mrs Beldoces,' he said, 'or rather Miss Gallicot. Now there's just one other little thing: You do as you like about it, of course, but if I were you I wouldn't try to get into touch with Bellamy. I've got an idea that the police may be plugged in on your telephone wire and we don't want to mix things up any more than they are, do we?'

She got up.

'I do not intend to spik to M'sieu Bellamy,' she said. 'I don' want to be mix in this thing at all. Eef I am asked, I spik the trut'. Eef not, I say nothing at all – you understand?'

He smiled at her.

'Perfectly,' he said. 'I think you're a wise little woman. Good-night, mademoiselle.'

They shook hands smilingly.

Callaghan sat in his fourth floor office in Chancery Lane and indulged in some constructive thought. In the outer office Fred Mazin balanced himself in Effie Perkins' old chair with his feet on the typing table, engrossed in a study of the next day's runners 'over the sticks' at Cheltenham.

Callaghan felt he could go ahead with his scheme. The first thing to do was to get the two hundred – or as much of it as possible – out of Bellamy. Bellamy was frightened. He'd probably have raised the whole sum.

It was a stone certainty that Gringall would have a couple of men tailing Bellamy. They would pick him up when he left his place in Pointers Mews and tail him to the Green Signal. Then they would get through to Gringall.

In the meantime Gringall would get the servant out of the Pointers Mews place on some pretext or other, and take a look round. He would find the grey homburg. That would settle it. He'd pull in Bellamy on something or other – probably a narcotics charge – and hold him so that he could complete sufficient evidence to arrest on the main charge.

Eulalie Gallicot would support the general idea. She would say that Bellamy had arrived at her apartment at twelve or twelve-five. The thing was that Bellamy must be made to say something else so that it appeared that he was trying to fix himself an alibi.

Callaghan thought that the process of making Bellamy say 'something else' would not be too difficult.

But he was curious about one thing: *At what time had Bellamy really arrived at Eulalie's apartment?* Eulalie had given Callaghan the idea that she had been 'rehearsed' in what she said to him – very well rehearsed.

Callaghan smiled a little grimly. He had an idea as to how he might find out about that, too.

He took out the little black notebook and made some notes. Then he looked at his watch. It was twelve-fifteen. He felt terribly tired.

He put on his hat.

'Guard the fort, Fred,' he said as he went out. 'Stay here till two o'clock an' then close down. I'll be seein' you!'

The Green Signal was like all the others. It was 'one of those places'. Started as most professional 'bottle parties' are, as a practical protest against grandmotherly regulations, it had developed into the usual centre for half a dozen different vices, constituted a meeting-place for the members of two or three different half-worlds who preferred to live during the night so that they might adequately hide their faces from the sun during the day.

Occasionally decent people came along with habitués to see what it was like. One visit usually was enough.

You approached it through a doorway off Pallard's Place, went up a flight of stairs, walked through a passage, knocked through the wall into the next house, went downstairs again, checked in on the ground floor and were then permitted to pass down into the basement.

The room was long and L-shaped – the end of the L turning off to the left. In the right-hand corner on a raised platform four reputed Mexicans - two came from Marseilles, one from Mile End, one from Lisle Street - beat out hot music on guitars, Spanish mandolins and other soul-stirring instruments.

Four tired waiters, whose eyes were rimmed with the blue of perpetual weariness, leaned against the walls when not rushing upstairs to put in an order for a client whose liquor had to be fetched (such is our law) from the wine merchants round the corner.

Not more than fifteen people were in the place. Most of them were women. You could take a look at them and give three guesses as to what they were and what they did. You might even be right three times.

Everybody looked tired. They looked like that because they were, most of them, trying steadily to escape from themselves and their own thoughts of themselves. Usually they failed and had recourse to the brandy bottle, the soft white powder that brought, with a good sniff, a sense of freedom for half an hour, or the hypodermic in the arm that got you out of one jag and pushed you into a more serious one - the problem as to where the next supply was coming from, and if that question were answered, who was going to pay for it.

Because, as your Sunday paper has probably told you, when a man or a woman dopes, somebody - usually more than one person, too, - pays for it dearly, even if the payment is not always made with money.

When Callaghan went down the stairs he saw Bellamy sitting at the table in the corner opposite. Callaghan took a look up the room and noticed that the other door - the one under the hangings at the end of the L - was unlocked. He could tell that by the way the hangings fell over it.

Bellamy was sitting on one side of the table, and a half-tight individual, who looked vaguely like Bellamy with the addition of a year or two, sat on the other. This, thought Callaghan, would be Percival. He was right.

Bellamy was in a bad temper consisting partly of annoyance but mainly of fear. He was sweating across the forehead, his hands were trembling, his face had that peculiar bluish tint which comes with continuous late hours and injections of morphine. He was drinking brandy.

Callaghan sat down.

'Don't let's waste any time,' said Bellamy jerkily. 'I don't want to waste time. I want to know what's going on. More especially I want you to prove what you say to me. I don't see why I should trust you particularly and I want to know where I am. I ...'

He would have gone on talking indefinitely. Callaghan stopped him by putting out a hand and grabbing Bellamy by the arm – hard.

He nodded towards Percival.

'Tell him to get out of here,' said Callaghan. 'I've got one or two things to say to you, an' I'm only goin' to say 'em to you – nobody else, see? An' if you don't want to be polite an' keep a civil tongue in your head I can always walk out of here an' leave you to stew in your own juice. Understand?'

Bellamy opened his mouth to protest, thought better of it, and spoke to Percival. Percival got up and walked out. Callaghan, watching his faltering exit up the stairs, thought that another six months would see the end of Percival. There is a limit to the amount of spirits which the human stomach and heart can cope with.

Callaghan lit a cigarette. He looked at Bellamy.

'Have you got the money?' he asked. 'All of it?'

'Look here ...' Bellamy began.

Callaghan stopped him.

'Just as you like,' he said. 'You can do what you like. You can either pay up an' shut up, or talk to yourself. I haven't come down here to listen to you.'

Bellamy dabbed his forehead with a verbena-scented handkerchief. Then he fumbled in the breast of his unbrushed dinner coat and brought out a packet of notes. He handed them to Callaghan almost despairingly.

Callaghan counted them and put them in his pocket. There were twenty ten-pound notes – two hundred pounds.

'All right,' said Callaghan.

He lit another cigarette deliberately, slowly, playing on Bellamy's strained nerves and tortured impatience.

'Now listen,' he said. 'I'm not goin' to mince matters with you – you're in a hell of a jam, an' when I say that you're in a hell of a jam, that's exactly what I mean. I'm not trying to frighten you, because you're not payin' me for that, but you've got to know the truth sooner or later.'

He leaned across the table. He spoke softly.

'You're suspected in the August Meraulton murder,' he said. 'I happen to know that the police are all but certain that you're the feller they're lookin' for. What they've got an' what they haven't got I don't know, but I do know one thing, an' that is that somebody or other has tipped 'em off that you were seen hanging about in Lincoln's Inn Fields at eleven o'clock or soon after.'

Bellamy turned a pasty white.

'My God,' he said. 'That's that damned Cynthis. That little ... So she's been talking, has she? Well, what was *she* doing there, that's what I want to know? What ...?' His voice began to rise.

'Shut up,' said Callaghan. 'What does that matter? I'm not concerned with her. I'm only concerned with tryin' to get you out of this. Now listen here an' don't start whimperin' an' cryin' all the damn time, because when you do you make me feel sick.

'After you left Lincoln's Inn Fields you went to see Eulalie Gallicot, didn't you? All right. Well, what time did you get there?'

Bellamy thought.

'I'm not quite sure,' he said finally. 'But it was soon after eleven. It might have been a quarter past eleven.'

Callaghan grinned inwardly. Here was a joke. Bellamy was going to say just what he wanted him to say. Bellamy was going to say that he got to Eulalie's at eleven-fifteen, and Eulalie would throw that story down by saying that he didn't get there until twelve or soon after. And the cream of the joke was that probably Bellamy was telling the truth.

'That's fine,' said Callaghan. 'That's all right. It looks as if the old boy was shot some time about eleven-fifteen or eleven-twenty.' (He made this up. He had no idea as to what the actual time of death was. The police surgeon's report had not been issued.) 'So you tell the truth. If anything happens, you can tell 'em what time you got to Eulalie's, an' she can confirm it. I suppose she *will* tell 'em that you got there at eleven-fifteen?'

Bellamy managed a smile.

'That's one thing I am certain about,' he said with a ridiculous touch of pride in his voice. 'Eulalie will tell them that too.'

Callaghan thought: So you've already been on the telephone to her about it, have you? And she told you that she'd give the right time as a matter of course, and since then she's been advised to add an hour on. Nice work.

He said: 'Well, it looks as if, with a bit of luck, everything's goin' to be all right with you. You've got a cast-iron alibi that can't be broken down.'

Bellamy began jittering again. His voice cracked at every third world.

'Who's trying to pin this thing on me?' he said. 'Who is it? It's that damned Cynthis, isn't it? It's that greedy ...'

'Steady on,' said Callaghan quietly. 'Steady on. Of course it's Cynthis. You know as well as I do that she shot the old boy herself, an' you know damned well why she did it. But you don't expect her to admit it, do you? She's got to save her neck if she can, hasn't she? All right. Well, what she says about you is one thing an' what they can prove is another. They've got to *prove* murder in this country.'

Callaghan smiled at Bellamy.

'D'you ever read poetry?' he asked. 'Have you ever read this bit:

'See how she twists an' turns in parlous straits.
"Finger your neck, sweet, the urgent hangman waits."

'I read that in an old poetry book once,' continued Callaghan. 'Well, I'll bet she's fingerin' her neck now, an' she don't like the feel even of her own fingers. An' they're softer than a rope, I'll bet.'

He pushed away the drink that Bellamy had poured out for him.

'All you have to do is to take it easy,' he said cheerfully. 'Just stick to your story. You've got a cast-iron alibi.'

Bellamy gulped down his brandy, nodded uneasily. The quartet on the platform, galvanized into a show of life by a raised eyebrow from Margualez the manager, began a tango that consisted mainly of a thin wailing on a Hawaiian steel guitar worked by the Mile End *maestro*. People got up and began to gyrate about the room. In the opposite corner a gentleman endeavoured to embrace his lady friend and was hit over the head with a handbag for his pains. Farther down the room another lady, her past brought poignantly before her by the appeal in the music, began to cry bitterly and most effectively for the benefit of the young-looking man in the tuxedo, who looked American and also as if he might, after a few more drinks, fall for a really good 'I was a good girl once' story.

Bellamy poured out another drink. From upstairs, from the direction of the passage, came the sound of really masculine voices, the tread of heavier feet. Callaghan, his eyes riveted on the angle of the stairway where it met the floor above, saw two large boots and a pair of blue trousers. He got up.

'I'll be back in a minute,' he said.

He walked quickly across the floor, turned into the top of the room, walked across to the hangings. He slipped through them and through the half-opened door behind as the police came down.

He stopped and peeped through the folds of the smelly silk

curtains. There were Gringall and two C.I.D. men, a couple of plain-clothes men who looked as if they'd come from Vine Street, and a Squad driver in uniform, standing in the middle of the dance floor.

Margualez was spreading his arms and expostulating.

'All right, all right,' Gringall was saying. 'There's no need to get excited. Perhaps this *is* a bottle party in the legal sense of the word, although where you got your music and dancing licence from I don't know. Maybe Vine Street'll want to know about that some time, after which you'll probably be a broken bottle party! In the meantime I want a few words with this gentleman.'

He walked over to Bellamy and looked down at him.

Bellamy finished his drink. Callaghan could hear the glass clicking against his teeth. Then he got to his feet unsteadily. He looked at the detective-inspector. He was almost crying.

'You're Bellamy Meraulton, aren't you?' said Gringall quietly. 'I'm a police officer. I'm arresting you on a charge of being in unlawful possession of drugs. There's no need to get excited, sir. Just come along quietly.'

Callaghan grinned. He closed the door softly, fumbled his way along the passage, found the door to the stairs leading to the street, walked quietly up and out into Viners Passage. He lit a cigarette and then made his way round the corner, past the two Squad cars. On the other side of the street was Jengel, leaning up against the wall.

Callaghan went over.

'What did I tell you?' he said. 'They've just pinched Bellamy on a narcotic charge. They'll hold him an' oppose bail till they've got what they want on the murder charge. The inquest on August Meraulton will be adjourned until Gringall gets his evidence against Bellamy complete.'

'Is that the lot, Slim?' asked Jengel.

'That's the lot,' said Callaghan. 'So long, Jengel.'

He walked twenty yards down the street, then crossed it, found the dark doorway and went in. There was a light on the stairs. Callaghan went up to the first floor and pushed open the door.

The room was a well-furnished office. In the opposite corner, set diagonally, facing the door was a large light oak desk. Behind it, smoking a cigarette and checking bills, sat Arnault Beldoces.

Beldoces was a large and handsome man. His shoulders were broad and his hair black, curly and oiled. His face was round and his big brown eyes gazed straightly on a world that he regarded with suspicious approval.

His black moustache was curled with hot irons every day, and his well-shaven face was slightly olive beneath the barber's talcum.

His clothes were beautifully cut. His shirt silk. His ties, from the Burlington Arcade, cost a guinea each.

'Hallo, Sleem,' he said easily. 'What happens? It is not often that I see you in zese days. You want somezing?'

Callaghan shut the door and walked across the room. He stood in front of the desk.

'Look, Beldoces,' he said, 'I know you an' you know me. You're a feller I don't like very much, an' I don't suppose you're very fond of me. All right. Well, Scotland Yard's just put the finger on your Green Signal dump. Whether it's a raid or whether they're just pickin' up somebody they want I don't know.'

Beldoces shrugged.

'My friend,' he said, 'these zings 'appen. Me, I am a philosopher. Everyzing comes right eef you wait and keep yourself calm. Joost anuzzer leetle fine.'

'Maybe you're right,' said Callaghan. 'Well, you can keep calm now an' answer a couple of questions. You can answer 'em quick an' you can tell the truth for once in your lousy life.

'I rang through to Eulalie Gallicot today. I know she's your wife, an' it's a pity that mug Bellamy didn't. All right. Well, I telephoned through to her because I knew that if she was tied up with you she'd get through an' ask you what she was to do.

'Well, she did, didn't she? An' I've got an idea in the back of my head that you tipped her off to tell me an' anybody else that Bellamy Meraulton didn't get round to her place until twelve or just after, whereas the truth is that he got there about eleven-ten or eleven-fifteen.

'Now, that's not worryin' me particularly. As a matter of fact, her sayin' that suits me down to the ground, an' I reckon she'll be sayin' it right now to some C.I.D. boy that Gringall's sent round there.

'But the thing I want to make certain of is whether it was you put her up to it or not. Well?'

Beldoces laughed.

'Sleem,' he said, 'you know me. I do not answer that sort of question. I jus' say nothing. Not one word!'

He laughed again, spread his hands gracefully.

Callaghan projected himself across the desk like a streak of lightning. His right arm, drawn back, connected with a thud against Beldoces' jaw. Almost immediately his left hand, held open and straight, after the manner of a judo expert, slashed across the heavy face in front of him, under the nose, sending a stream of blood down over the silk shirt and collar.

Callaghan, lying across the desk, brought his left elbow after the hand, smashing with the crook of it against the fat neck and jaw in front of him.

Beldoces went over sideways in his chair. Callaghan shot over on top of him. Beldoces, with an effort of his huge shoulders, threw the other off, stretched back his neck, got up. He turned, snarling, and faced Callaghan.

Callaghan stepped back, extended himself, up on his toes, feinted that he was going in with a head punch. Beldoces threw his left hand up to catch it, struck out blindly with his right. Callaghan side-stepped to the right, caught the wild punch with his left, stepped in with a double 'Carpentier' punch on Beldoces' jaw that wasn't good enough because there wasn't enough weight behind it, sensed the fact, brought his elbow up and over after it and smashed the point of it into his opponent's eye. Beldoces' head went back. Simultaneously Callaghan dropped his head and smashed it into the fat stomach in front of him.

Beldoces went down with a wheezy gasp.

Callaghan went on top of him, straddling him, kneeling on his bicep muscles, sticking the knee point on the muscle joint, rolling with his legs until Beldoces began to sweat with pain.

'Listen, you greasy louse,' said Callaghan softly. 'You're goin' to talk, an' you're goin' to talk quick. You answer yes or no, or I'm goin' to work the nose trick on you. Now, then, was it you who put Eulalie up to ditchin' Bellamy over that alibi at her flat? Come on, yes or no!'

Beldoces said nothing. He was in agony. A whimper escaped from his tightened lips.

Callaghan put his thumb squarely on Beldoces' nose and pushed, pushed until the nose was flat. A scream broke from the foreigner. He twisted and wriggled under the torturing thumb.

'I tell you,' he gasped, 'I tell you. Yes. I tell 'er to do eet. I tell 'er!'

Callaghan removed his thumb.

'Good,' he said. 'Now you tell me somethin' else.'

He stopped talking, cocked his head ... listened. Then he jumped backwards away from Beldoces, spun towards the door, became casual, felt for his cigarettes.

The door opened. Gringall came in. Beldoces, bleeding, his nose the colour of a piece of raw steak, got to his feet, staggered to an arm-chair.

'Good-evening, Slim,' said Gringall. 'Been having a little chat with the proprietor?'

Callaghan grinned.

'Yes,' he said. 'We were just talking ...'

He moved over to the door.

Gringall looked at Beldoces and then at Callaghan as the latter put his hand on the doorhandle.

'And you're the fellow who was talking about third degree,' he said.

Callaghan could see that his mouth was twitching.

'Well, good-night, Slim.'

'Good-night, Gringall,' said Callaghan.

He closed the door behind him, stood listening. He heard Gringall begin to talk.

'I've just been looking in at the Green Signal,' said Gringall. 'I've taken Bellamy Meraulton on a drugs charge - unlawful possession - and I want to know if you know where's he's been getting the stuff ...'

Callaghan walked quietly down the stairs.

CHAPTER EIGHT

What the Eye Doesn't See!

A gleam of winter sunshine came through the drawn curtains of Callaghan's room in the Axford Private Hotel, and, lighting squarely on his face, awakened him.

He rubbed his eyes and sat up. Then he rang for some tea, and while he was drinking it allowed his mind to dwell on the present situation of things in the Meraulton murder case.

Whatever he was going to do had to be done quickly. Gringall was not going to be the mug for very long. Faced with Bellamy's denials of knowledge of the grey homburg hat, or how it even got into the flat at Pointers Mews, Gringall was going to find out where that hat came from. It would take him perhaps two days to trace it, after which the knowledge that Callaghan had gone, within a short time of its purchase, to see Bellamy, would tell Gringall all he wanted to know.

He would know that Callaghan had planted the hat on Bellamy. He would know that he, Gringall, had been pushed into bringing the 'unlawful possession of drugs' charge against Bellamy, merely as a pretext for holding him, by Callaghan. He would know that Callaghan had deliberately pulled a red herring across the path of the forces of law and order, and he would promptly come to the conclusion that Callaghan had not only faked the alibi for Cynthis Meraulton, but was going to the most extreme lengths to keep her out of the case.

She would be more suspect than ever.

Gringall would go out to find Cynthis Meraulton with every possible assistance that he could get from anywhere. He would flood the press with her photographs, advise every hall porter, night porter, railway porter and every other possible source of information to look out for her.

Cynthis Meraulton would see the papers, know that Callaghan had led her up the garden path, dislike him even more than she had in the first place, and would probably take a walk round to Scotland Yard merely for the purpose of inviting inquiry and proving that she was *not* running away. A very pretty little situation, thought Callaghan, with a yawn.

Well, he thought, he had two days ... possibly three ... certainly two. And there was another factor to be reckoned with, and that factor was Bellamy.

Bellamy would first of all be frightened. When he found that the drugs charge was merely a 'front' put up in order to hold him as a suspect for the murder, he would be furious. He would probably begin to talk. He would tell Gringall that he had himself seen Cynthis in Lincoln's Inn Fields. True, this would constitute an admission that he had been in Lincoln's Inn Fields himself, but he would rely on his alibi with Eulalie. Eulalie would let him down over that, and Gringall would find himself wondering which of the two - Cynthis or Bellamy - had killed August Meraulton.

He might even lead himself to believe that they'd both done it!

Callaghan got himself out of bed and sat in an arm-chair admiring his new blue silk pyjamas. He rumpled his thick black hair and pondered on the difficulties of a policeman's life - especially when it came to proving murder, which must be proved without any reasonable shadow of doubt.

He put on his dressing-gown, took himself to the bathroom, bathed, shaved and returned. He fumbled in his clothes and produced the money he had collected up to date.

Out of the original five hundred pounds paid by Cynthis Meraulton on her first visit, there was left two hundred and eighty pounds. In addition to this there was the three hundred pounds he had collected from Willie Meraulton, plus the two hundred that he had got from Bellamy the night before - seven hundred and eighty pounds. Callaghan thought that he hadn't enough for what he wanted to do, that he'd have to get some more from somewhere.

He had already considered this possibility and had some ideas as to where it might come from, but he thought that the process of getting it was going to be remarkably tough.

He went carefully through the banknotes, checking on the numbers, putting them in his little black notebook.

Then he dressed, and his mind went to Cynthis Meraulton's maid. He wondered just how smart or otherwise this young woman was. He imagined that the police had already been on to her at her mistress's Victoria Street flat, asking her where Cynthis was, and generally finding out anything that was going. Callaghan grinned to himself, knowing that the girl couldn't give any information, because she didn't know anything.

All the same, he thought, he would wander round and see her.

But he'd got to work fast, because once Gringall was wise to his game in throwing suspicion on Bellamy he'd be after him. There were two or three different charges that Gringall could get him on. There was a very nice old-fashioned one (from the 1896 Act) – 'perverting the true course of justice' – which would suit Gringall just as well as anything else.

Callaghan visualized himself picking oakum, and grinned a trifle ruefully.

He went down to breakfast.

While he was waiting for it he wandered out into the lounge and into the telephone call-box. He rang through to Revenholt, asked him if he'd got anything yet.

Revenholt laughed into the telephone.

'I've got plenty, Callaghan,' he said. 'You'll say I've earned that other eighty.'

'We'll see about that,' Callaghan answered.

He told Revenholt to come round to the Axford at once.

Revenholt looked at Callaghan across the table. He looked fresh and well turned-out. His eyes were clear and bright. Callaghan found himself wondering why it was that people always looked different to what they were really like inside.

Revenholt produced a sheet of paper.

'It was fearfully easy,' he said, 'and quite interesting.'

He lit the cigarette which Callaghan offered him.

'Three and a half years ago,' he said, 'Paul Meraulton bought no less than four companies which had been originally registered donkeys years ago. That is to say he bought the names of these companies. You know how that's done? A company is registered and does some business and goes broke. It goes into liquidation and is wound up. Well, anybody who likes to come along and pay the Liquidator's fees – which in these cases were very small – can have the assets of the company and revive it. The assets of the company usually consist of a few bad debts and the title of the company.

'Well, this is what Paul did: For the sum of about one hundred and twenty pounds he bought four old companies which had gone into liquidation and been wound up for years. Here are their names.'

Revenholt pushed the slip across the table. Callaghan read:

The Connecticut Export and Trading Co. Ltd., The Freshwater and Ilworth Trust Co. Ltd., The Endeavour Coal Finance Syndicate Ltd., The Greater Atlantic Bond Co. Ltd.

'Paul Meraulton bought the first two companies early in 1934, and the last two at the end of the same year,' Revenholt went on. 'I thought you'd like to know who the directors and shareholders in these companies are, so I did a little more searching. Here is what I found:

'In each and every case Paul Meraulton is the managing director, and the only other shareholders – who are also directors – are Bellamy, Percival and Jeremy Meraulton. The registered address of the four companies is 22 Greeneagle Street, Russel Square, which consists of a third floor office, containing a desk, a telephone and a few books. Paul Meraulton goes there about once a fortnight and stays for an hour – to see if there is any correspondence, I suppose.'

Revenholt gave himself another cigarette.

'Is that what you wanted?' he asked airily.

Callaghan grinned.

'That suits me very well,' he said. 'Nice work, Revenholt.' He got up. 'There's just one other little thing you can do for me,' he said, 'an' then you can go an' see Darkie an' collect the eighty-pound balance that's comin' to you. Here's the thing: Jeremy Meraulton has got a girl – a Spanish-American girl, they tell me. Now I want to know where this woman is. Maybe she's with Jeremy at that place he's got on this side of Oxford – the Show Down, they call it – but maybe she's not there all the time. Perhaps she comes up to town to do a little shoppin'; maybe she stays up here for a day or so sometimes. Find out. I want to get that girl when she's on her own. I want to have a little talk with her on the q.t. D'you think you could find that out for me?'

Revenholt nodded.

'That shouldn't be difficult,' he said. 'I can contact somebody who'll know someone employed at the Show Down, and they'd be able to tell me. Or,' he added darkly, 'there are other ways.'

'All right,' said Callaghan. 'You find out, an' if you can find out by this afternoon, you telephone through to my office in Chancery Lane at four o'clock. If I'm there I'll talk to you, an' if not an' you've got some address where I can get at this Mayola Ferrival – that's her name – you tell Fred Mazin, who's keepin' an eye on things at the office, to make a note of it an' let me know when I contact him. Got that? An' directly you've put the address through, you can touch Darkie for that eighty. All right?'

'That's excellent,' said Revenholt. 'I'll get it as soon as I can – for my own sake, if not for yours.'

He shot one of those flashing smiles – all teeth and good humour – which had temporarily deluded more than a few discontented women, took his hat and went off.

Callaghan stood looking after him, smiling.

Callaghan sat in the lounge of the Axford Hotel until twelve o'clock thinking, smoking cigarettes and drinking coffee. Then he packed his bag, paid his bill, took a taxi to Victoria Station and left his suitcase in the luggage-room.

He wandered down Victoria Street slowly, walking on the side of the street opposite Greenford Mansions, where Cynthis Meraulton had her flat. When he arrived in the vicinity of the flat he stood in the crowd at the bus stop, watching the building, seeing if there was anyone who looked like a plain-clothes man hanging about. Then, satisfied, he walked over, went up to the first floor and rang the bell.

He liked the look of the girl who answered the door. She was about twenty-two years of age, a red-head with the clear skin that usually goes with that colouring. She had frank eyes and a humorous mouth. She looked a trifle worried.

'Good-mornin',' said Callaghan. 'Are you Miss Meraulton's maid?'

She nodded.

'But she's not here,' she said, 'and I don't know ...'

Callaghan stopped her with a grin.

'I know you don't, he said. 'My name's Callaghan. I'm a member of the firm of solicitors who act for Miss Meraulton, an' I want to talk to you.'

She stood aside.

'Please come in, sir,' she said.

He went in, crossed the hall and went through the door which the maid held open. Inside he turned and faced her. His face shone with benevolence, honesty, friendship and what-will you.

'What's your name?' he asked.

'Jenny Appleby,' she said.

She stood waiting.

'Listen, Jenny,' said Callaghan quietly. 'You read the papers, don't you? All right – well, you know what's happened, and you know that Miss Meraulton has gone away, although you don't know where she's gone to.'

He lit a cigarette and smiled at Jenny, who was awaiting further information with her mouth open. He sensed that she was the sort of girl who would be thrilled by a good movie, that she had a sense of the dramatic.

He dropped his voice.

'My firm – I – am out to protect Miss Meraulton, Jenny,' he said. 'And we know who are her friends and who are her enemies. We know that you are one of her friends.'

'I'd do anything for Miss Cynthis,' said Jenny. 'She's the best friend I ever had. She ...'

'I know,' said Callaghan wisely. 'I know all about it. She's told me all about you,' he went on, lying with his usual smoothness.

He sat down and indicated that she should do likewise. Jenny sat as near the edge of her chair as she could without slipping off.

'I expect you've had some callers, haven't you, Jenny?' asked Callaghan winsomely. 'I expect Mr Gringall from Scotland Yard's been round here, hasn't he? He told me he was going to come round and have a little talk with you.'

She nodded.

'He was round here last night,' she said. 'He asked me if I knew where Miss Cynthis was. He asked me about her going away and if I knew where she'd gone to. I said I didn't and that anyhow if Miss Cynthis had wanted me to tell people where she was going to she'd have told me herself.'

She tossed her red head.

'Good girl,' said Callaghan. 'What else did he ask?'

'He asked me some funny things,' said the girl. 'He asked me if I knew whether Miss Cynthis had a pistol. I told him she had, that she'd had one for years – one that her father used in the War. But I said that it was only a little one.'

Callaghan nodded. That wasn't so good, he thought. August Meraulton had been killed with a 'little' pistol – a .22.

'I could see what he was getting at,' Jenny went on, 'so I told him something else. I told him that Miss Cynthis hadn't any ammunition for it, that it was just a relic of the War.' She paused. 'I didn't know then that she *had* got ammunition for it. I didn't know there were any bullets in the place until this morning when Mr Willie came and took them away.'

'Ah,' said Callaghan smiling. 'That was just the sort of nice thing that Mr Willie would do, isn't it?'

He lit another cigarette.

'Tell me about Mr Willie coming round and taking the bullets away,' he said. 'Do you think that there was a chance that anyone saw him coming here?'

She shook her head.

'He came in by the tradesmen's entrance,' she said. 'He asked if anyone had been round. I told him about Mr Gringall, and he looked terribly worried. When I told him about telling Mr Gringall about the pistol and that I'd said that there wasn't any ammunition, he said, "Thank God" - just like that. He asked right away if he could go into Miss Meraulton's room for a moment. I said of course he could, and he went in and went straight to the drawer - the bottom drawer where the pistol was kept - and turned out the things that were in it - Miss Cynthis used to keep a lot of old trinkets and boxes there - and after a minute he found it. There was a box of bullets - a little square box.'

Jenny dropped her voice.

'Mr Willie put the box in his pocket,' he said, 'and told me to forget that he'd ever taken it away. He said that I wasn't to tell any one except you; he said that if you came round and asked me what had happened I was to tell you about Mr Gringall coming here and about the box of bullets and that he'd taken them.'

Callaghan nodded.

'You're a fine girl, Jenny,' he said. 'Now *I* want to ask a favour. There's nothing like making absolutely certain. Can I go and take a look in that drawer, too?'

'Why, of course, sir,' she said. 'It'll be all right for *you* to look.'

She led the way to the bedroom.

Callaghan turned out the drawer. It was filled with trinket boxes, lengths of material and brocades, old gloves, the hundred-and-one things that a woman keeps without quite knowing why.

Callaghan was methodical. He took every box out of the drawer, every piece of material, every glove. He turned everything inside out, examined every box.

Then he looked at Jenny with a grin. Shaking a length of crepe de chine, something fell out. He held it out to her. It was a .22 bullet.

'You can't be too careful,' he said. 'Cartridges always fall out of the silly cardboard boxes they pack them in, because they're heavy, an' when the box gets turned upside down one or more come out. Give me a hand, Jenny. I'm goin' through all these drawers.'

They searched the chest of drawers, the dressing-table drawers, everywhere. There were no more bullets.

Callaghan put the bullet in his pocket.

'Tell me something, Jenny,' he said. 'Do you ever remember either Mr Paul, Mr Percival, Mr Jeremy or Mr Bellamy coming into this room – being in here alone?'

She thought for a moment.

'Yes, I do,' she said. 'It was about three months ago. Mr Jeremy came here to see Miss Cynthis, but she was out. He said he'd wait for her to come back. I was busy in the kitchen pressing a frock and he put his head in and asked if he might look around the flat, said he admired it. I said of course he might. He came in here, and he was here for some time.'

Callaghan smiled.

'That's fine,' he said. 'Well, Jenny, you've been a real friend. Miss Cynthis will thank you for all this one day. Now all you have to remember is to forget that I ever came here or that Mr Willie came here either.'

He picked up his hat.

'Don't you worry,' he said. 'Everything is goin' to be marvellous, an' in the meantime I think I'll be wise, too, an' go out by the tradesmen's entrance as well. *Au revoir*, Jenny. We'll be meeting again.'

He followed the girl to the back of the flat, and went down in the hand-worked tradesmen's lift. Outside he took a quick look round, but there was no one in the street. He tipped his hat slightly over his left eye – a sure sign of satisfaction – and strolled in the direction of Victoria Station.

At the station he went into a telephone box. He rang through to the Meraulton Estates Office, asked for Willie. He gave his name and waited.

Willie came on the line. His voice sounded tired. He spoke slowly.

'Mr Meraulton,' said Callaghan softly, 'I just wanted to tell you that that was a fine bit of work you did at the flat at you-know-where – takin' that little box away, I mean. I thought of the same thing myself an' went there this mornin'. It might mean something to you, an' then again it mightn't, when I tell you that the girl around there told me that some two-three months ago Jeremy was in that room – alone. Understand?'

'I understand, Callaghan,' said Willie. 'Thanks for ringing up. How is everything and everybody?'

'*Everybody's* fine,' Callaghan answered. 'I was with everybody last night, and she understands perfectly that the thing for her to do is not to try and get in touch with you – or anybody else in the family. Just so's there shouldn't be any slip-up about that, I took the liberty of tellin' her that you'd be in Edinburgh for a few days. I said I'd be talkin' to you an' try an' get your telephone number, but I don't think I'll even do that.'

He extracted a cigarette from his case with one hand.

'In fact, Mr Meraulton,' he said, 'I've got hopes about this case. I've got hopes that I may sort of stumble on something or other within the next forty-eight hours or so, something that will pin this thing down. Anyhow I'll keep in touch with you from time to time, an' if by chance you shouldn't hear from me, don't worry. I may have to go out of town for a day or so.'

He lit the cigarette.

'There's just one thing that's worryin' me a bit, Mr Meraulton,' he said. 'I tell you quite frankly I'm still worryin' about Cynthis. There may be a pretty strong *circumstantial* case againt her in a day or so, an' even circumstantial evidence has to be reckoned with in these days.'

He took a long puff at his cigarette and inhaled.

'Why didn't she come an' see me when you first told her to,' he said, 'which would have been about eight days ago, long before any of this business got goin'? Why didn't she do it? Hadn't she got any money?'

'That wasn't the reason,' said Willie. 'I don't know why she didn't do as I asked. It couldn't have been the money, because she knew perfectly well that you'd need money before taking the job on, and she also knew that she was to get the money from me. It was here for her whenever she wanted it.'

'Silly girl,' muttered Callaghan.

'Silly girl is right,' Willie went on. 'I pestered her every day to go and see you, said I would take her myself if she would only make a definite time, but something or other turned up each day to prevent her - you know what women are. Also, I don't think she was looking forward to the interview very much.'

Callaghan laughed.

'I *know* she wasn't,' he said. 'I don't think she liked me at all. Anyhow it was lucky you got her to come when you did. That was better than not comin' at all. At least we've been able to do *something*.'

'That's as may be,' said Willie, 'but if she'd come when I asked her to in the first place all this business wouldn't have happened. She only came when she did because I insisted.'

Callaghan exhaled, filling the telephone box with smoke.

'Never mind,' he said. 'Better late than never.'

His voice became a little more friendly.

'I'm damn sorry for you, Mr Meraulton,' he said. 'But you keep your pecker up. Somehow or other we'll keep the flag flyin' an' one day all this business will just be a memory. So long, sir.'

He hung up and threw the cigarette stub away.

Then he walked over to Stewart's Restaurant and ordered a double portion of lamb chops with mint sauce. The chops to be very well done.

Life could be worse, he thought.

It was two-thirty.

Callaghan came out of Stewart's Restaurant and walked across to the station. He went into a telephone call-box and rang Scotland Yard. He gave his name and asked for Detective-Inspector Gringall.

Gringall came on the line.

'Hallo, Slim,' he said cheerfully. 'That was a nice job of work you did on Beldoces the other night. I didn't know you could hit as hard as that!'

Callaghan grinned.

'Oh, that isn't anythin',' he said. 'I was tryin' to get some information in a blackmail case I've got, an' that fat slob got funny, so I socked him.'

Gringall grunted. He sounded dubious.

'I rang up because I may have to go off for a day or so,' said Callaghan. 'An' I didn't want you to think that I was running away or holdin' out on you or anythin'.'

Gringall laughed.

'I wouldn't think that about you, Slim,' he said. 'Oh, no!' His tone was sarcastic. 'By the way,' he went on, 'Bellamy Meraulton's telling all sorts of fairy stories about you.'

'Really,' said Callaghan airily. 'Such as ...?'

'Such as you took him for two hundred pounds. Absolute blackmail, he called it, and that you told him that you believed Cynthis Meraulton killed the old boy, and a lot of other stuff like that.'

Callaghan laughed.

'Bellamy's an awful liar,' he said. 'But then, these dopes always are, aren't they, Gringall?'

'Possibly,' Gringall replied.

He changed his tone.

'I'm trying to trace that hat we found in Bellamy's place,' he said. 'You knew I'd look for that hat, didn't you? Well, I'm doubtful if August Meraulton ever bought or wore that hat we found at Bellamy's place. I'm having its sale traced. I shall know tomorrow or the next day. Unfortunately it's a rather common type of hat, and there's no maker's name on the inside band.'

Gringall paused for a moment and coughed.

'If by any chance we find that someone else bought that hat and planted it on Bellamy, if we do find that, then I should like to have a word with you, Slim.' His voice hardened. 'So I take it you'll be in town in, say, two days' time.'

'Definitely,' said Callaghan. 'Although what the hat an' where it came from has got to do with me I *don't* know. However,' he went on, 'I'll tell you what I'll do: I reckon I'll be droppin' in to see you in about two days' time anyhow. I reckon I'll want to talk to you then.'

'All right,' said Gringall. 'The only thing is, I wonder if I'll want to talk to you.'

Callaghan laughed into the transmitter.

'I'll promise you one thing, Gringall,' he said. 'When I want to talk to you, you'll listen. By heck you will – and like it!'

He hung up the receiver.

Outside he took a taxi and drove to his office in Chancery Lane. Fred Mazin was half asleep over a racing form book in the outer office.

Callaghan went into his own room, took off his hat, put his feet on the desk and prayed that Revenholt would come through.

He wondered what he would do if Revenholt didn't come through.

He thought about this for some moments. Then he removed his

feet from the desk top, unlocked a drawer in his desk and took out a well-kept Luger pistol. It was fully loaded. Callaghan inspected it, put it in his hip pocket, thought again, took it out and looked at it.

'I'm always givin' it,' he muttered to himself, 'to somebody or other. Maybe one of these fine days I'll have to take it.'

He put his pistol back in the drawer and locked it.

'An' if you've got to take it, you've got to take it,' he concluded.

He put his feet back on the desk as the telephone rang.

CHAPTER NINE

The Lady Friend

It was Revenholt. His voice came casually through the telephone in answer to Callaghan's hallo.

'You're in luck, Callaghan,' he said, 'and so am I. If you want the Ferrival woman very badly you can get her tonight.'

Callaghan said: 'When an' where?'

'I'll tell you,' Revenholt went on. 'After I left you this morning I did some quiet thinking, and I remembered a man – he's in service with some friends of mine – who'd once put a relative, who had a weakness for flipping the pasteboards and losing the family shekels on the green cloth, on to this 'Show Down' place. It's about seven miles on the other side of High Wycombe.

'I went round and had a word with my butler friend, and he was able then and there to get through to *his* friend, who acts as a sort of unofficial maître d'hotel at the Show Down, and get a few points – quite in confidence, of course – on the beautiful Mayola.

'She knows all the answers, apparently; she's as hard as nails. She acts as hostess down at the Show Down and occasionally introduces visitors with heavy pocket-books down there. Sometimes she goes in for a little high-class blackmail for a change. Her method is to find some old boy who's feeling a little playful and lead him up the garden path. Apparently she has rather a way with old gentlemen. And she always takes care that some one else knows all about it, some one, that is, who – just as the old gentleman is beginning to get tired of things – intimates that it would be useful for him to come across with a few hundreds, otherwise his wife might like to hear a few amusing little stories as to what he's been at.

'The old boy usually pays up. They never ask too much money, and it's usually worth while to pay.

'That's Mayola's side-line. There's no doubt she runs it in conjunction with Jeremy. Apparently she's pretty fond of Jeremy, that is as much as a you-know-what like her can be fond of anybody. She's also pretty good at singing a hot number. She does a turn sometimes at the Show Down just to liven things up a bit, and she also does one now and again on an extension night at one of the London night joints. She's doing one tonight. I'll come to that in a minute.

'Jeremy's a tough proposition. Apparently he was kicked out of the Army (His Majesty having no further use for his services) for having a too unique system of shuffling cards when playing poker. He then got a job over in Buenos Aires being secretary to a rather mysterious sports club that used to do a little dope running. He was nearly jailed there on two occasions, and only got out of a very nasty jam because he's very quick on the uptake. Apparently Jeremy doesn't like any of his brothers very much, but he has a certain respect for Willie. Jeremy has no delusions about himself. He knows he's no good and rather likes the idea, and he thinks, apparently, that Paul, Bellamy and Percival are as bad, but *don't* know it. He despises them for that.

'He thinks Willie is the only male member of the family who's got brains enough to be honest, and he rather envies him for that virtue.

'But remember what I told you about his being tough. It seems as if he'll stop at nothing when he gets going.'

Callaghan grunted.

'That's fine,' he said. 'Now where do I contact Mayola?'

'She's in town tonight,' said Revenholt. 'There's an extension at the Noughts and Crosses Club – just off Cork Street – and she's singing there. She'll do her turn about midnight, and when she's done it she drives herself back to the Show Down. Sometimes she takes one or two mug gamblers with her and sometimes not.'

He coughed diffidently.

'Now,' he went on, 'do I touch for that eighty?'

'Yes,' said Callaghan, 'you do. I'll telephone Darkie to send it along to your address by express messenger. You'll get it this evening.'

'Thanks a lot,' said Revenholt. 'I can do with it. Is there anything else I can do? I'm as keen as mustard to turn over a few honest pennies.'

Callaghan thought for a moment.

'I don't think so, Revenholt,' he said. 'Thanks all the same. I think I'm through with you.'

'Righty-ho,' said Revenholt. 'Then it only remains for me to collect my eighty and take a trip across the Channel and see what I can do to 'em at Monte. Perhaps I can win myself a thousand!'

'Maybe,' said Callaghan. 'That, or a thick ear!'

He hung up.

He sat for a few moments looking at the telephone; then he got up and walked into the outer office.

'Fred,' he said, 'walk round to the corner to the tea an' coffee shop. Go in an' buy something – some cigarettes – anything – and grab a couple of those sheets of rough paper they use for wrapping things up in. Bring 'em back here.'

Fred nodded. Callaghan went back to his own room and telephoned through to Darkie, told him to send the eighty pounds to Revenholt.

Five minutes later Fred Mazin came back with the paper. It was rough white stuff commonly used for wrapping foodstuffs in.

Callaghan folded one of the sheets and tore it into four, making it the size of an ordinary sheet of writing paper. Then he placed a sheet of carbon paper on top of it, and two sheets of ordinary typing paper over that. He placed these in the typewriter, typing through the two sheets of paper, through the carbon paper on to the wrapping paper. He wrote:

Somewhere in London.

Dear Mr Calligan,

I have herd that you are working for Belamy Meraulton. If you are you might be interrested in knowing about the man that the Yard are asking after. I mean the man who was seen near the morterary on the night of the murder. In case you do not alreddy guess I will tell you that this is the man who took the will out of old Merault on's watch-case. Now you know as well as I do that all the Merault on boys know that this will does them all out of getting any money at all, but if this will was to get lost they would still get there dough under the first will. Well I am the one who has got that will and if you like to cash in with five hundred of the best I will hand it over to you and they can burn it or do what they damn well like with it. If that will is found they wont get a sou. If you like to get the five hundred nicker you can get hold of me by showing this letter to Willie the Lug down at Tom Peppers place and he will tell you where you can find me. And I'm not even asking you to keep your mouth shut about this becos praps I know as much about you as I want to.

Ta ta Slimmy boy,

Sammy the Shiek

P.S. If I don't get that five hundred nicker in three days I'm going to send the will to Gazeling the solicitor so the boys had better cash in quick.

Callaghan perused this missive, folded the paper two or three times and then searched in the wastepaper basket for an envelope addressed to himself that had arrived that morning bearing a bill. This envelope, after the manner of its kind, was cheap and unsealed.

He inserted the note he had just written, stuck down the flap of the envelope and then slit it along the top, opening it in the ordinary way.

He now scrutinized his handiwork which bore the appearance of a letter, complete in envelope, addressed to himself.

It was half-past eleven.

Callaghan, who was sitting at one of the small tables at the end of the dance floor at the Noughts and Crosses Club, lit another cigarette.

Before him were the remains of an excellent supper.

On the floor, dancing to the soft and 'hot' music of a band of six, were all those very tired and disinterested people who go to the Noughts and Crosses, and who, having got themselves there, seem to spend most of the time wondering why they *are* there and gazing vacantly about in the hope that something will happen to give them a moment's escape from the boredom in which they seem to have been born and lived.

Callaghan, stubbing out his cigarette, lighting another, drinking the whisky and soda before him, then ordering another, did all these things mechanically.

His mind was concentrated on the ramifications of the Meraulton Murder Case; on his own position in it; on Gringall and the ideas that would be forming slowly and surely in Gringall's head; on Cynthis Meraulton and the trouble that might ensue from that direction within the next twelve hours, on Mayola Ferrival and on Jeremy Meraulton.

Percival didn't matter. Percival was just a stooge; just a shadow of Bellamy; the complete and absolute 'yes man' to Bellamy; hanging around on the chance of getting his drinks paid for, without sufficient backbone or mentality to be dangerous to anyone except himself.

Now the dance floor was clear, the band silent. From the tables about that of the private detective came the soft chatter, representative of the minds of the talkers, that can be heard in most dance clubs that specialize for people who have money and who believe that late hours are necessary for a good time . . .

'. . . I said to him, "Don't be a damned fool," I said. But you know, Vicky, once he's made up his mind that he's going after a girl, well, he goes after her and he doesn't mean maybe, either . . .' Then a woman's voice: '. . . He's got to marry her. I don't care what he says or does, he's just got to. If he doesn't there'll be trouble . . .' A man's: '. . . Of course the jolly old cheque bounced back, old boy. Scriven's cheques have always been made of rubber, an' any money-lender who's mug enough to take his bill is just askin' for trouble ...'

Callaghan, listening vaguely, permitted himself to think that the Noughts and Crosses Club might make a good stamping ground for him and his business. There ought to be 'cases' for him in the Noughts and Crosses Club. The people who belonged to it were the sort of people who had money, who got into mischief.

Suddenly, and for no apparent reason, Callaghan found himself thinking that he was rather bored with people who had too much money, who got into mischief. He wondered if he were feeling out of sorts. It wasn't like him to feel like that. He had not come to realize that it was the Meraulton case, his own connection with the Meraulton case, everything connected with the Meraulton case that was slowly but surely bringing to his mind a clearer realization of just how *he* stood in regard to the world at large; just what the world at large would think of *him*.

He smiled, stubbed out his fifth cigarette in the last half-hour and ordered another drink.

The orchestra broke into a 'chord on,' the leader, small-moustached, slim-waisted, looking as nearly as possible like the film star of the moment, advanced to the edge of the band platform.

'Ladies and gentlemen,' he said. 'It is my pleasure to present to you a star from Paris, Beunos Aires and New York. A lady who can put over a hot number that's just nobody's business. Ladies and gentlemen – Mayola Ferrival – the Argentine Nightingale!'

The band crashed into a fuller chord on. The curtains to the right of the band platform drew open. The lights went out and a steel-blue spotlight picked out Mayola as she walked to the centre of the dance floor.

Callaghan looked her over appreciatively. She had lots of eveything, he thought. She was tall and not *too* slim. She was more than attractively curved and every movement spelled sex – and Mayola knew how to move.

Her body, beautifully poised, moved quietly and rhythmically to the beat of the music. The band, taking close time from the exaggerated gestures of their leader, slowly increased the tempo of what had sounded like a blues, but which now began to get hot.

Mayola began to sing. She sang in a soft, vibrant voice that held promise of much reserve of power. She sang a number – a cleverly-written number – whose every word and every line held a double meaning. The innocent expression on her face, marked even more definitely the carefully pointed suggestive vulgarity of her song.

Mayola was good – damn good.

Her gown was black, slit half-way up to the thigh, showing lovely ankles and legs; her body, sinuous now with the quicker music, brought a new light into the eyes of the tired men who watched her, an amused or envious expression into those of the women with them.

Callaghan looked at her face. The clearly cut features, chiselled mouth, well-set ears, expressed character – and strength. Her eyes, dark, glowing, showed a steely glitter that was caught and reflected by the spotlight as she turned this way and that. Her rounded chin curved on each side of her oval face into a clearly defined high jaw-line.

Mayola was tough all right, thought Callaghan. Into his mind came the modernized version of an old song: 'You can always tell a man by his friends – his lady friends!'

He looked round him. Standing near was a waiter who caught his eye. Callaghan signalled, ordered a sheet of notepaper and an envelope. When they were brought he unscrewed his fountain pen and wrote a note:

Dear Miss Ferrival,

It is urgent and important for me to see you immediately. I have information that should interest Mr Jeremy Meraulton a great deal. Perhaps you can spare ten minutes in private.

Yours,

S. Callaghan

He gave the note to the waiter as the lights went up.

She sat looking in the dressing-room mirror, watching Callaghan sitting back in the corner of the room. He knew he was being watched, assessed. He set his face accordingly, fumbled with his hat, sent a quick, admiring glance at the curve of her hips as she leaned forward.

She turned round on her stool, smiled.

'Well,' she said easily, 'what is it, Mr Callaghan?'

She looked at him, still smiling.

'What is it that is so important to Mr Jeremy Meraulton?'

Callaghan thought that her voice was as good as the rest of her. She spoke English almost perfectly, with the merest trace of a foreign accent, a trace that lent added charm.

He put his hat on the floor beside him, folded his fingers.

'I'm in a bit of a jam, Miss Ferrival,' he said. 'I don't know whether I'm doin' right or wrong in comin' an' talkin' to you like this, but I thought it would be better to do that than go down an' see Mr Jeremy at the Show Down an' get flung out on my ear for my trouble!'

She laughed.

'So you think it better to take the chance of coming here and getting flung out – as you call it – from the Noughts and Crosses?'

He laughed, too.

'That's one way of putting it,' he said. 'But I wasn't only thinkin' of that. I'd heard that you were a friend of Mr Jeremy's, an' there's one thing I do know, an' that is that sometimes – especially on a job like this – a woman can be a damn sight more intelligent than a man.'

She nodded, picked up a long gold cigarette-case from the dressing-table and took a cigarette, then offered one to him. He took it, lit them both.

'I'm goin' to be quite straight with you, Miss Ferrival,' he said. 'I'm a private detective – Callaghan Investigations is my firm. Well, we've been doin' some work on this Meraulton case, first of all on behalf of Miss Cynthis Meraulton' – he watched her eyes, saw them flicker – 'and afterwards on behalf of Mr Bellamy. We weren't able to be quick enough to prevent Mr Bellamy from bein' taken on that drugs charge, but between you an' me an' the doorpost, I don't think they'll hold him very long, because that drugs charge was just a fake. They suspected him of the murder, an' by tomorrow or the next day they'll know they were wrong – so they'll give him bail on the drugs charge an' let him go.'

She nodded. She took a deep breath of cigarette smoke and allowed it to escape through red, prettily pursed lips.

'I'm not particularly interested in Bellamy,' she said. 'Anything that happens to him means nothing to me. But, tell me, if they don't suspect him, who *do* they suspect?'

He grinned.

'If it's not him it's got to be her,' he said. 'Cynthis, I mean. They know that both she an' Bellamy were in Lincoln's Inn Fields at eleven o'clock. Well, I don't know what time that murder was done, but it's a stone certainty that it was done between half-past ten an' a quarter past eleven. So they reckon that she did it. They've probably got other reasons for thinkin' that, too.'

He finished his cigarette and lit another.

'Cynthis Meraulton came to see me the night that murder was done,' Callaghan went on. 'I suspected her from the start myself, an' I think she did it all right, but private detectives aren't paid to think too much sometimes, Miss Ferrival. All right. Well, I expect you've read the papers an' I expect you've noticed – an' Mr Jeremy will have noticed, too – that the police are tryin' to find a man who was seen in the vicinity of the Ensell Street Mortuary on the night of the murder, after August Meraulton's body was taken there.

'I wondered what the hell somebody would be doin' round at the mortuary, an' I've found out that owin' to some mistake or other the body was left alone for a bit. It's a certainty that this feller – the one they want – took something off the body, an' so they think that he's had something to do with the murder in some way or another, that he was paid by the murderer to do the job. Well, I thought that, too, an' by heck, I was right!'

He felt in the breast pocket of his jacket and produced the letter that he had written to himself a few hours before.

He handed it over to her.

'You read that, Miss Ferrival,' he said, 'an' you'll find that it's signed by some feller callin' himself Sammy the Sheik. Well, I don't know who Sammy the Sheik is, but it looks as if he knows me, an' that I would know him if I knew what his right name was. You read that letter an' you'll know just as much about it as I do.'

She read the letter. She read it through quickly, and then again, slowly. Then she handed the letter back to Callaghan, turned to the mirror again and began to arrange her hair with long white fingers.

'Five hundred pounds is a great deal of money, Mr Callaghan,' she said softly.

'You're right,' he said. 'But it's not a great deal of money when you come to consider that if this Sammy the Sheik does what he says, an' sends that will he's got – the one August Meraulton told the Meraultons about, the one that did them out of every bean – to the solicitors, well, nobody is goin' to get a penny. I reckon that spendin' five hundred pounds in gettin' that will an' destroyin' it would be money well spent – at least I would reckon it was if I was Jeremy Meraulton.'

She nodded into the mirror.

'I'm rather inclined to agree with you, Mr Callaghan,' she said. 'And what about you? Are you doing this just for love, or wouldn't you want some money, too – that is, of course, if Jeremy found he was at all keen on this very interesting proposition?'

Callaghan coughed.

'Well, Miss Ferrival,' he said. 'I looked at it this way. I reckon I'm goin' to get myself into a bit of trouble with the police over this business anyway. You see, I've been a bit too keen on lookin' after Miss Meraulton's interests to be very popular with the police, an'

I reckon that the thing for me to do is to get my hands on a nice little sum an' get out.

'Well, I've got a few hundreds an' I reckoned that if Mr Jeremy was interested in this Sammy the Sheik business we might be able to do a deal like this. Supposin' he was to give me two hundred an' fifty, well, I reckon I could get that will off Sammy the Sheik for that. It's all very well him askin' for five hundred, but he probably expected to be haggled with a bit, an' I think that when he sees two hundred and fifty pounds he'll want to grab the dough while the goin's good an' he'll hand over that will.'

He got up and stubbed his cigarette butt out in the tray on her dressing-table. He looked at her in the mirror. She looked up at the same moment. Their eyes met. Hers were smiling.

'I thought,' Callaghan went on, returning to his chair, 'that if I got the will for two hundred an' fifty an' brought it along to Mr Jeremy so that he could know he was goin' to get his share of the Merault money under the first will that old August made, then I thought that he would probably feel like handin' me the other two hundred an' fifty for myself just so's I could take a little holiday before the Yard start askin' me a lot of questions about Cynthis Merault.'

He stopped speaking, bent down and picked up his hat.

She turned round on the stool and faced him.

'I first met Jeremy Merault in Buenos Aires,' she said. 'He was doing a little business with a Spanish gentleman – a rather fat Spanish gentleman. This Spaniard thought that Jeremy was a fool. He tried to – what do you call it – double-cross. That's the word. He tried to double-cross Jeremy.'

She took another cigarette.

'Jeremy killed him,' she said quietly, looking at Callaghan.

Callaghan looked shocked.

'Quite right, too,' he said. 'I hate double-crossers. They never do anybody any good. Not even themselves.'

She smiled.

'Well, Mr Callaghan,' she said. 'I think that you and your letter, and your unknown friend Sammy the Sheik – charming name that – interest me a great deal. It is possible that Jeremy may be interested, too. I have to sing another number in fifteen minutes time, after which I am driving down to the Show Down. We have a late party there tonight, just a little card playing and some music.'

She got up, stretched herself sinuously.

'Perhaps you'd like to come down with me, Mr Callaghan,' she said. 'I think that possibly you and Jeremy might like to meet and talk a little business. Would you like to do that?'

Callaghan got up. He was smiling.

'That's fine, Miss Ferrival,' he said. 'That's absolutely fine. I'm very glad I came along to see you. I wasn't certain whether I was doin' the right thing, but now I know I was wise.'

'There is a proverb which says he who hesitates is lost,' said Mayola prettily. 'I *never* hesitate. Neither does Jeremy.'

She put out her hand.

'*Adios*, Senor Callaghan,' she said. 'Return for me here at one o'clock please. We will go down together. It is a charming drive. The country roads at night are so quiet and pleasant.'

He took her hand. He thought for a moment that the pressure on his fingers was unduly prolonged.

'I'll be back, Miss Ferrival,' he said, 'at one o'clock. Till then, *adios* – as you said – *Senora.*'

Callaghan went into the telephone call-box at the top of Cork Street. While he was waiting for Darkie to answer he looked at his watch. It was twenty to one.

He could hear Darkie yawning at the other end of the wire.

'Hey, Darkie,' he said. 'Here's a little job for you to case. This feller Paul Meraulton. Well, this one's got some office – a third-floor place near Russell Square – the address is 22 Greeneagle Street. I want you to have a look at that place tomorrow. Find out all about it. If there's a caretaker there, what the outside door-lock's like. If there's a back entrance. Maybe I want to have a look around that office tomorrow night. You got that? All right, well, when you've done that, you find out where Paul Meraulton's livin'. His private address. I'll ring you through some time tomorrow in the late afternoon or the evenin'. You stick around in your place all tomorrow afternoon an' evenin'. Don't you go out. See?'

'Right,' said Darkie. 'How you goin', Guv? You all right?'

'I'm fine,' said Callaghan. 'I reckon in a couple of days I'll be very well indeed - or pinched - or dead. I don't rightly know which. So long Darkie!'

He hung up.

Outside the call-box he flagged a passing taxi and drove to the Vere Street all-night Post Office. He wrote and dispatched a wire to Cynthis Meraulton. He thought she'd have to be kept quiet for a bit:

To the Occupant Flat 14a Delvine Court
Apartments South Kensington
Everything fine and in order arranging
for you to see Willie tomorrow case
practically all over bar the shouting. -
S. Callaghan

This done, he went back to his waiting cab and told the man to drive to the Noughts and Crosses Club. He stopped on the way and bought a ham sandwich at an all-night snack bar.

He got back into the cab with the sandwich, continued on his way, eating the sandwich very slowly so that he should not get indigestion.

CHAPTER TEN

The Show Down

Mayola swung the wheel and the Bentley swerved into the almost hidden driveway between the trees. Callaghan, sitting in the passenger seat beside her, felt a tinge of admiration for the way in which she handled the powerful car. Mayola, he thought, would be pretty good at handling cars, situations - and men.

The driveway was uphill and dark, but she drove surely and fast, swerving here and there to take a bend in the narrow drive or to miss some obstruction that even Callaghan's keen eyes could not distinguish.

She pulled up in an open space bordered by trees at the side of the house. She looked sideways at Callaghan. In the dim light from the dashboard bulb he could see her smiling.

'Here we are, Mr Callaghan,' she said. 'Here is the Show Down, and I hope you'll like it.'

She switched out the lights and got out of the car.

Callaghan got out and stretched. Before him, dark and ghostly, the house, antique and rambling, showed up vaguely against the night sky.

Together they walked towards the side door, their feet crunching on the gravel.

Callaghan, feeling in his pocket for a cigarette, wondered just how far he was from the last act in the Meraulton drama; whether he was to be a part of it; whether Jeremy was going to fall in with the scheme of things or start something else, something that would necessitate more planning, more schemes.

She took a key from the pocket of her fur coat, opened the door and entered. As Callaghan stepped in beside her she shut the door and switched on the light.

He found himself in a large square hall, well furnished and attractive. From somewhere in the house came the sound of soft distant music. From a passageway on the left-hand side of the hall came the soft tinkle of glasses. Suddenly a woman's voice sounded as a door opened, then a man's, then came the sound of laughter, then the door shutting, then silence.

Callaghan grinned.

'This is a hell of a place,' he said. 'What a little gold mine if it was run properly!'

She smiled at him.

'It *is* run properly,' she said. '*We* run it properly – or improperly.'

She laughed softly.

He smiled back at her.

'I wouldn't mind runnin' a joint like this with a woman like you,' he said. 'It ought to be fun – profitable fun. It might be amusin' too.'

'You think so?' she said, touching a bell in the wall, then slipping out of her coat. 'You seem quite sure of yourself, Mr Callaghan. You take it for granted that I would like to be in partnership with you.'

She stopped suddenly and turned towards him. He could see a gleam of mischief in her eyes.

'You're sure you want to go through with this, aren't you?' she said. 'You're sure you want to see Jeremy? You wouldn't do anything that you might regret afterwards?'

Callaghan grinned.

'If I'd ever regretted the things I've done in my life,' he said, 'I'd be wearin' sackcloth an' ashes as a permanent lounge-suit!'

She laughed softly.

'All right,' she said. 'You've had your chance. I just don't want you to think that I've pushed you into anything.'

Callaghan shrugged his shoulders. Just then a man came out of a service door on the right of the hall and stood waiting.

'I'm going along to the corridor room, George,' said Mayola

Ferrival. 'Will you tell Mr Jeremy that I'm there, and that Mr Callaghan is with me?'

Callaghan thought: So she telephoned Jeremy. He's expecting me. This Mayola doesn't take any chances.

He took off his coat and hung it, with his hat, on the stand in the corner of the hall, then he followed her down the right-hand passage, which led obliquely through the house.

Jeremy came through the red velvet curtain that cloaked the door beside the bookcases.

Jeremy was tall, broad and straight. His shoulders were square. His hair was black and his moustache carefully curled. His eyes were large, very blue, very antagonistic.

His beautifully cut dinner coat hung on him as if it had been poured over him. His linen was immaculate.

His hands, swung on long arms that hung easily at his sides, were big, the fingers spatulate, the fingernails flat.

Jeremy was dominant, strong, clever. Callaghan, looking quickly at him, thought: Here's a dangerous feller, by heck. Here's a man who'll stand no nonsense and who would think nothing of killing – that is if he could get away with it, and very likely if he couldn't. Here's a man who'll stop at nothing. Just the sort of man who'd have a woman like Mayola ... Well, here we go ... Now we shall see something.

Callaghan sat in a big chair on one side of the open fireplace, Mayola Ferrival on the other. Jeremy looked at Callaghan for a moment and then went to the sideboard, opened it and brought out a set tray on which stood a decanter, syphon and glasses. He poured out three stiff drinks, brought the tray to the table in the centre of the room, set it down, carried glasses to the woman and then Callaghan. Then he stood in front of the fire, his back to it, looking down sideways at the private detective.

Callaghan looked up at Jeremy and smiled – a little odd smile. Mayola, looking over the rim of her glass as she drank, thought

Here are a couple of so-and-so's if you like. God, what a pair! One of them all muscle, weight and cunning, the other all sinew, nerve and probably damned brilliant under that grin. I wonder which of them is going to get away with this. Anyhow it's going to be good to watch. I think the odds are a trifle on Jeremy. Callaghan's too far in to be able to fight properly.

Jeremy began to speak quietly.

'Well, Callaghan,' he said, 'Miss Ferrival came through to me on the telephone and gave me the gist of her conversation with you at the Noughts and Crosses. Very interesting, I must say. I told her I'd like to have a talk with you down here where we shouldn't be disturbed.'

Callaghan nodded and brought out his packet of cigarettes. He lit one and inhaled deeply.

'I don't see there's much to talk about, Meraulton,' he said. 'If Miss Ferrival told you what we talked about at the Noughts and Crosses Club, then it looks to me as if the only thing to be decided is whether you are goin' to hand over the money or not; whether I'm to try an' get my hands on that will of your uncle's or leave Sammy the Sheik – whoever he may be – in peace an' let him send it along to the lawyers.'

Jeremy began to smile. The smile illuminated his face with a certain cruelty. Mayola, half-amused, sent her eyes flashing from Jeremy's face to Callaghan's, then back again. She was enjoying herself.

'That might be so if Sammy the Sheik were the beginning and end of this business,' said Jeremy. 'But five hundred pounds is a great deal of money to hand over to a man like Mr Callaghan, who is – if you will excuse me saying so – not a person of any great reputation.'

'All right,' said Callaghan. 'Well, we don't have to talk about it at all, do we?'

He sent a stream of smoke trickling out of his nostrils.

'Another thing,' he went on coolly, 'who the hell are you to talk about reputation? I think for a man who's been kicked out of the

Army for cheatin' at cards you've got a damn nerve to talk to me about reputation; an' if you want to go on talkin', my advice to you is to keep a civil tongue in your head.'

Mayola's smile widened. This was going to be *very* good.

Jeremy flushed. The flush, beginning at the cheeks, encompassed the whole of his face, spread downwards to his neck. He controlled himself with an effort.

'Very well,' he said. 'We will not discuss reputations, either yours or mine. We will discuss Sammy the Sheik. Will you tell me, Callaghan, what guarantee I have if I hand over the sum of five hundred pounds, that this rather vague and nebulous individual will give you the will, and what guarantee have I that, if and when you have got it, you'll hand it over to me?'

Callaghan grinned.

'You haven't got any guarantee,' he said. 'That's the joke. You just have to take a chance; but it wouldn't be the first chance you've taken, would it, Meraulton? Another thing is, I'm not askin' you to hand over five hundred pounds to me. I know these fellers. I reckon that if Sammy the Sheik sees two hundred and fifty – maybe two hundred – he'll be glad to get his hands on the money and to hand over that piece of paper. All right. When I hand it over to you, you give me the balance bringing the sum up to five hundred. I can't see anything wrong with that.'

Jeremy went to the sideboard and got himself a small cigar. He pierced and lit it carefully.

'Tell me, Callaghan,' he said. 'Have you got any ideas about this Sammy the Sheik? Have you any ideas as to who he might be? Hasn't that clever brain of yours the remotest notion as to the identity of Sammy the Sheik?'

Callaghan shrugged.

'He might be anybody,' he said. 'I've no ideas as to *who* he is, but I've got ideas as to what he might be. Doesn't it stand to reason that if Miss Cynthis Meraulton could consult one private detective – me – then she could have consulted another one? There are one or two so-called private detectives in this country who aren't private detectives at all. They're just first-class honest-to-goodness crooks. They're the sort of people who would be glad to take a fifty-pound note just for doin' a little quick work at a mortuary gettin' that will, especially if they knew just how important it was to you Meraulton fellers.'

Jeremy nodded. He examined his cigar carefully.

'Well, let me tell you something, Callaghan,' he said. 'Possibly you haven't any ideas as to the identity of Sammy the Sheik, but I have. I have very definite ideas!'

Callaghan looked interested.

'You don't say!' he said.

'Yes, I *do* say,' said Jeremy. 'I have a definite idea that Sammy the Sheik is no less a person than Mr Slim Callaghan of Callaghan Investigations, who thinks he's on an easy way to get himself another five hundred pounds in addition to anything he's already got from my charming half-cousin Cynthis for doing his original job of corpse-robbing.'

Callaghan began to laugh. He laughed for some time.

'Why don't you stop bein' so damned dramatic, an' such a first-class God-damn idiot?' he said. 'Why don't you use your brains? Wouldn't it be easy, supposin' I *was* Sammy the Sheik, for me to have told Cynthis that unless she cashed in with more money I was goin' to hand that will over to one of you fellers? Don't you think she'd have paid plenty for that?'

Jeremy's face was white. His big blue eyes began to glitter. Mayola moved appreciatively in her chair. She knew that Jeremy had all the brakes on, that he was dying to throw himself on that coolly recumbent figure in the chair, to smash at the insolent face that was mocking him. Possibly in a minute or so he would. She ran her little red tongue over her lips in deliciously sadistic apprehension.

'That *would* be easy for you if you were Sammy the Sheik,' said Jeremy. His voice was ice-cold. 'And I see no reason to believe why you should not have already done it. It would be just like Mr Callaghan to have soaked Cynthis for every penny he could get his grasping fingers on, and then, having collected to the limit from her, to come along to me with this proposition. Incidentally, why come to me? Why not go to Percival, to Bellamy, or Paul? Why am I honoured?'

Callaghan shrugged again.

'It's pretty obvious, isn't it?' he said. 'Percival hasn't got a bean and can't get a bean except the chicken feed he gets from Bellamy. Bellamy's broke. I had his last two hundred quid,' he went on reflectively, noting with pleasure the quick flash of eyes between Mayola and Jeremy. 'Bellamy paid me two hundred to try an' get him out of bein' pinched an' I slipped up on it. I just couldn't manage it.'

He inhaled, then threw his cigarette end away.

'As for Paul, I haven't got round to him yet,' he said. 'An' I don't see why I should even want to. I don't suppose Paul's got any money. But I reckon that you would have *some*, or that anyway you could get some pretty quickly. You take the mugs you get down here for plenty, I've been told.'

He took out his packet of cigarettes.

Jeremy put up his hand.

'I shouldn't bother to light that cigarette if I were you, Callaghan,' he said. 'Not for a minute, anyhow.'

He threw his cigar into the fire.

'I think the time has come when we can do a little straight talking,' he went on. 'I think you're a liar, Callaghan, an insolent liar. I've stood here and listened to more insults from you than I've ever had to listen to before without doing something about it. I was able to do that because at the back of my mind was an idea that I was *going* to do something about it.

'I'm going to give you some advice. If you're a wise man you'll take it. I believe that you are Sammy the Sheik. Alternatively, if you are not Sammy the Sheik, you know who he is, all about him, where he is and where he has got that will hidden. I don't propose to pay you five hundred pounds or five hundred pence while there's the slightest chance of these ideas being correct. Do I make myself plain?'

'I understand, if that's what you mean, Meraulton,' said Callaghan. He was still grinning. 'I don't like you and I don't like your lady friend. I think you're a pair of lousy swindlers; but if you think that you can frighten me, you try again. I've put a proposition up to you, an' you can either accept it or not, just as you damn well please, an' I tell you that I'm not particular as to whether you accept it or not. Maybe I've already found out what I wanted to find out.'

Jeremy smiled at Mayola. It was an evil smile. Her eyes flashed back at him.

'It's quite on the cards,' said Jeremy, 'that I may eventually be forced to do business with you, but I'm going to try something else first.'

He pressed the bell button at the side of the fireplace. Mayola got up. She smiled sweetly at Callaghan.

'I think I'll be getting along,' she said. 'There are one or two things I have to do, and it is *so* late. *Au revoir*, Mr Callaghan. If I were you I'd still listen to reason. It's not too late, you know!'

She walked across to the door and opened it. As she did so a door under the hangings on the other side of the room opened. Three men came in. They were big ugly men - bruisers. Callaghan looked them over carefully. He was concentrating on remembering their faces for the future.

Mayola closed the door behind her. The three men came into the room and stood by the table, looking at Jeremy.

'Well, Callaghan,' said Jeremy. 'We'll soon know whether or not you know where that will is, whether you have it yourself. But I think I ought to tell you that you'll save yourself a great deal of inconvenience if you talk now, if you tell me where that will is, or if you have it with you, produce it.'

Callaghan was still smiling. He lay back in his chair, relaxed.

'I don't know Sammy the Sheik,' he said. 'I don't know who he is. I don't know where the will is; an' even if I did I wouldn't walk round the corner to get it for you for one penny under five hundred pounds. And where do we go from there?'

Jeremy felt in his pocket and produced a cigarette-case. He selected a cigarette, lit it. He threw the match away and motioned to one of the men who stood by the table.

'Get to work on him,' said Jeremy. 'He's asked for it. Let him have it.'

Jeremy came back into the room. He was smoking a cigarette and held a small cup of black coffee in his hand.

Callaghan lay in the corner of the room. His head was propped in the angle of the oak wainscotting. A thin stream of blood ran down one nostril, trickled over his chin on to the floor.

Both his eyes were black, his face bruised. One hand was cut and was bleeding slowly. One side of his jaw presented a grotesque sight. It was semi-dislocated, the joint having been knocked half out of its socket.

All this, however, did not bother Callaghan very much. He was unconscious.

Jeremy stood in front of the fire and began to drink his coffee. He looked at the tallest of the three men who stood grouped about Callaghan looking down at him. One of them was swinging a piece of rubber tubing in his hand, a piece of tubing badly bloodstained.

'Did he talk?' asked Jeremy.

The man grunted.

'Not a word,' he said. 'Not a bloody word; from the moment we got started on 'im, 'e ain't said nothin'. Sort of grinned at us most of the time. I was afraid to go any further with 'im. We don't want to do 'im in altogether, so I told 'em to lay off.'

Jeremy nodded. He pointed with a finger towards Callaghan's jaw.

'His jaw's dislocated,' he said. 'You'd better knock it back.'

One of the men put his hands behind Callaghan's head, held it up off the wainscotting. The big man bent down and measured the distance with a careful eye. Then he swung his right arm, crashed it against Callaghan's unequal jaw.

There was a click as the ball joint cracked back into its socket.

'Put him in the chair and get some water,' said Jeremy quietly. 'You'd better get him a spot of brandy, too. He's tougher than I thought.'

There was almost a note of admiration in his voice.

Very vaguely the mist began to recede from before Callaghan's eyes. He lay in the chair, his head propped up against the high back, his brain fighting to come back to a realization of the present. When he tried to open one eye the electric light almost blinded him, and he closed it again wearily.

His body felt like one immense bruise. His right hand was cut, and one finger of his left, which had been bent backwards, was sending shooting pains up his arm.

He began to remember things, but lay there quite still, coming back slowly, trying to reassess the situation, trying not to worry about the hundred aches which shot through his battered body.

Somebody held a glass to his mouth. He felt the rawness of the brandy as it ran over his dry tongue, down his parched throat. He gulped and gasped, but the spirit began to revive him. He remembered Jeremy and his bruised lips drew back over his teeth.

He lay there, his eyes closed, wondering what the next move in the game would be, wondering what Jeremy would try now.

He heard Jeremy talking. The voice, cold and incisive, seemed to come from a distance.

'Well, Callaghan,' said Jeremy, 'even if we haven't got any information from you, we have still taught you not to be insolent to your betters.'

He signalled to the big man.

'Take him away,' he said, 'and give him a good clean-up. Then when he's presentable bring him back.'

They seized Callaghan under the arms and half carried, half assisted him out of the room.

Jeremy, finishing his coffee, began to curse softly.

He was very disappointed.

Callaghan, steadier on his feet, stood before the washbowl in the lavatory, dipping his head into cold water, bringing it out, then dipping it again. He had done this for five minutes and was beginning to be able to think clearly, to produce within himself an unutterable hatred for Jeremy and Mayola and everyone else.

He took a piece of soap and began to wash his hands. Looking about him, he saw that he was in a lavatory with two doors. One led to the passage outside where the bruiser stood leaning against the wall smoking a cigarette just out of sight of Callaghan. The other to an adjoining bathroom. Callaghan dried his hands on a towel, moved warily and wearily towards this door. He looked in. On the brush-tray across the bath he saw a bath-brush, a mahogany brush with a twelve-inch handle. Callaghan slipped quietly into the bathroom, picked it up, weighed it in his hand. It was heavy enough, he thought. He put the brush into his right-hand hip-pocket, leaving the handle sticking out; then he moved back to the other room, began to splash in the water for the benefit of the man outside in the passage. Then he put on his coat, went outside.

The man looked at him with a grin.

'That's better,' he said. 'But I bet you ain't feeling so cocky as you was before you got down 'ere. Come on, this way.'

Callaghan followed him back along the oblique passage to the room he had just left. Jeremy was still standing in front of the fire. He motioned Callaghan to a chair, handed him a whisky and soda. Then he nodded to the man, who left the room, closing the door behind him.

'Well,' said Jeremy, 'it looks as if I've got to talk business with you, Callaghan, but I've satisfied myself about one thing: I'm certain that if you'd known where that will was you would have told.'

Callaghan grinned. The process hurt his cut lips.

'Maybe,' he said, 'and maybe not.'

'I want that will,' said Jeremy, 'and I'm perfectly honest about it. I want it by fair means or foul. I intend to have it.'

'There's only one way you'll get it, Meraulton,' said Callaghan, 'and that's by payin' over that money I asked you for.'

Jeremy lit a cigarette.

'I'm beginning to believe that you're right,' he said. 'I think you realize now that it wouldn't be to your advantage to double-cross me. You might get even more knocked about than you have been tonight.'

He put his hand inside his coat and produced a wallet. He handed Callaghan a wad of banknotes.

'There are 250 there, Callaghan,' he said. 'When you bring me August Meraulton's will – the one he was carrying in his watch-case the night he was murdered – and remember I'm very conversant with his signature – I'll give you another 250. I think I'm overpaying you,' he went on, 'but, as you so rightly observed earlier tonight, I have got to take a chance.

'I'm giving you till ten o'clock tomorrow night to get that will and to be back here with it. If you're not here by then I'm coming after you, and what's happened to you tonight will be nothing compared with what will happen to you then. I don't think there is anything else to be said, is there?'

Callaghan got up slowly.

'I don't think so,' he said, 'except' – he grinned wryly – 'I've got an idea that I wish I'd done this business over the telephone instead of comin' down here.'

He counted the notes with stiff fingers, saw they totalled 250. Then he folded them up and with his right hand went through the motion of putting them into his hip pocket.

But he did not do so. His right hand behind him, under his coat, gripped the handle of the bath-brush. He moved round the table, pretending to be unsteadier, weaker than he was, pretending to support himself with his left hand.

Then, as he faced Jeremy, he jumped forward. The brush came out of his pocket, descended with a fearful thud on Jeremy's head.

Jeremy crumpled up. He subsided on the carpet. He was right out.

Callaghan kneeled down, opened his coat, took out the pocket-book, examined it. Inside were more notes – £150's worth of them. Callaghan grabbed them, stuffed them in his pocket.

Then he got up, walked over to the door, looked down the passage. He saw no one. He moved quietly along until he reached the side hall, listened for a moment again. He crossed the hall, opened the door, closed it quietly behind him and began to stumble down the driveway back towards the road.

CHAPTER ELEVEN

Nothing Like the Truth

The Victoria traffic rumbling past the Hotel Excelsis (Family and Commercial: Bed and Breakfast 4/6) awakened Callaghan.

He opened his eyes, closed them again wearily, concentrated on the business of opening them again; finally, with a groan, sat up and rang the bell.

When the slatternly chambermaid - wide-eyed at the sight of Callaghan's face - had brought his tea, he sat on the edge of the bed and drank it. This done, he walked over to the mirror on the dressing-table and looked at himself.

Both his eyes were badly discoloured. His right jaw-socket had a lump on it as big as a walnut. One eyebrow, badly cut, was beginning to heal, and there was a two-inch laceration on the left-hand side of his throat.

Every inch of his body possessed its own particular ache, and his right-hand knuckles were almost dislocated. That punch had hurt some one, anyhow!

He reflected that Jeremy's bruisers certainly knew their business, that possibly they had ample opportunities for much practice at the Show Down!

He went to the bathroom and let the taps run. The hot water felt good. Callaghan allowed his mind to wander on Jeremy, who had proved conclusively one or two things which were worth the hat and coat which had been left hanging in the side hall at the Show Down.

His sense of humour came to his rescue. Lying back in the bath, relaxed, he began to grin. Anyhow that coat and hat had cost Jeremy £400.

His bath finished, he shaved, ordered more tea, and as he drank it, went through his wad of banknotes, making notes of the numbers, checking again and again. He had in all £1180 worth of notes, which he accounted for in his notebook:

Group 1.	Received from Cynthis Meraulton (original payment, supplied by Willie Meraulton)	£500
	Less expenses for Darkie, Revenholt and himself	£220
		£280
Group 2.	Further advance from Willie Meraulton	£300
Group 3.	From Bellamy Meraulton	£200
Group 4.	From Jeremy Meraulton	£400
		£1,180

A nice round sum.

Callaghan finished dressing slowly, went downstairs, returned the borrowed razor, paid his bill and left the Hotel Excelsis. He walked slowly towards Victoria, stopping on the way to buy himself a new overcoat, hat and gloves. At the station cloakroom he retrieved his suitcase.

This done, he took a cab back to the Axford Hotel in Orchard Street and engaged a room. He sent up his suitcase, went into the phone-box and called Scotland Yard. One minute later he was talking to Gringall.

'Good afternoon, Gringall. This is Callaghan speakin'. How're things with you?'

He heard Gringall grunt. Then:

'Look here, Callaghan, don't you think it's time you stopped playing silly games that are liable to get you into trouble? I don't want to get really tough with you, but unless I know within a couple of hours where Cynthis Meraulton is I . . .'

'Listen, Gringall,' interrupted Callaghan, 'I'll bet all the tea in

China that you know as well as I do just where Cynthis Meraulton is. If you don't, then there must be somethin' radically wrong with our police system.

'What you mean is you know damn well where she is, but you've been layin' off her because you think that the clever thing for you to do is to leave her alone just to see what her next move is, an' if she's goin' to contact any of the Meraulton boys. An' your reason for doin' this is because you've come to the conclusion that there was more than one person concerned in the murder. Well, don't worry. Maybe I'm goin' to hand you this thing on a plate. Anyhow I'll be with you in twenty minutes if you want to talk things over ... Well?'

Gringall grunted again.

'If you've got anything to say, I'm listening,' he said.

He hung up.

Callaghan rang the Delvine Court Apartments and spoke to Cynthis.

'Now don't be angry,' he said, smiling into the telephone transmitter. 'I know that you're fed-up an' that you want to see Willie, an' that you're beginnin' to distrust me an' believe all sorts of things. Well, suppose we take it easy for just a little while longer.

'Here's the position: Everything's absolutely all right; but I've just got to settle one or two little things. I'll be workin' most of this afternoon, this evenin' an' maybe a bit of tonight, but I give you my word that I'll be with you somewhere round about midnight, an' don't be surprised if I bring Willie with me.'

He chuckled.

'I'll tell you somethin' else, too,' he said. 'Maybe when you see the way I've handled this case you'll probably want to make me best man at the weddin'. Willie'll be agreeable, I can promise you.'

Her voice was cold.

'I'll expect you not later than midnight,' she said tersely. 'If you don't come, or if there are any more excuses or delays, I shall get into touch with Scotland Yard first thing in the morning.'

'All right, madame,' said Callaghan, 'that's a bet.'

He was still smiling when he replaced the receiver.

Gringall faced Callaghan across the desk. Detective-Sergeant Fields, a pad in front of him, sat at the end of the desk and nibbled a pencil. Not the least of his accomplishments was an ability to write over ninety words a minute in shorthand.

Callaghan took out his packet of cigarettes and gave one to Gringall. Then he relaxed in his chair.

Gringall grinned at him sourly.

'Somebody took a nice sock at you last night, by the looks of you,' he said.

Callaghan nodded.

'Three "somebodies,"' he said. 'I've never been knocked about like it in my life before. Those fellers were really tough. However,' he continued ruminatively, 'perhaps it was worth it.'

He exhaled a cloud of smoke, looked at Gringall through it.

'I'm not makin' any statements, Gringall,' he said. 'So you can tell Fields there to put that pencil down. Maybe I'll have something to say to you later today. Maybe you'll stick around here or leave somebody here who can get at you.

'What I'm doin' now is to have a little quiet talk with you.'

Gringall looked at him.

'What sort of quiet talk is this one?' he asked. 'Is it going to be like the last one?'

Callaghan grinned.

'Don't get fed-up, Gringall,' he said. 'Before I'm through with you, you're goin' to admit that I'm your best friend. Just now you've got somethin' ranklin' in your mind. You've got the idea in your head that I led you up the garden about Bellamy Meraulton, that I planted that fake blood-stained hat on him. Well, I don't admit it, but supposin' I did? You're goin' to see that it doesn't matter, providin' it helps. By the way,' he went on easily, 'what happened to Bellamy?'

'He's out on bail on the drugs charge,' said Gringall. 'Apparently he'd been getting the stuff from Beldoces. But Bellamy cleared himself of the murder charge easily enough. We found the taxi driver who took him to Lincoln's Inn Fields and dropped him there at five minutes to eleven. We found the other taxi driver who picked him up in Holborn afterwards and drove him on to Eulalie Gallicot's place at five minutes past eleven. The Gallicot woman told us a pack of lies in the first place. Said she was frightened and that you put her on to it. It looks as if you've got a lot to answer for, doesn't it?'

Callaghan grinned.

'Why don't you get down to the brass tacks of that Gallicot business, Gringall?' he said. 'What you really mean is that because you pinched Bellamy as a suspect he told you about seein' Cynthis Meraulton in Lincoln's Inn Fields, an' because Gallicot told you that I'd got her to fake the time when Bellamy really got around there it looks to you just as if I'm still tryin' to keep Cynthis Meraulton out of this, doesn't it?'

He flipped the ash off his cigarette.

'Listen, Jigger,' he said. 'You've got too much brains to believe that the Gallicot dame told that lie just for *me*. Not on your life. She said what she said because Beldoces told her to say it long before I got around to her. By the way,' he continued, 'since we're talkin' so frankly, at what time *was* the old boy really murdered?'

'Definitely before a quarter to eleven,' said Gringall. 'Probably at half-past ten or thereabouts. That's as near as we can get.'

Callaghan nodded.

'That's about it,' he said, as if talking to himself. 'I'd say ten-thirty.'

He took another cigarette.

'Look, Gringall,' he said. 'You know how it is. A private detective can do a lot of things that a policeman can't. He can create a hell of a lot of situations that would get a C.I.D. man kicked out in no time. Well, maybe that's what I've been about.

'Now I like you. I think you're a good feller. I guessed you'd have found Cynthis Meraulton by now, an' I reckon that the reason you've laid off her was what I said over the telephone. You're givin' her her head for a bit. Well, I think you're wise.

'Now, I'm goin' to make a bargain with you, an' by all that's holy I'm goin' to keep it. Within the next eight hours – if things go right with me – I'm goin' to have this case cleaned up an' cleaned up the way *I* want it done.'

He smiled pleasantly at them both.

'Take it from me,' he went on. 'There's only one way to handle this case, an' there isn't a policeman on earth who can do it. If I get what I want you'll get your killer – man or woman, or both – but if I don't, then I reckon the Meraulton murder is just goin' to be another of those unsolved crimes with a lot of suspicion an' no proof.'

He produced his little black notebook.

'Listen, Fields,' he said. 'You write down the numbers of the groups of banknotes that I'm goin' to give you. An' when I'm gone you check up on 'em an' do it quick. Here they are.'

He read out the four groups of numbers. Fields, after a quick nod from Gringall, wrote them down.

Callaghan got up.

'I'm goin' now,' he said, 'but I'll be seein' you, Gringall, maybe sooner than you think. So long!'

He shot a quick grin at Gringall, picked up his hat, walked out of the room.

Fields looked at his chief, his eyebrows raised.

Gringall shrugged.

'It's a funny thing,' he said. 'You can say what the hell you like about that fellow, but every time I see him I like him a bit more. He's got something – even if it's only nerve!'

Fields nodded.

'Aren't we going to put a tail on him, sir?' he said. 'Maybe he'll go off again for another little jaunt. You don't want to lose him *now*!'

Gringall looked at Fields and smiled.

'Your psychology's wrong, Fields,' he said. 'Callaghan knows damn well that I *know* that *he* planted that hat on Bellamy Meraulton. He knows damn well that I *know* that he was the man who got into the Ensell Street mortuary and took that will out of the old boy's watch-case. *He knows I know it,* and he knows just what's going to happen to him if he takes one more chance with me.'

He got up and stretched.

'Callaghan's got brains,' he said. 'I'm going to let him use 'em!'

It was ten o'clock.

Callaghan, standing in the Russell Square telephone box, called through to Fred Mazin, who was keeping guard at the Chancery Lane office.

'Hallo, Fred,' he said. 'This is Callaghan. I'm expectin' a visit from a Mr Jeremy Meraulton. This feller is expectin' to get somethin' from me – a will I promised to get for him. He's a tough customer an' he can be very nasty.

'If he comes around you tell him to wait. You tell him that I said he was to wait for me, that I'll be back. Tell him that if he waits I'll give him that will tonight as promised. So-long!'

He waited for a minute and then rang Darkie.

He said, 'Callaghan here. Did you find out about that office of Paul Meraulton's – the one near here, at 22 Greeneagle Street?'

'Yes, guv,' said Darkie. 'I did – an' you ain't got a dog's chance. It fronts on to the main street, an' the back door's in full view of the houses in Mervyn Street, so that ain't any use. There's two night watchmen on the premises an' all the offices have doors leading off the corridors with special locks on 'em. I should say you've got as much chance of bustin' in there quietly as you have of jumpin' straight up to heaven. See?'

'I see,' said Callaghan. 'All right. Did you get Paul Meraulton's address?'

'Yes, I did,' replied Darkie. 'He lives close to the office. Melleville Apartments, Glasbury Street. Telephone number is Museum 88976, an' 'e's usually there. 'E don't go out very much.'

'Right, Darkie,' said Callaghan. 'Well, you stick around. I'll probably be wanting you again tonight.'

He hung up, left the call-box, stood on the pavement and lit a cigarette, thought for a moment. Then he went back into the box and dialled Museum 88976. He asked for Mr Paul Meraulton.

After a few minutes a voice came through. It was brusque and incisive – a well-controlled voice, thought Callaghan.

'Is that Mr Paul Meraulton?' he said. 'Good evenin'. I don't suppose you've heard of me – my name's Callaghan, of Callaghan Investigations. I'm rather sorry to trouble you, Meraulton, but I'd like you to meet me at your office building in Greeneagle Street in five minutes, an' just so that we don't waste any time arguin' on the telephone, let me tell you one or two things.

'First of all the game's up. It's wide open, an' the best thing you can do is to get out of this country as quick as you can. Well, maybe that doesn't sound so easy to a man who's broke, but if you want to get your hands on a thousand pounds an' make a quick getaway you can do it if you do what you're told.'

There was a long pause. Then:

'And just exactly what am I to be told?' said the voice.

'I'm tellin' you to get round to your office in Greeneagle Street right away,' said Callaghan. 'I'll meet you round there. I want to inspect the books of those funny companies you four Meraulton boys run. After that I want to have a little talk with you, and if you're sensible you may still be able to get away with it. Well ... what are you goin' to do?'

There was another pause. Then Meraulton said:

'Well, as a beginning, I'm going round to Greeneagle Street to take a look at you, Mr Callaghan. When we've talked a little more I'll decide as to whether we can do any further business together.'

Callaghan grinned.

'Wise man,' he said. 'I'll be seein' you.'

Paul Meraulton sat at the desk in front of the open safe. Before him, open, lay half a dozen account books. He looked across the small office at Callaghan, who was sitting in a corner lighting himself a cigarette.

Meraulton ran his tongue over dry lips. His face was drawn and one finger was beating a tattoo on the edge of the desk. He was frightened.

'How did you get to know about this?' he asked.

He motioned towards the account books.

'Just by puttin' two an' two together without makin' five of 'em,' said Callaghan. 'I had a friend of mine check up on you an' he told me that you spent a certain amount of time at Somerset House, that you earned six pounds a week an' spent sixty.

'Well, a feller doesn't hang around Somerset House for nothin', does he? Somerset House means Company business – especially as you used to go to the Companies Registry. So I thought I'd see if any of you fellers were interested in any companies, an' the check-up showed that you were – all four of you – the only shareholders in four old companies that you'd bought up an' refloated.

'Well, I asked myself what for, an' the answer was easy.'

Callaghan drew down a lungful of smoke, sent it out, as usual, through one nostril, then the other.

'It was a clever idea, Paul, an' I've got to admit it. You four knew damned well that old August Meraulton was sick of the lot of you, that he'd never consent to lettin' you have any money while he was alive, an' you also knew that there would be some money comin' to you from his estate – that is if he didn't alter his will – so you think of the Company idea. Hidin' behind those four companies, you've been able to get money out of the Meraulton Estates and Trust Company because old August Meraulton thought that he was lendin' money to four legitimate tradin' companies. The poor old mug didn't know that he was simply lendin' the dough to four Meraulton boys that he'd have seen in blazes before he'd wittingly have lent 'em a penny!'

He blew a smoke ring, watched it sail across the room.

'The old boy thought your dud companies were legitimate

ones. When his money went out he saw your phoney Debentures and Share Certificates come in. I just wanted to see your books because I wanted to make certain, an' now I'm certain ...'

He shrugged his shoulders expressively.

Paul Meraulton got up. He stood looking at Callaghan.

'You know too much for me,' he said. A thin smile wavered about his mouth. 'How much more do you know?'

Callaghan looked at him. There was something very near a sneer on his lips.

'I know pretty well all there is to be known, Meraulton,' he said. 'Enough to put you away for a considerable time.'

Meraulton walked over to the window and looked out on to the quiet street.

'What was that you said on the telephone about making a getaway?' he said. 'About my being able to get my hands on a thousand pounds.'

'I mean what I said,' Callaghan grinned. 'Have you got a typewriter here?'

Meraulton nodded.

'All right,' said Callaghan. 'You go over there an' sit down at the typewriter. You're goin' to make a full confession an' you're goin' to sign it. When you've done that I'm goin' to hand you one thousand pounds, an' you can get out of here just as quick as you like. If I was you I'd take a boat to the Argentine – or one of the Greek Islands. They tell me it's very hard to get people extradited from either of these places.'

'How do I know you're telling the truth?' mumbled Meraulton. 'How do I know you'll give me the money?'

'You don't,' replied Callaghan. 'You're goin' to take the chance. But if you don't get over there an' get busy I'm goin' to ring up my friend Mr Gringall at Scotland Yard, an' in about one hour you'll find yourself in a nice cell in Brixton. Now, which is it to be?'

Meraulton hesitated for a moment. Then he walked over to the typewriter and took the cover off. He put a sheet of paper in the machine.

'What do I say?' he said. 'How do I start?'

Callaghan got up. He was grinning. He walked over and stood behind Meraulton.

'I'll dictate,' he said, 'an' you can write it down. Now, then ... "*This is a confession made voluntarily by me, Paul Meraulton ...*"'

Callaghan's voice went on and Meraulton's fingers tapped on the typewriter keys until the thing was done. Callaghan took out his fountain pen.

'Just sign it at the bottom,' he said, 'and put the date on it.'

He watched Meraulton do this, then, taking the pen from his fingers, wrote underneath: 'Witnessed S. Callaghan, Callaghan Investigations.'

He folded the sheets of paper, put them in his pocket, then brought out his packet of cigarettes. He gave one to Meraulton, took one himself.

'I reckon you need that,' he said.

He put the cigarettes away and produced the wad of banknotes. He began to count off notes until a little pile to the value of one thousand pounds lay on the corner of the table. He put the balance of £180 back into his pocket.

'There's your money,' he said. 'Now get out, an' if you're wise you'll get out quickly.'

Meraulton picked up the money.

'Are you going to keep quiet about this for a few hours?' he asked.

Callaghan grinned.

'You're a crook, Meraulton,' he said. 'An' I never make bargains with crooks, if I can help it, that is! You get out while the goin's good. Maybe they'll get you an' maybe they won't; that's a chance you've just got to take.'

It was a quarter to twelve.

Callaghan, half-way up the stairs to his office in Chancery Lane, began to cough. Continuing on his way, he told himself that old one about cutting down his cigarettes to fifty a day.

Fred Mazin was in the outside office. Sitting on the other side of the room reading a newspaper was Jeremy Meraulton.

'You get out, Fred,' said Callaghan. 'I'll attend to Mr Meraulton, an' another thing: you needn't come up here tomorrow. I reckon I'm through with you for a bit.'

'O.K.,' said Fred Mazin.

He took his hat, gathered up his racing edition and the form book and disappeared.

Callaghan looked at Jeremy. He was grinning.

'Come inside,' he said.

He unlocked the door of his own room, went inside, switched on the light. Then he sat down at his desk.

Jeremy stood in the doorway. His lips were twitching. He looked ominous.

'I don't want any argument with you,' he said. 'I've got to admit I've a certain respect for you, Callaghan. You turned the tables on me last night and you were lucky to get away with it!'

Callaghan was still grinning.

'I was,' he said simply. 'An' I was even luckier to find a lorry driver down on the main road who gave me a lift back to London, otherwise I'd probably be walkin' now.'

He lit a cigarette.

'Well,' he said. 'What is it you want – your money back or the will?'

'I want the will,' said Jeremy. 'I promised you the money, and you can keep it. If you've got the will, hand it over. If you haven't, I'm going to beat you into little pieces.'

'You don't say so,' said Callaghan.

He was leaning back in his chair, enjoying the situation. He stayed like that for several seconds, then:

'I'm goin' to do you a very good turn, Jeremy,' he said. 'I'm not only goin' to give you the will, but I'm goin' to give you a tip that'll do you a bit of good!'

He opened the drawer in front of him, fumbled about in the

corner and produced the piece of gold copy paper on which August Meraulton had typed his will.

He threw it across the table to Jeremy.

'Take a look at it an' you'll see that that is the old boy's signature right enough,' he said. 'Well, are you satisfied?'

Jeremy examined the paper.

'I'm satisfied,' he said.

He smiled a little.

'All right,' said Callaghan. 'Now I'll tell you what you're thinkin'. You're thinkin' that all you've got to do is to destroy that will an' that when you've done that you'll be O.K. because under the first will that the old boy made you all got an equal share.

'Well, if you're thinkin' that you're wrong. That will isn't twopennorth of good to any one. Mind you, I'm not sayin' that that isn't August Meraulton's will. I'm just sayin' that it's no durn good whether you destroy it or not!'

Jeremy was still smiling. He held the piece of copy paper between his finger and thumb. With his other hand he produced a cigarette lighter. He set fire to August Meraulton's will and watched it burn. When he had finished he looked at Callaghan.

'That's that,' he said. 'Now just what were you saying, Callaghan?'

Callaghan lit a cigarette.

'I'm goin' to tell you something that nobody else knows,' he said. 'I'm goin' to give you something to think over. Something that's going to make you feel like nothin' on earth. Here it is:

'Everybody – the police, and you an' all the rest of you, an' probably all the rest of the country who's bothered to read the papers – have got an idea in their heads that August Meraulton was killed by somebody who wanted to get their fingers on that will.

'*Well I know he wasn't! An' the reason I know that is because I'm the feller who got into the Ensell Street mortuary an' took that will out of his watch-case.*

'So I know he wasn't killed because somebody wanted to take

that will off him. If they killed him for the will they'd have taken it. They wouldn't have left it for me to take. Work it out for yourself, Jeremy. The old boy was lyin' there in Lincoln's Inn Fields for nearly an hour after he'd been murdered an' the will was on him the whole time, an' the murderer didn't even bother to take it.'

Jeremy looked across the desk at Callaghan. His eyes were wide. His big hands twitched spasmodically.

Callaghan began to laugh.

'All the while your lousy thugs were knockin' me about last night I was consolin' myself with the fact that the laugh was goin' to be on you,' he said.

He got up, walked round the desk.

'You're supposed to have brains, Jeremy,' he said. 'An' I thought that Mayola had 'em, too. Did you think that I was such a damn fool to come down to the Show Down to do business with you when I could have done it on the telephone, if I hadn't had a reason?'

Jeremy put his hands in his pockets.

'Well, what was the reason?' he asked.

'I wanted to see just how far you'd go to get your hands on that will that you've just burned,' said Callaghan. 'I wanted to see if you were an accomplice in the murder of old Merualton. Now I know you're not.

'Maybe you don't quite understand. Maybe I can make it a bit clearer. Listen: The murderer of August Meraulton didn't even bother to take the will because he knew that takin' it wouldn't do him any good. If you'd been in on the murder job you'd have known that, too. The fact that you went to the trouble of first of all beatin' me up to try an' get it an' then payin' me money to try an' get it showed me that you didn't know a damn thing about that murder.

'An' that's what I wanted to know!'

Callaghan picked up his hat.

'By the way,' he said, 'there's something else might interest you.

Paul's ratted on you. Paul's told the full story about that fake company swindle you boys pulled on old August, and now made a run for it. Somebody told me tonight. So it looks as if the game's up, doesn't it, Jeremy?'

Jeremy said nothing. He had picked up his hat. He was watching Callaghan.

'If I were you,' said Callaghan, 'I'd just run along nicely and go into a huddle with your lady friend Mayola about what you're goin' to do. It looks as if life is goin' to be a bit tough for you four Meraulton fellers, doesn't it?'

Jeremy still said nothing. He turned on his heel and walked out of the office. Callaghan listened to his footsteps as he descended the stairs.

Callaghan waited for a few minutes. Then he went over and locked the door. Then he took from his pocket half a dozen closely written sheets of paper which represented his work between the time he had left Gringall in the afternoon until the time had come for him to telephone through to Darkie.

He folded up these sheets, pinned them together and placed them with the confession he had taken from Paul Meraulton in a stout envelope which he took from the drawer. He addressed this envelope to Detective-Inspector Gringall, at Scotland Yard. Then he put it back into his breast pocket, switched off the light, closed and locked the office doors and went down the stairs.

He was still grinning.

CHAPTER TWELVE

Including Kidnapping

Callaghan turned into Chancery Lane and began to walk towards the Holborn end. It had begun to rain, and he turned up his coat collar, kept in the leeway of the wall.

As he walked he began to think of the night when the Meraulton case had started. It had been raining then. He ruminated on the question of rain, cursed quietly to himself at the thought of the nights he would spend walking up and down Chancery Lane, going to or from the office, settling a case or looking for one, bribing somebody with a fiver or trying to get his hands on a fiver for himself.

He realized with something akin to surprise that he was sick of being a private detective. Callaghan Investigations gave him a pain in the neck. He, Callaghan, gave himself a pain in the neck.

There was no ending to the business of being a private detective. He wondered what happened to them when they got old, when they were too tired to go running around town getting old ladies and gentlemen out of trouble, snooping about, talking to the lousy people, the near crooks, the complete crooks that made up the rather extraordinary panorama of the life of a private investigator.

Of course there were men who had got away with it in a big way – Pinkerton – now there was a successful man for you with a big organization, a nation-wide organization in the States where a private dick with a good reputation meant something.

William J. Burns was another. Callaghan, fumbling for the inevitable cigarette, wondered why the devil he was thinking about successful private detectives. It was all the tea in China to a bad egg that he wasn't ever going to be like that. The best he could do would be to 'get by.' If you could 'get by' you were doing pretty well, some people said. But who the hell was going to be satisfied with that?

Fumbling for a match, his fingers encountered the £180 in notes in his trouser pocket. That was a devil of a lot of good, wasn't it? One way and another he'd got £1180 out of the Meraulton case and could have stuck to it, and played along with Gringall. But he'd parted with a thousand to Paul just because it was indicated, and to tell the truth, necessary.

Darkie would want another £80 for his work, and the boys would want a bit, Fred Mazin and the other boys who'd helped. By the time he was through with the job he'd make a fifty-pound note clear – if he were lucky.

But he knew why he'd handled it the way he had. He just wasn't keen on admitting the fact that he'd fallen for a woman, and fallen hard. Cynthis Meraultons didn't come across the path of Slim Callaghans every day in the week. He'd fallen for her like a sack of coke the first time he'd seen her. She had everything that he liked in a woman and probably a lot more than he knew about or guessed. He shrugged his shoulders.

He turned off Holborn into a narrow street, walked along until he came to a dark cul-de-sac, turned in and knocked on the ramshackle door at the end. A minute later it opened and a very old and wizened face looked out.

'Hallo, Slim,' said the owner of the face. 'How's things? Want somethin'?'

Callaghan grinned.

'You didn't think I'd come round here to ask what the time was, did you, Grandpa?' he said. 'You give me one of those little bottles of easy knock-out drops an' I'll give you a pound note.'

The old man screwed up his face.

'I usually get a fiver, Slim,' he said. 'A pound don't get very far these days.'

'I'm payin' a pound,' said Callaghan. 'An' don't make the dose too stiff. I just want to use it on a handkerchief.'

'All right,' said Grandpa. 'I'll do it for you, Slim, but I wouldn't do it for anybody else. How long do you want it to work for?'

'Two hours or so,' said Callaghan.

'Then you want chloroform,' said Grandpa. 'It ain't no good me givin' you that ether mixture if you want it to go two hours. You wait, I'll get a bottle.'

Callaghan waited, drawing on his cigarette, tapping with his foot on the doorstep.

Five minutes afterwards Grandpa returned with the bottle.

Callaghan paid his pound, said good-night and walked to the garage in Lamb's Conduit Street. He paid an account of nearly four pounds against which they had been holding his car, and took possession of it with a cynical survey of its antiquity. It was a 1929 saloon with tyres worn flat and a permanent wheeze.

He got in and looked at his watch. It was a quarter to one.

He drove westwards.

Callaghan stood in the middle of the floor and looked at Cynthia Meraulton. He looked her over with the same calm appraisal that he had used on the night of their first meeting.

She had seated herself on the other side of the fireplace. She was wearing a figured crepe-de-chine day gown with black satin court shoes and beige stockings. Callaghan thought that every time he saw her she looked colder, more desirable.

Stacked up against the wall were two kit bags, ready packed. A black coat with a fur collar, a small hat and gloves lay beside them.

Callaghan grinned apologetically. His fingers in his overcoat pocket twisted the chloroform bottle, fumbled with the handkerchief with the cotton wool inside it that lay beside the bottle.

'I'm always apologizin' to you for something, I know,' he said grinning cheerfully. 'But my business is a funny business. It doesn't always go the way you want it to go.'

She looked straight at him.

'Mr Callaghan,' she said, 'I think that you are a liar, and not a particularly good one. You said that you would be bringing Willie with you tonight. That was a lie. You said that he was, or had been, in Edinburgh; that was another lie.'

Callaghan shrugged.

'One lie's as good as another sometimes, madame,' he said. 'But how did you know about Willie?'

'He telephoned through this evening,' she said. 'He told me that you had asked him not to contact me, but naturally he was worried. If it hadn't been for you, for your continued trickery, he would have been here before.'

'Fine,' said Callaghan softly. 'How did he know you were here? Still, I reckon I can answer that one. Gringall told him, I'll bet a quid!'

She looked amazed. Her eyes, searching, looked at him with a mixture of curiosity and contempt.

'Gringall,' she repeated. 'Isn't that the police officer in charge of the case? Isn't he the reason why you got me to come here, so that he shouldn't be able to find me. How could he have told Willie?'

'Gringall's known you've been here for some time,' said Callaghan. 'But he hasn't done anything about it. He knew he could get you if he wanted to. Gringall's no fool.'

She said quietly:

'I don't suppose he is, and I don't suppose you are, either. It seems to me that the only people who are fools are Willie and me – and possibly Bellamy – Bellamy, that poor, drink-sodden, dope-ruined person that you subjected to the indignity of arrest merely in order to get some more money for yourself. You seem to have done pretty well out of the Meraulton family, Mr Callaghan.'

Callaghan smiled.

'Not too badly,' he said. 'By the time I'm through I shall be doin' quite well. You see I haven't rendered my final account yet. But tell me something: Where did you get that information about Bellamy? Has he been talking, too?'

'What would you expect?' she said contemptuously. 'Bellamy arrested on a charge which he knows merely conceals a serious suspicion of murder naturally talked to save himself. He was forced to talk about me, forced to throw further suspicion on me in order to obtain his freedom.'

'Maybe,' said Callaghan, 'but still you realize ...'

'I realize that you're thoroughly dishonest,' she said. 'I realize that you have used all the trouble that has been brought on all of us – even the death of August Meraulton – to get money and still more money. In order to keep things going your way you have not scrupled to do anything that suited your own ends. Well, Mr Callaghan, this is the end of you. Your little act is over.'

Callaghan smiled again. His smile was quiet, vaguely superior, almost maddening.

'No, it isn't,' he said. 'By heck it isn't! My little act isn't over by a hell of a long way. An' I'd like to tell you something else, madame, whilst I'm on the job. You seem to be damn satisfied with yourself in this business. Maybe you've got a great deal of sympathy for yourself, an' maybe you think you've been given a tough time merely because you've been kept out of the way an' not allowed to see your boy friend. Well ... what of it?

'I suppose it never occurred to you that when you came around to my office to see me that first time you were startin' something that you've got to finish, even if I have to stick by you to see that you do. I didn't ask you to come to Callaghan Investigations in the first place, did I? You did it to suit your own book. Why in the name of blazes didn't you disclose the fact that you were a lily-white innocent without any brains in your head when you came round? You tell me that.'

Callaghan paused and lit a cigarette.

'You've got to realize that I'm not in the habit of receivin' visits late at night in my office from perfectly innocent young women,' he said. 'I've always reckoned that if young women were perfectly innocent they didn't have to do things like that.'

He allowed the smoke to trickle out of one nostril. His eyes never left her face. She was sitting as if petrified, speechless.

'There was just one thing I didn't think of,' he went on. 'I didn't think that any woman could be so damn brainless as you are. If I had I wouldn't have got myself in the jam that I did over you – a jam that I've been tryin' to get myself out of ever since.'

'I see,' she said, slowly and bitterly. 'So you've been thinking of Mr Callaghan all the time. I've always disliked you from the moment I set eyes on you, but I had a faint idea that you might have one good quality, that you might be loyal; apparently I was wrong there, too.'

'Maybe an' maybe not,' said Callaghan. His lips twisted up into a cynical grin. 'An' that is a point that I don't propose to argue with you here an' now. I'm just tellin' you that you puttin' on that damn fool act in my office even took me in that you'd got something to be good and frightened of, an' so I start fakin' alibis for you an' gettin' myself in bad with one an' all.

'All right. Well, one bad things leads to another. Because I fake that alibi, I get pulled in by Gringall before I've got time to do anything or fix anything, an' I have to start something else. I had to get time, so I pulled that fast one an' planted some fake evidence on Bellamy that got him pinched. Well, that's how it was, an' if I was in the same position tomorrow I'd do it again.'

'I expect you would, Mr Callaghan,' she said. 'And I expect that you'd use exactly the same method on anyone else that you wanted to get money from. Even if I believed that it was necessary for you to implicate Bellamy, I still think it was low and beastly of you to get that money from him, money which you got under a false pretence of protecting him after you'd carefully arranged that *nothing* could protect him.'

Callaghan spread his hands.

'That was a little bit fast, I grant you,' he said. 'But still you've got to admit that it was clever. It takes Callaghan of Callaghan Investigations to be as clever as that!'

He stood smiling at her. She got up. She was trembling with rage.

'Please leave here at once,' she said. '*Get out, do you hear?* I never want to see you again. But I would like to tell you one thing before you go: When I see Mr Gringall I propose to tell him the whole of my experiences with you, of the lies, trickery and deceit which you have used on every one with whom you have come in contact. You once told me that your reputation at Scotland Yard was not very good. Well, when they've heard what I've got to say you'll find it will be infinitely worse. I wouldn't even be surprised if you find yourself in prison!'

She stood in front of the fireplace, one arm on the mantelpiece Her lips were trembling with rage. Her whole person radiated a furious indignation.

Callaghan thought that she looked superb.

'Now,' she said, 'please get out. Don't talk any more because, if you do, I shall ring and have you turned out!'

Callaghan found another cigarette in his left hand coat pocket brought it out and lit it.

'No, madame, you won't,' he said. 'You won't do that because I'm goin' to show you that that would be the last thing in the world that Willie would want you to do.'

He inhaled. He was still watching her closely.

'You're not feelin' so good about me,' he went on. 'Bellamy's been at you, an' told you a lot of nasty bits about me, an' Willie has been through an' you've found out that I've told you one or two little fairy stories about where he was an' why you two couldn't meet.

'Well, I admit all that, an' maybe I admit some of the other things an' maybe not. But there's one thing I would like to say an that's this.

'I can see you're all packed an' ready to leave here. I suppose you're goin' to meet Willie. Maybe you two are plannin' a quick marriage, but I still think that you're goin' to agree with me when I say that before you get married you ought to clear yourself of any suspicion of havin' had anything to do with this murder.'

She raised her head disdainfully.

'That is for Willie to decide,' she said, 'and he has decided.'

'I see,' said Callaghan. 'He's decided to get married to you before this thing's cleared up. Well, all I can say is I don't think much of you for doin' it. I think you're pretty good when it comes to tellin' people like me just how lousy we are, but when it comes to doin' the right thing yourself you're not so good!'

She was almost speechless with rage. She controlled herself with difficulty, spoke with a little gasp.

'Exactly what do you mean by that?' she said.

'I mean that I expect Gringall to make a serious arrest tomorrow mornin', said Callaghan quietly. 'I think the person he's goin' to arrest will be a very good-lookin' and, at the moment, angry young woman by the name of Cynthis Merаulton, an' I say that if you marry Willie with that hangin' over your head you're not the woman to tell me where *I* get off the tram!'

She gazed at him in amazement.

'Listen,' said Callaghan. 'I told you just now that I'll bet that Willie got your address here from Gringall. Well, Willie probably knows that Gringall's goin' to get you tomorrow, so he does the right thing an' thinks his job is to marry you first. You know – hero stuff, you read about it in books.'

She sat down suddenly. Then she put her head between her hands. Callaghan watched her, his face serious.

'I'd like you to know that I'm not leadin' you up the garden path this time,' he said. 'An' I'll prove it to you. Listen to this –'

He walked across the room to the telephone. He turned and looked at her as he dialled the number. She was still sitting with her face hidden.

Callaghan listened. He heard the dialling tone buzzing regularly. He thought it wouldn't be so good, just at this moment, if Willie happened to be out or somewhere where he couldn't hear the telephone ringing.

He experienced a sense of relief when he heard Willie's voice.

'This is Callaghan,' he said. 'I'm at Delvine Court – with Cynthis, and she's not likin' me very much at the moment. She thinks I've double-crossed everybody on this business, including you.'

Willie did not speak. Callaghan went on:

'I had to tell her that I think it would be damn silly of you two to get married,' he said. 'I told her just now that it looks to me as if Gringall will be gettin' busy tomorrow, that he might want a *very* detailed statement from her, that he might even go so far as to arrest her. I've known stranger things.'

'I know . . .' Willie's voice was troubled. 'I know, Callaghan,' he repeated, 'but all the same, whatever happens I think that the best thing is for us to get married. Cynthis needs a friend now more than ever before. I can at least show her that I have the most perfect trust in her.'

Callaghan grinned amiably into the telephone.

'I know,' he said. 'I can guess how you're feelin', but the thing I'm concerned with just at this moment is how much trust have *you* got in me?

'You know this has been a pretty tough job from the beginning, an' you know that I've done my damnedest right the way through to play this thing the way you wanted it, an' I'm tellin' you that I think it will be mad for you two to start anything fresh until we've got some of this business straightened out.

'Let Gringall do what he wants to do, let him get busy and clear the job up an' then you can get married every day and twice on Sundays.'

Willie hesitated.

'Look here, Callaghan,' he said. 'I believe you've done one or two odd things since you've been working on this case, but I believe that your motives have been fairly straight – except that I don't think you should have got that money from Bellamy. He's been raising the very devil about it. He told Gringall; he told Cynthis. Don't you see that all that has only made things worse for her in Gringall's eyes? It made it appear that you were doing anything, going to any lengths, to stop him getting into touch with her.

'I realized that and that's why I told him where she was. I knew it wasn't any good trying to evade the issue any longer.

'But we're going to be married tomorrow morning. We've made up our minds on that point. Whatever happens we're going to see it through together.'

Callaghan nodded wisely at the telephone.

'All right, Willie,' he said, 'if you two people have made up your minds then you'll have to get ahead with it. But you take a tip from me. You get married directly the Registrar's office opens in the mornin'. The reason I'm advising that is because Gringall may take it into his head to make a move some time tonight, or very early tomorrow mornin'.'

He fumbled for a cigarette.

'If you're goin' through with it the wise thing would be for Cynthis to come straight round to your place now,' he went on. 'I've got my car outside, an' I'll bring her round. I want to have a little talk with you anyhow. There are one or two things that I think we ought to discuss. Perhaps you'd like to have a word with the lady on the telephone, an' tell her that you think I'm to be trusted to take her round to your place.'

Willie laughed softly.

'Put her on the line,' he said. 'You know, Callaghan, it's natural that she should distrust you a little bit. When a woman's in love she becomes hypersensitive. I think you've been doing what you consider your best, and I'll tell her so.'

'Thank you,' said Callaghan. 'I'll get her.'

He held the receiver out to the girl.

'Willie's on the line,' he said. 'He wants to talk to you.'

He went over to the fireplace, stood there, watching her, thinking.

She spoke to Willie. After a minute she hung up.

'Perhaps I've been a little bit unfair,' she said. 'But most of the things I said to you were true.'

Callaghan shrugged. His grin was amused, but his eyes were angry.

'It doesn't really matter, does it?' he asked. 'From now on you won't be afflicted with me – you'll have Willie lookin' after you.'

He walked over to the bags and picked up her coat, helped her on with it, handed her the gloves.

As he did so a suggestion of the perfume she wore came to his nostrils. He twitched his nose a little and smiled - a deprecating little smile. Then he picked up the bags and led the way towards the corridor.

Callaghan's antique car began to behave strangely when they got to the region of Hyde Park Corner. It coughed and wheezed and rattled. Once or twice, owing to Callaghan's quiet application of the choke it seemed that it would stop altogether.

Cynthis Meraulton said nothing. She sat beside him and looked straight ahead. Instinctively, he knew that she wanted to say something, that she was finding it difficult.

They passed the traffic lights at Hyde Park Corner. Callaghan should have turned into Park Lane, but he did not. He went straight on.

She looked at him in the darkness.

'You've missed your turning,' she said. 'You should have gone into Park Lane.'

He made an exclamation of annoyance.

'So I should,' he replied. 'I was thinkin', I suppose. Never mind, we'll turn up Down Street.'

A minute later he turned the car into the dark recesses of Down Street. Three-quarters of the way up is a small dark passage. Expertly, Callaghan shot the car into the passage, switched off the engine.

'What is this?' she said. 'Is this some new idea? Is this some other clever scheme which Mr Callaghan has thought out since we started? Please go on to Willie's flat, otherwise I shall get out.'

Callaghan smiled. His right hand was busy in his pocket.

'Listen, madame,' he said. 'I told you tonight that I didn't like this idea of your gettin' married tomorrow mornin'. I didn't like it then an' I don't like it now. But as you're all bein' so damned obstinate there's only one thing for me to do an' here it is!'

Suddenly his left hand shot out and about her shoulders, up to her face. She attempted to turn away from him but could not. She realized vaguely that he was very strong.

She became aware of a sickly and sweet smell. She struggled for a moment and then relaxed, fell back against the side of the car, unconscious.

Callaghan put the chloroform pad back into his pocket. He shot a quick glance round the passage and backed the car into Down Street. He turned down into Piccadilly and drove straight down towards the Circus. Then through Shaftesbury Avenue, Holborn, the Gray's Inn Road to Hunter Street.

He pulled the car up outside Darkie's place, got out, rapped on the door.

After a moment Darkie appeared.

'Hey, Guv.!' he said. 'I'ad an idea we'd see you around 'ere.'

Callaghan grinned at him.

'It looks as if you were right, doesn't it?' he said. 'Is Fred here or young Wilpins or any of the boys?'

'Fred's 'ere,' said Darkie.

'All right,' Callaghan indicated the car. 'You'll find Miss Meraulton in the car. I've had to give her some knock-out drops. Go an' get your missus down. We've got to get her inside an' your wife had better put her to bed for a bit. She won't be feeling so good when she gets out of the chloroform.'

Darkie disappeared. Callaghan went back and stood by the car.

Callaghan stood in the centre of Darkie's small sitting-room, smoking a cigarette.

He took the £180 in banknotes out of his pocket and handed the wad to Darkie.

'Eighty pounds of that is yours, Darkie,' he said. 'Fifty of the balance goes to the boys and you'd better keep the other fifty for me. Give it to me when I ask for it.'

He turned to Fred who, under the dim light, was still trying to work out the chances of some fancied quadruped with the aid of his inevitable 'form' book.

Callaghan took out of his pocket the envelope addressed to Gringall, containing his notes and Paul Meraulton's confession.

'Now listen, Fred,' he said. 'Don't make any mistake about this.'

He looked at his watch.

'It's two o'clock,' he said. 'Now, here's what you've got to do. You get along into the Gray's Inn Road and pick up the first cab you find. Drive along to Scotland Yard an' ask to see Mr Gringall. Say you've got an urgent message from me. An' you don't want to see anybody else either. If Gringall's gone home say you want his private address or get 'em to phone through to him. He'll turn up quickly enough if he knows I want him.

'When you get him give him this envelope. If, by some odd chance something's happened to Gringall an' he's not available you give the envelope to Detective-Sergeant Fields and tell him to open it. When you've done that you can go home to bed.'

Fred Mazin took the package.

'O.K., Guv,' he said.

He picked up his hat and walked out.

Darkie produced a cigarette from behind his ear. His eyes fixed on Callaghan's face were serious.

''Ow's it goin', Slim?' he said. 'Is it all right?'

Callaghan grinned.

'We'll soon know,' he said.

Darkie nodded.

'An' what do we do about the girl?' he said. 'My missus wants to know what we're goin' to say to 'er when she comes out of those knock-out drops you give 'er. Maybe she'll be a bit rorty.'

Callaghan shook his head.

'She'll sleep for some time when she does come out,' he said. 'You don't have to worry. Another thing is that I expect Gringall will be around here before very long.'

Darkie raised his eyebrows.

'Wot?' he exclaimed. 'Blinkin' police comin' round 'ere.' He laughed. 'I'll get the red carpet out for 'em,' he said. 'An' when they come what do I say to 'em, Guv.?'

Callaghan threw his cigarette stub into the fireplace, produced another. He lit it, then picked up his hat.

'When Gringall comes round,' he said slowly, 'you give him my love. He'll understand. So long, Darkie!'

He turned and walked out of the room. Darkie heard the front door close quietly behind him.

He stood, scratching his head.

Callaghan walked into the telephone box at the intersection at Gray's Inn Road. He dialled Willie Meraulton's number.

He was smiling - a peculiar tight little smile that showed his white teeth.

Willie came on the line.

'Listen, Willie,' said Callaghan. 'I'm afraid I've rather taken things into my own hands again. I'm sorry, but I thought it was necessary. Cynthis is with some friends of mine. She decided that it was her duty to see Gringall before she got married. She thought it wouldn't be doin' the right thing by you to marry while she's under suspicion.

'But that isn't the main thing,' he went on. 'The main thing is this: That will that the old boy was carryin' around in his watch-case didn't matter a damn. Not a tinker's cuss. You see, the old boy made another will - a later one. He made it on the day he was murdered, probably in the afternoon.

'An' he was pretty clever about this one. He made two copies and signed 'em both. I suppose he was afraid one might get lost. Well, one of 'em's disappeared all right, but I've had a bit of luck. I've found the duplicate. I've got it in my pocket now. It's in a sealed envelope, an' written on the outside are the words "signed duplicate of the last Will and Testament of August Meraulton," in the old boy's handwriting.'

Callaghan paused for a moment. Took a long drag at his cigarette.

'Now, I think you ought to have that duplicate,' said Callaghan, letting the smoke trickle out of his nostrils. 'You're the one that the old boy would want to have it. I thought maybe you'd like to come around to my office in Chancery Lane an' get it.'

He stopped speaking. There was a pause.

'What time will you be there?' said Willie eventually.

'I'll be there at three o'clock, sharp,' said Callaghan. 'I'll be seein' you, Willie.'

He hung up the receiver.

CHAPTER THIRTEEN

Exit Paul, Exit Jeremy

Detective-Sergeant 'Lucy' Fields put his hand in front of his mouth and hoped Gringall wouldn't see him yawning. Gringall didn't like people who got tired easily.

Fields, chewing the end of his pencil, looked at the sheet of his official shorthand book as it lay before him on the end of Gringall's long desk.

Written on the top of the page was 'Jeremy Meraulton. Arrested. Conspiracy to Defraud. Statement on Examination.'

Fields thought the Meraulton case was one hell of a case. Nothing happened and then, suddenly, all sorts of things began to happen. Fields wondered just how much Gringall knew, just how much he pretended he didn't know. The Jigger was a clever devil, thought Fields.

Jeremy Meraulton stood on the other side of Gringall's desk. A detective-constable stood beside him. Jeremy's big hands were hanging straight down by his sides. His brain was realizing something rather near to hopelessness. The idea occurred to him that it was extraordinarily quiet, and then he remembered suddenly that it was very late at night, and that here, in Scotland Yard, in this remote office, it would *have* to be quiet.

Jeremy thought that he had been a fool to go back to the Noughts and Crosses just on the chance that Mayola would be there. He realized bitterly that he would never have gone there except for the suggestion from Callaghan... 'If I were you I'd just run along nicely and go into a huddle with your lady friend Mayola about what you're goin' to do ...' Jeremy could hear

Callaghan saying those words, and like a fool he had done just that thing – walked into a trap like an insane rabbit.

Standing there with the feeling of hopelessness growing stronger with each second, Jeremy began to think quickly about Callaghan, to realize that Callaghan was a much more clever person than he, Jeremy, had realized, that Callaghan was not only very quick on the uptake, but that he was also a person of a certain courage. Jeremy remembered the beating that Callaghan had taken down at the Show Down. He certainly could take it. He had taken it. Now it looked as if he was going to be the cause of Jeremy 'taking it'!

And it would have been so easy to have made a getaway. If only he hadn't thought of talking it over with Mayola – who would probably smile that slow smile of hers when she heard what had happened – he might still have got out.

But the suggestion had come from Callaghan, and, like a fool, he'd followed it ... just like a rabbit.

Jeremy bit his lip.

Damn Callaghan!

The detective-constable was speaking:

'In accordance with an instruction received from Inspector Myse at Vine Street, I telephoned through to inform the night officer at Scotland Yard that an anonymous telephone call received at Vine Street Station about twelve thirty-five had suggested that Mr Gringall might like to know that Mr Jeremy Meraulton would probably be contacting a lady by the name of Miss Mayola Ferrival at the Noughts and Crosses Club. The same anonymous speaker also suggested that Mr Gringall might like to know that Mr Jeremy Meraulton might be able to give Mr Gringall some interesting information about four old companies that had been re-floated by Mr Paul Meraulton for the purpose of fraudulently obtaining money from the Meraulton Estates and Trust Company. The caller went on to say that he believed that Mr Jeremy Meraulton might try to leave the country immediately, and that Mr Gringall would probably not desire this, having regard to his own investigations into the August Meraulton murder case.

'I later received an instruction,' the detective-constable continued, 'from Inspector Myse to go at once to the Noughts and Crosses Club and contact Mr Jeremy Meraulton if he were there. I went to the club and I saw Mr Meraulton. I told him that I was a police officer and asked him to accompany me to Scotland Yard as Detective-Inspector Gringall would like to ask him one or two questions.

'He said . . . "Damn Callaghan. He's responsible for this. Damn him!" He then turned to Miss Ferrival and said: "Now I've got it. That damned Callaghan has got Paul to squeal. Paul's got away with it whilst I get taken!"

'I took Mr Meraulton to Vine Street and, in accordance with another instruction received, I went immediately, accompanied by Detective-Constable Ferris, to the Melleville Apartments, Glasbury Street. There we found Mr Paul Meraulton in the act of packing his clothes. I informed Mr Paul Meraulton that there was, at Scotland Yard, a warrant for his arrest on a charge of conspiracy to defraud. I searched him and found on him one thousand pounds in bank notes. I brought him to Scotland Yard.'

Gringall looked at Jeremy.

'That's how it is,' he said.

He lit his pipe carefully.

'Now, if I were you, Mr Meraulton,' he went on, 'I'd make it as easy for yourself as possible. Maybe you can throw a little light on one or two small points. If you can so much the better for you. If you can't or don't want to . . .' Gringall shrugged his shoulders.

Jeremy said nothing.

'This afternoon,' said Gringall, 'a certain Mr Rupert Patrick Callaghan, usually called Slim Callaghan, left the numbers of certain groups of bank notes in his possession with me. We find that several of these numbers tally with those on the notes taken tonight from Mr Paul Meraulton when he was searched. Have you any sort of explanation in your mind for that?'

Jeremy smiled.

'That's easy,' he said. 'Perfectly simple. Callaghan told me tonight that Paul had talked, that he had made a confession. I suppose Callaghan paid him to.' He stopped smiling. 'I suppose it's also amusing to realize that Callaghan got some of that money from me.'

Gringall smiled now.

'Not only from you,' he said, 'but from Miss Meraulton, Mr Willie Meraulton, Mr Bellamy Meraulton – as well as Mr Jeremy Meraulton.' The Jigger's smile broadened. 'In fact,' he went on, 'it rather looks as if Slim Callaghan has been collecting money from the Meraulton family for the purpose of bribing Paul Meraulton to make a confession.'

The Jigger drew on his pipe.

'Paul was a fool,' he said. 'He ought to have kept his mouth shut for a little longer, in which case he might have faced only one charge instead of two.'

He blew a perfect smoke ring.

'I'm beginning to believe that Callaghan is even more clever than he looks at first sight,' he concluded.

Jeremy spoke bitterly.

'And I suppose Callaghan telephoned through and told you,' he said. 'I suppose he gave Paul away in just the same way as he put you on to me!'

Gringall shook his head.

'No,' he said. 'Callaghan knew that would be unnecessary. He probably guessed that we'd had Paul under observation ever since *we* discovered about those companies. That's one thing I do like about Callaghan,' said Gringall pleasantly. 'He does show that he thinks we have a little intelligence here at the Yard which is very pleasant in these days when most people seem to believe that we're quite solid above the neck.'

Jeremy sneered.

'Callaghan's quite a hero, isn't he?' he said. 'Well, perhaps I can put a spoke in *his* wheel. It might interest you to know,' he went on, 'that Callaghan was the man who got into the Ensell Street mortuary and stole the will – the one on gold copy paper – from my uncle's dead body. He told me so himself tonight!'

Gringall nodded gravely.

'I knew that,' he said. 'But since you're being so frank, Mr Meraulton, perhaps you'll be good enough to tell me where that will is – that is if you know?'

'I don't know,' said Jeremy. 'I don't know and I don't care. I xpect that Callaghan destroyed it. I expect somebody paid him o!'

Gringall looked surprised.

'Why should *he* want to destroy it?' he asked. 'And while we're n the question, Mr Meraulton, who do *you* think would be the nost likely person to want that will destroyed? I would suggest hat the person who wanted that will destroyed would be the erson who murdered or assisted in the murder of August Meraulton!'

Jeremy was silent for a full minute. He realized that he was alking too much.

'How should I know why he would want to destroy it,' he said ventually. 'Why should I know anything about what Callaghan vants to do or wants not to do? I prefer to mind my own business!'

Gringall nodded. He opened his desk drawer and took out a locument.

'Jeremy Fane Gresley Meraulton,' he said. 'I have here a varrant for your arrest on charge of Conspiracy to Defraud the Meraulton Estates and Trust Company. I should tell you that part f the money found on your brother Paul Meraulton – under rrest on the same charge – tonight, was in the form of bank notes riginally obtained by fraud from the Meraulton Estates and Trust Company, and handed by you for some consideration nown to yourself to one Rupert Patrick – commonly known as Slim" – Callaghan. I have to caution you that anything you may ow say may be used in evidence against you.'

Jeremy said nothing.

'Take the prisoner away,' said Gringall.

Fields stirred his coffee.

'I suppose Callaghan's got that confession,' he asked. 'I wonder what he's going to do with it?'

Gringall smiled at him.

'We'll see,' he said. 'I expect it will come along here sooner or later.'

Fields grinned back at his chief.

'I've got an idea that you've a soft spot for Callaghan, sir,' he said. 'What's he playing at? What's happened to him all of a sudden? He seems to be making some first-class breaks for us!'

Gringall nodded.

'I'm wondering about him myself,' he said. 'But I've got an idea. You know,' he went on, 'it would be a damn funny thing if Callaghan got the idea into his head that that fake alibi he tried to work on us about Cynthis Meraulton had made things look very bad for her, that it had corroborated other points in the evidence against her.

'It would be a damn funny thing if Callaghan had got keen on the girl - and by what I understand she's what is commonly known as a peach - and was simply rooting around, working himself to pieces so as to get her in the clear. Anyhow,' he concluded, 'I've got an idea that Slim's got a devil of a lot up his sleeve. He's a clever devil.'

Fields nodded.

'Even so,' he said, 'supposing he has got the confession? You knew that they'd been defrauding the old boy. You've known that for some time. But does it get us anywhere - in the murder case I mean?'

The Jigger refilled his pipe.

'Use your brains, Fields,' he said. 'Haven't you heard of that old proverb "when thieves fall out, honest men have a chance to come into their own"? It looks as if Callaghan's heard of it.

'There's no evidence in the murder case. There was never a case that I've ever been connected with where there was less.

'Look at it. August Meraulton has an appointment at his office with somebody or other somewhere beween ten-fifteen and eleven o'clock. We don't know whether he goes to his office or not. All we know is that there's been some sort of disturbance there, that the door is left open and that the street door is left open.

'The old man is shot through the head at close range, either on the spot where he was found or he was moved there after he'd been shot.

'We know that Cynthis Meraulton went to the office in Lincoln's Inn Fields at eleven o'clock. Bellamy saw her. But we know that she didn't get her car out of the garage until a quarter to eleven. It's true, of course, that she might have killed the old boy about ten twenty-five, and still had time to get back to her garage and then drive back to Lincoln's Inn Fields, so as to give herself a clever alibi.

'But we can't get at Cynthis and we can't find out anything at all from her - not in the beginning I mean. And the reason we can't do that is because Callaghan has got the girl hidden away. Well, I didn't like him for doing that in the first place, but I think I'm grateful to him now, because I'm certain that whatever the girl had said would only have produced more chaos. I believe that Callaghan thought she might have said too much or too little. He wanted time. He knew that later we would find her if we wanted her.

'But we've no evidence on the murder. We can only *think* about all these things. We haven't any proof whatsoever. We have no evidence direct or circumstantial. We know she quarrelled with August Meraulton, but so have most of the other people he's come into contact with.

'The worst thing against her is the fact that Callaghan deliberately faked the time she went to his office. He lied like a trooper about that. The girl, Effie Perkins, was telling the truth. I know that and Callaghan knows it. But that still doesn't mean a thing. It's all very well our knowing what Cynthis Meraulton did *after* eleven o'clock, but we still don't know what she did between ten and a quarter to eleven. Her maid doesn't know. She was in the kitchen and she doesn't know what time Cynthis Meraulton went out. So much for Cynthis.

'At one time it looked as if we had a case against Bellamy. The only case we ever had against him was as phoney as the deuce. It was all faked – Callaghan faked it. He faked it to get time to give himself a chance to think up something, or to do something – Heaven alone knows what! But we know that Bellamy didn't get to Lincoln's Inn Fields until close on eleven, that he was only there for a minute or two. So much for Bellamy.

'All the rest of 'em have alibis. All the Meraulton boys were with Willie at his club, trying to get money out of him. The room where they met was in a passage where there was a pass door out to the street, and you can say if you like that one of 'em went out, killed the old boy and came back again, but the fact remains, if they all swear they were there together, that evidence has got to count and we can't rebut it with mere theories.

'We can *prove* nothing. We know that half a dozen people hated the old boy – Bellamy especially. We know that Cynthis had a row with him just a while before, and we can think a whole lot more things, too, but we can't *prove* a damned thing, and Callaghan knows it!'

Fields raised his eyebrows.

'Callaghan . . .?' he queried.

Gringall looked at him in disgust.

'Haven't you got it yet?' he said. 'Remember the proverb I quoted – "When thieves fall out, etc." Hasn't it struck you that Callaghan has very successfully stirred up the Meraulton crowd to such an extent that the whole four of 'em will try an' save their skins at the expense of the others? Bellamy, pulled in, squeals on Cynthis, because he believes she's squealed on him. Paul, pushed into a corner, makes some sort of confession which should be damned interesting when we see it. And now, Jeremy – he'll probably talk tomorrow.'

Gringall finished his coffee.

Fields put his pencil away.

'I get all that, sir,' he said. 'But there's still one thing I don't get. And that's this: Where does Callaghan come into all this? What's he doing? What does he think he's going to do?'

The Jigger put his pipe away. Then he looked at Fields with a broad grin.

'Search me,' he said. 'God knows, I don't, but whatever he's doing or whatever he's done, I'll bet a month's pay it's going to be good! In the meantime,' he added, 'you can send for some more coffee.'

Gringall had just finished his third cup when the desk telephone rang to tell him that a Mr Fred Mazin was waiting to see him in connection with the Meraulton case. Five minutes later the Jigger was opening the envelope that Callaghan had addressed to him. When Mazin had gone the C.I.D. man read carefully through the confession made by Paul. He tossed it over to Fields.

'That clears that up,' he said. 'I was expecting Callaghan to pull something rather spectacular tonight. Now, let's look at the rest of this stuff.'

He pulled the desk light nearer. As he did so, he glanced, more from force of habit than anything else, at his wrist-watch. It said a quarter to three.

Gringall settled down to read:

Dear Gringall,

It is not very often that I have the pleasure of writing to C.I.D. officers, and so I'm getting a bit of a kick out of this. Maybe you know as much as I do, and maybe you don't. I think you don't!

Anyhow I'm going to take the liberty of giving you a few pointers on the Meraulton case. I'm also going to explain just why I've handled this job the way I have, and if, when you've read this, you want to have a big laugh at me getting sentimental in my old age, well, go ahead.

I expect that it's struck you just as forcibly as it has me that there isn't any real or concrete evidence in the Meraulton case – certainly not enough for you to make a pinch on. There isn't even any CIRCUMSTANTIAL *evidence that matters a damn, and when a policeman hasn't even that, it looks as if it's going to be too bad for him doesn't it?*

I realize, just as well as you probably do, that whoever it was killed old August had made up his mind that he was going to do the job in such a way that he wasn't going to be caught. Even now, if he has any luck, he won't be caught. Because this fellow was clever enough to realize these salient facts: first, that if there isn't a motive for a murder, the police can't take any definite steps against ANYBODY *without laying themselves open to a good kick in the pants if they happen to be wrong, and second, that if you can get two or three people suspected in a murder job, all of whom are obviously not working on any prearranged scheme, then it's a stone certainty that evidence (if any) against one is going to be cancelled out by evidence (if any) against the others, and so the upshot of the job would be that although the police might have a devil of a lot of suspicion against this person or that person, they wouldn't have sufficient concrete proof of any sort whatsoever to make an arrest. Our murderer knows that.*

That's your position at the moment. You can't do a damn thing, and that's where I come into this job, because, not being a policeman, when I have suspicions I can create circumstances that either corroborate or break them down. Personally, I'm out for something that will make your mouth water. I'm out for a real, honest-to-goodness confession from the murderer, and with a lot of luck I'm going to get it.

Here are the things I want you to know: Every bit of apparent evidence in this case points to Cynthis Meraulton having done the old boy in. But if you use your brains, you will see that the main thing against her is that she came round to my office on the night of the murder; that she'd been in Lincoln's Inn Fields somewhere (roughly) about the time of the murder; that she knew the old boy was going to be there; that she'd quarrelled with him over his trying to stop her from marrying Willie and because he'd given her mother a bad time.

But the salient fact is that she DID *come round to see me. She came round to see me because Fingal had told Willie that I was the sort of person who would be O.K. to look after her if somebody tried to frame a murder charge on her. Think that out.*

You'll probably want to know why I planted that blood-stained hat on Bellamy. You probably think I did this to gain time. You'd be partly right. But I also did it to follow on the logical sequence of events that I was intended to follow. Get this: Cynthis Meraulton was suspect because she'd been in Lincoln's Inn Fields, and therefore I was entitled to suspect Bellamy because he had also been there. The interesting point, to my mind, was why was Bellamy there? Possibly you asked him, after you pinched him on that drugs charge, and maybe he told you. If he didn't, I think I can. I'll bet you any money you like that Jeremy got Bellamy to go down to Lincoln's Inn Fields to keep watch and see if old August Meraulton turned up at his office at eleven o'clock. That's why Bellamy was there.

You and I both know that August Meraulton must have got to Lincoln's Inn Fields much earlier, that it was quite useless for Bellamy to get there at about three minutes to eleven and wait for the old boy, because August had already been to the office.

BUT BELLAMY WASN'T TO KNOW THAT. BELLAMY BELIEVED THAT THE OLD BOY WAS GOING TO GET THERE AT ELEVEN O'CLOCK, OR SOON AFTERWARDS.

Why did he believe that? You try working that question out, and see where it gets you!

Maybe you're wondering why I touched Bellamy for that 200 just after I'd planted evidence on him that was going to get him arrested. If Fields has checked up on the groups of bank note numbers I gave you this afternoon – I think you can answer that one for yourself.

I went around and played that big act with Eulalie Gallicot, because I knew that Bellamy had gone on, after he'd left Lincoln's Inn Fields, to see her. So I went along there just to see if somebody was trying to get her to fake the time that he got there, SO AS TO THROW FURTHER SUSPICION ON HIM. *You realize that it was only because you were lucky enough to find two taxi-cab drivers who were able to give you the right times that you knew that Bellamy must be innocent in the murder charge.*

Eulalie agreed to MY *demand that she fake the time because she thought I was working for the same person that had instructed her, through her husband Beldoces, to do the same thing. It was only afterwards that she would know she was wrong there, but it still wouldn't make any difference. Now, who would her original instruction have come from?*

Here's another point: I wondered why you were able to send a Squad car to just the right place, at just the right time, on the afternoon I went to see Bellamy, and plant that hat on him. You told me that a policeman had seen me, but I knew that was all bunkum. I'd gone there in a closed cab, anyhow! You knew I was going to be there, because somebody (no name was given, I'll bet), telephoned through to the Yard and told you. And who do you think that was? Can you work that out? I know that there was only one person who could have done it.

The fact that Paul Meraulton has been running those four fake companies is another pointer. We know why those companies came into the story. They were started by Paul to enable the four Meraulton boys to get money out of the Estates and Trust Co., without the knowledge of August Meraulton. All that is very interesting, but it isn't half as interesting as the fact that somebody must have been keen to see that this money was repaid sometime, and if you bring that brain of yours (I'm not being funny, I think that you HAVE *got brains!), to bear on the subject, and you care to think about this business from the point of view of* HOW WAS THE MONEY GOING TO BE REPAID *then you'll have another step towards the murderer.*

After I'd done a certain amount of talking to Cynthis Meraulton, I was more than certain that I was heading in the right direction. I've got a very good memory for conversations, and after I'd had a couple of talks with Cynthis, I came to the conclusion that either she was a first-class liar (which I wasn't inclined to believe), or that she was quite innocently playing a line which she had been intended to do from the start.

You realize, of course, that when she came to see me the first time, at my office, I believed that she had murdered August Meraulton. That was why I tried to fake that alibi for her – which was about the silliest thing I've ever tried to do in my life. Effie Perkins didn't know that she was doing both you and me a good turn when she went along and saw you and told you the actual times that Cynthis came and went. I'm very much obliged to Effie about that, and one day, if I ever see her again, I'll buy her a nice bunch of roses or raspberries – whichever she prefers.

I told Cynthis that I thought Bellamy was the murderer, not because I believed that to be true, but because I wanted to see whether she'd be surprised or whether she would feel entitled to think that Bellamy had killed the old man. She wasn't surprised, so I knew that somebody or something had been working on her mind to the effect that he had. This told me a bit more.

Another interesting point: Arnault Beldoces is Eulalie Gallicot's husband. Eulalie Gallicot is (or was) Bellamy's mistress. Beldoces is the man who has been supplying Bellamy with drugs. He is also the man who instructed Eulalie to give the wrong time of Bellamy's arrival to the Police. He is also connected with the Meraulton boys, who use his night clubs.

Now, it's a certainty that Beldoces isn't the sort of man to do anything for anybody, unless he gets well paid for it. But we know that the Meraulton boys hadn't any money to speak of. They were always trying to get some for themselves. There's another point for you to work on.

I've got to admit that I've kept you badly in the dark about one point. I'll make a clean breast of it now.

You went along to take a look round Cynthis Meraulton's flat but you didn't find anything. So you couldn't have looked very well, could you? I went there after you, and made a very close search. I found a .22 bullet which had fallen out of a box of ammunition that had been kept in one of the drawers in the room. The whole box was there but you didn't find it. Willie Merauiton found it. He'd been along there before me and grabbed it. In doing so, one of the cartridges fell out of the box.

This will indicate to you that Willie, at this time, concluded that you were actually going to arrest Cynthis, and he wanted to make certain that you didn't find too much evidence against her. I've still got that cartridge, and if it's possible, I'll let you have a look at it one day.

Now, about Jeremy. You know damn well that I was the mysterious man who got into the Ensell Street mortuary, and grabbed the gold copy paper will out of old August's watchcase. I wrote a letter to myself from some fake person called Sammy the Sheik, saying that Sammy had the will and was prepared to sell it. I passed this letter on to Jeremy through Mayola and he was prepared to go to the trouble of first of all beating me up, and secondly, paying me good money to get his hands on that gold paper will.

That told me all I wanted to know about Jeremy.

My next thing was to plan to take a look at Paul and see whether Paul was prepared to stay here in this country and face things out, or whether, when he discovered that I was wise to the company business, he'd be prepared to take the £1000 which I'd collected and take his hook. When I know about this, I shall have even another point for or against the murderer. If I succeed with Paul I shall try and get a confession from him which I shall send to you with these notes.

Well, Jigger, I suppose you want to know why I've played it this way, and why I'm prepared to take the chance I'm going to take fairly soon, if things go the way I expect they will.

I suppose I've broken the law in half a dozen places. I've done that before in odd ways (you remember our little conversation about those fake alibis of mine in previous cases!) and I expect I've laid myself open to about a dozen different charges of one sort or another.

Well, it's the old story of CHERCHEZ LA FEMME! *I've met a lot of women in my time but I've never met one who looked like Cynthis*

Meraulton. I once told her that I'd go to hell for her and the joke was that she thought I was telling just another lie! Women are like that.

I'm a man who's never bothered to look at himself very much. I suppose I've never had the time or inclination, but the Meraulton case has done one thing. It has taught me that I'm fed up with this game and that there's something to be said for being a two pound a week clerk and knowing that you're going to get the two pounds at the end of the week!

There's another thing to be said for doing a job like that, too. If you do meet a woman and fall for her you can still kid yourself that you've got a chance with her even if it's only a day-dream.

But in my job you can't even indulge in a day-dream. Just imagine a man like Slim Callaghan kidding himself that he'd got a chance with a girl like Cynthis Meraulton!

All right, the sob stuff is now over, and I want you to concentrate pretty carefully on the stuff I'm writing down now. Here's what I plan to do, and here's what I want you to do ...

Gringall read on for a few moments. Then, with an exclamation, he pushed the papers into his desk drawer. Fields, watching him, got up.

'Telephone downstairs and tell them to have a Squad car round at the entrance,' snapped Gringall. 'We're going round to Callaghan's office in Chancery Lane, and we're going fast.'

He grabbed at his hat. As he ran for the door he looked at his watch.

It was ten past three.

CHAPTER FOURTEEN

The Hangman Speaks

It was a quarter to three.

Callaghan, coughing, climbed up the stairs to his office. He told himself, as usual, that he would have to cut down his cigarettes, then thought, almost simultaneously, that perhaps it would not matter very much whether he cut them down or not.

The idea seemed to amuse him.

Inside the outer office he switched on the light and locked the door behind him. Then he crossed to the inner office, hung up his hat and coat in the darkness, switched on the desk light and slumped down into his chair.

He stayed there for a moment thinking. Then he opened a drawer and took out a long envelope. He walked into the outer office, looked about him and eventually found what he was looking for – a copy of the *Evening News* left behind by Fred Mazin. He tore the two front sheets off the newspaper, folded them carefully, put them into the envelope, and wrote on it, 'The Last Will and Testament of me, August Meraulton.' He wrote the words in a scrawly handwriting, to look as near that of the dead man as possible.

Then he stuck down the envelope, put it in the top drawer of his desk.

He unlocked the bottom drawer of the desk, took out the Luger pistol, looked at it for a moment regretfully, then replaced it and locked the drawer. He did this with a peculiarly hopeless expression that was almost humorous.

He got up, walked to a cupboard in the corner of the office, and took out a heavy wooden box, rather like an attache case. He took this box into the opposite corner – the corner on the right-hand side of the desk, fiddled about for a moment or two; then sat down in his chair.

He took out his packet of Player's, saw that he had only three cigarettes left. He lit one and put the other two on the desk in front of him within easy reach.

He pulled the desk light into an appropriate position, took a piece of writing paper and began to write a letter to Cynthis Meraulton. The letter was brief. When he had finished it he read it through carefully, grinned sheepishly, tore it up into very small pieces, and threw them into the waste-paper basket.

There was a knock on the outer office door.

Callaghan walked into the outer office and opened it.

Willie Meraulton stood outside. He smiled when he saw Callaghan, and took the pipe he was smoking from his mouth. Callaghan could see that Willie was worried.

'I'm glad you're punctual,' he said. 'I've got two or three things to talk to you about and I want to get them right in my mind before morning, because it looks as if things are going to happen at last.'

Willie nodded seriously, and put his pipe back into his mouth. Callaghan closed the outer door and led the way into the inner office. He stood at the door, allowed Willie to pass, closed the door quietly.

Willie Meraulton sat down in the chair in front of the desk. Callaghan threw away the stub of the cigarette he was smoking and picked up one of the two that he had laid on the desk. He lit it and stood in his favourite position, leaning up against the wall.

Willie knocked out his pipe into the palm of his hand. He got up and threw the ashes into the waste-paper basket.

'I think you've been very clever, Callaghan,' he said, without looking at Callaghan, 'to find out about that other will – the one you say my uncle made on the day that he was murdered. Are you sure you're right? There's no possibility of a mistake?'

Callaghan shrugged.

'There's always the possibility of a mistake,' he said. He

grinned. 'Life wouldn't be half so amusin' if people didn't make mistakes. But I don't think I've made a mistake this time.'

Willie sat down again and began to fill his pipe. Watching the steadiness of the fingers that pressed the tobacco into the bowl, Callaghan was smitten with a sudden queer admiration for Willie's coolness. Willie had nerve all right.

Callaghan sat down at his desk. The light from the lamp illuminated the top of the desk, leaving the faces of both men in the shadow.

'There's something you ought to know, Willie,' said Callaghan. 'You read in the papers about the fellow who was seen hanging about Ensell Street on the night that your uncle was murdered. Well, this fellow stole the gold copy paper will out of the old boy's watch-case.'

Willie looked surprised.

'How extraordinary,' he said. 'Wasn't the murder done merely to get possession of that will? If the murderer didn't take it he must have been the fellow who went to Ensell Street and stole it. He failed to get it when he killed August, so he was forced to try again. Perhaps he had no opportunity on the first occasion?'

Callaghan shook his head.

'No,' he said. 'That doesn't wash. In any event, *I* was the man who stole that will. I got into the mortuary and took it. I wanted to have a look at it.'

Willie's eyes were wide with astonishment.

'I can't make you out, Callaghan,' he said. 'Where is that will – what have you done with it?'

Callaghan settled himself back in his chair. He was beginning to enjoy the situation.

'I sold it to Jeremy,' he said. 'I got four hundred pounds out of Jeremy, and sold it to him. I watched him burn it in this office.'

'You did what?' exclaimed Willie. 'You must be mad. That was criminal! What was the purport of this will?'

'Oh that . . .' said Callaghan casually. 'Well, the old boy revoked all previous dispositions and left the whole of his fortune and estate to Cynthis Meraulton.'

'My God!' Willie's voice shook with anger. 'And you sold that to Jeremy! You robbed Cynthis of her fortune in order to sell that will to Jeremy for four hundred pounds! You'll have a lot to answer for, Callaghan. You'll pay for all this dearly even if you have made a few hundreds out of the Meraultons.'

Callaghan stubbed out his second cigarette and lit the third and last one. Willie had not lit his pipe. He was sitting holding it clenched tight between his teeth, watching Callaghan's face.

'I've heard something like that before,' said Callaghan. 'Cynthis told me that I'd been doin' pretty well out of the Meraultons, but I didn't take very much notice of that. Thinking what she did think, she was entitled to say it I suppose.'

He drew the smoke down into his lungs.

'Nobody's done well out of the Meraultons,' he said eventually. 'I got a few hundreds out of them – £1180 to be exact. I gave £1000 of that to Paul for the confession I got out of him, an' I'm prepared to bet a fiver of the lousy fifty pounds that I might eventually make out of this business – if I'm lucky – that he didn't get it either. I bet I know who's got it.'

Willie put his pipe into his pocket.

'Who's got it?' he said.

His voice sounded a little thick.

Callaghan looked across at him. He was smiling broadly.

'Gringall's got it,' he said. 'I'll bet all the tea in China to a bad egg that Gringall pinched Paul tonight. If he did he searched him. If he searched him and found those notes, he'll check up with the numbers of the notes I gave him this afternoon. He'll realize where that money or most of it originally came from.'

Willie drew in his breath with a little hissing sound.

Callaghan got up and leaned against the wall behind his desk, his cigarette hanging from the corner of his mouth.

'You're a damn clever feller, Willie,' he said. 'You've given me a helluva lot of trouble over this business. I thought that I was pretty smart but when it comes to thinking out a really first-class scheme embodying everything that there is on the Newgate calendar I take my hat off to you!'

Willie's voice was still cool and bitter.

'I don't think I understand you,' he said. 'I think you're trying something else on. Just as you've tried something on with Cynthis and Jeremy and Bellamy.'

Callaghan looked down at his wrist watch. The time was ten minutes past three.

'That's the funny thing about it,' said Callaghan. 'I'm a bad feller with a bad reputation, an' you're a good feller with a good one. That was the thing that first put me wise to you. You see, when Cynthis Meraulton came round here with that funny story of hers, I believed that she'd murdered old Meraulton. I believed – as you intended me to believe – that you had the idea in your head that she *might* do such a thing and were trying to protect her from the consequences.

'I fell for the idea. I faked an alibi for her. But pretty soon I realized that I'd done a damn silly thing. I realized that she was innocent of anything to do with the murder. When I thought that, the first thing I asked myself was why such a good feller as you are should send the girl he's in love with to a bad feller like me!

'I'll tell you why you sent her here. You knew I had a reputation for fakin' alibis. Maybe, when Fingal was tellin' you about me he also told you I was broke. The night Cynthis came around here I hadn't eaten for a day, or smoked for eight hours. I was very glad to see some money from anywhere.

'I've got a damn good memory,' Callaghan continued coolly. 'When I came to see you the day after the murder, you said that the first suggestion that Cynthis might be in some sort of danger from your brothers was made some days before the murder. That was a lie. The suggestion never came from her. It came from *you*, and your reason for makin' it was to put the idea in her mind that it might be necessary for her to be looked after by somebody – somebody who was as smart as your brothers – me, in fact.

'You told me something else too. You said that you'd wanted her to come around and see me days before. That was a damn lie. You were clever enough to think up a scheme by which she wouldn't come round and see me until the night of the murder. I'll tell you how you did it.'

Callaghan threw the stub of the last cigarette into the ash tray. Then he put his hands into his pockets, and tilted his chair back. Willie was sitting forward in his chair, his hands clasped, his eyes like pinpoints of fire.

'You told that poor kid,' Callaghan went on, 'that I was the sort of feller who wouldn't do anything without money. You told her that it wasn't any good her coming round to see me unless she *had* money. All right. When I was talking to you the day after the murder you told me that you'd given her the five hundred pounds just as soon as you'd made inquiries from Fingal about me – days before the murder day.'

Callaghan grinned broadly.

'That was another damn lie, Willie,' he said. 'I'll tell you what you did. You drew the five hundred pounds and put it in an envelope, and you kept it in your office. Possibly Cynthis asked you about making the appointment with me and you stalled her by tellin' her that you hadn't got the money, that you were gettin' it. You know as well as I do that you only sent her that money on the day – late in the day – on which you *had* to kill old August, and you made the appointment for her on the telephone that evenin' so that she should come around to this office immediately she'd been round to Lincoln's Inn Fields and found that the old boy wasn't waiting for her as he should have been.'

Callaghan tilted his chair forward.

'You knew as well as I did that the fact that she came around here immediately after she'd left the Square would damn her in the eyes of the police.'

Willie laughed easily.

'How very interesting,' he said. 'And perhaps you'll be good enough to tell me just how I knew that Cynthis would be going to

Lincoln's Inn Fields to meet my esteemed uncle on that particular night?'

Callaghan's eyes narrowed. Then he recovered his temper and relaxed.

'Yes, I'll tell you,' he said. 'An' I'll tell you a damn sight more, too. If you like to sit back an' keep quiet for a minute I'll tell you the whole damn thing from start to finish. You know it already, but it might be a good thing for you to know that somebody else knows it, an' that very soon the whole damn country will know it.'

He leaned forward over the desk. He looked straight at Willie. He was smiling, but there was something terribly hard in his eyes. For a moment Willie Meraulton, looking at him, realized the strength of this tousled-haired private detective, this cheap-jack who had been pushed into a murder case to play an unimportant part, who had stolen all the limelight and who was now proceeding to cast himself for the leading role.

'I once read a bit of poetry,' said Callaghan. 'It was called *The Urgent Hangman*. I always remembered a bit of it. It went like this:

'See how she twists and turns in parlous straits.
"Finger your neck, sweet, the urgent hangman waits."

'You remind me of that bit of poetry,' Callaghan went on grimly. 'You thought you were goin' to be the urgent hangman, didn't you? You thought you were goin' to put the noose round somebody's neck – you didn't care whether it was her neck or Bellamy's, so long as it wasn't yours. But you weren't goin' to put an actual rope around their neck. You were just goin' to put a rope of suspicion, one that would be good enough to make people – including the police – think that they *might* have done it – either of 'em – but not be able to prove it. So long as you were kept out of it, everything was goin' to be fine.

'But I've managed to alter that. There's only one urgent hangman in the Meraulton case, an' that's me, an' I'm damned urgent, I'm tellin' you!'

Willie began to laugh softly. He sat there quite coolly and laughed. Callaghan stole another glance at his watch. It was three-twenty. His ears straining to catch the slightest sound heard nothing at all. He cursed quietly to himself, wished that he had a cigarette.

'All right, Willie,' said Callaghan. 'You want to hear, an' so I'll tell you. I'll tell you the true story of the murder of August Meraulton, an' although I may be slightly wrong on one or two little points, that don't matter, because in the main I'm dead right.'

Willie yawned.

'Fearfully interesting, Callaghan,' he said. 'But there's one question I must ask you before you begin this dramatic tale: Can you by any chance *prove* what you think? Can you do that, or are you by any chance doing what the police seem to have been doing – that is merely theorizing and hoping that something would come along that looked like some *real* evidence?'

Callaghan shrugged.

'I can't answer that now,' he said. 'Maybe you'll be able to answer your own question for yourself. In the meantime perhaps you'll admit that this is a good *theory*:

'The Meraulton boys – Jeremy, Paul, Percival and Bellamy – are broke. They can't get any money. Old August hates 'em like the devil and won't give 'em any. But he likes you an' he trusts you. He must have, otherwise he wouldn't have allowed you to run the Meraulton Estates and Trust Company, the business that looked after his property and money.

'You made out that you were the good boy of the family, but you weren't. You were as bad as the rest of 'em, and they knew it. They told you that they had to have some money, an' that if they didn't get it they'd talk to the old boy about you. So you had to do some quick thinkin'.

'You got a good scheme. You got Paul to buy up four old companies and re-float them. Then you began to lend money to these companies. If August ever took a look at the books – which he did occasionally – he would merely find book transactions with these companies, and against the money that had gone out he would find credit entries of stocks, shares and mortgages bought from, or taken up with, these companies.

'You probably did damn well out of this yourself. The money that you got out of the Meraulton Estates and Trust didn't all go to the quartet. I bet you stuck to most of it.

'There was always the chance, of course, that the old boy would go snooping about and find out. But you knew he was a sick man, an' you hoped that he'd die before he did find out, after which you could have straightened things out with the share of money that came to you and the quartet from the estate.

'Then all of a sudden the old boy throws that dinner-party and tells the lot of you that he's made a new will. He tells the other four that unless he decides to alter this new will – which he's carryin' about in his watch-case – they'll all find themselves left out in the cold.

'As a matter of fact he was challenging you as well as them. I've got an idea that the old boy had just begun to get a little bit suspicious of you. Probably you thought so, too.

'Then he did something that proved it. He told Cynthis that he would not allow her to get married to you. This was a few days before his death, and so far as you were concerned it was a danger signal. You realized that something had got to be done and done pretty quickly. You knew that the fact that the old boy had made the new will would constitute a damn good motive for one of the quartet trying to put him out of the way, so you tell that story to Cynthis about her bein' in danger, an' you mention my name an' tell her that she's to come an' see me directly you can get the money to give her – the money that I'll want an' insist on havin' before I'll do a damn thing.

'Then you stick around watching like a cat, watching to see if old August does know anything, or whether it was just your nerves.'

Callaghan pushed his chair back. He was dying to smoke. His

mouth felt dry and his head had begun to ache a little. He realized suddenly that he had been living on his nerves for days, that he felt all in.

Opposite him, in the shadow, sat Willie, a big huddled form. The head and neck pushed down into the overcoat collar, and two abnormally bright eyes staring straight into his own.

'Well, Willie,' he said, 'how does it sound? How am I doing?'

Willie smiled.

'I love your *theories*, Callaghan,' he said. 'Go on. I'm interested.'

Callaghan nodded. His ears, straining, caught an infinitesimal sound from the outer office. He ran his tongue over his dry lips and hoped he was right.

'All right,' said Callaghan. 'Now you've got everything all set, and we come to the day of the murder. You've arranged to go to the theatre with Cynthis, but suddenly the balloon goes up. August Meraulton rings you up at your office and tells you that he's wise to the whole damn bag of tricks. He tells you that you're a lousy swindler, a cheat, a thief, and that he's glad that he's prevented Cynthis from marrying you.

'You probably put up an act. You probably tell him that you've got a first-class explanation for everything, and eventually the old boy orders you to call at his office – his private office – in Lincoln's Inn Fields at eleven o'clock that night.

'Then he hangs up, and you sit back and do a little bit of thinking. The first thing you wonder is whether old August has told Cynthis anything about this. That's the first thing you've got to find out. So you telephone through to her and ask her if she's still keen on going to the theatre. When you were telling me about this you said that *she* telephoned *you*, that she had a headache. That was another damn lie, an' you told it just because I was wise enough to point out to you that I wasn't goin' to discuss this matter with her, but I did, an' she told me what had really happened.

'She said that she couldn't go to the theatre with you because she had an important appointment at eleven o'clock. She didn't say anything else, but that remark told you all you wanted to know. It told you that August had been through to her and told her to come to his office at Lincoln's Inn Fields at eleven o'clock. You guessed that he hadn't told her anything else.

'You knew what he intended to do. He intended to confront you with her in his office and to show her just what a cheap, swindling liar you were, to show her what a good turn he'd done her in refusing to allow her to marry you.

'All right. Well, now you've got to get a move on, haven't you? You know that Cynthis is goin' to Lincoln's Inn Fields at eleven o'clock, so you say that you are very worried about her and that it's absolutely necessary that she gets along and sees this feller Slim Callaghan, even *if she goes after her appointment* at eleven o'clock, that you will telephone through an' make an appointment for eleven-fifteen or eleven-thirty an' that you will send round the five hundred pounds that this Callaghan will want for his services – the five hundred that you've had stuck in your desk drawer for a week or so, waitin' for this to happen.

'You then get in touch with the Meraulton quartet. You tell them that the balloon's gone up, and that they've got to come round to your club and talk things over at a quarter to ten. You take a private room at the club somewhere near the side entrance. Jeremy, Paul, Percival and Bellamy arrive, and you let them know more or less what's happened. You also tell them that you've heard that Cynthis is goin' round to see the old man in Lincoln's Inn Fields, and that you expect that there'll be some sort of trouble. You tell them that you're going off to try and find Cynthis to talk to her before she goes round to see the old boy, to try and get her to straighten things out.

'You go off. It's about ten o'clock. You're banking on the fact that the old boy will have followed his usual habit of going out of his house in Knightsbridge and taking a cab down to his office, that he will have arrived there early.

'You went out of the club by the side door an' drove your car down to somewhere near Lincoln's Inn Fields, leaving it somewhere where it wouldn't be seen. You walked along to the office and went upstairs. You were lucky; the old boy was there, and the time was about half-past ten.

'August told you just where you got off the tram. He waved the gold copy paper will – the one he'd been carrying in his watch-case – in front of you, told you he was going to destroy it, told you why. You had your own reason for not wanting that will destroyed.

'You didn't waste a second. You shot the old man dead. You picked him up, knocking a chair over in the process, carried him downstairs, across the dark street, and pushed him over the short railings on the west side of the gardens. You got over yourself, carried him across the gardens, and after putting the copy paper will back into his watch-case pushed him over the railings on the other side. On your way back across the gardens you threw the pistol into the shrubbery. You weren't worrying about finger-prints; you'd got gloves on.

'You drove back to the club like mad. You got there about twenty to eleven. You say that you haven't been able to find Cynthis, and you get that poor fool Bellamy, who is dying to get away to see Eulalie Gallicot, to promise to drive to Lincoln's Inn Fields to wait until five past eleven to see if she does go to see August, and telephone you if she does. As this is on Bellamy's way, he agrees.

'You wanted him to see Cynthis arrive. This, with her visit to me afterwards, is going to implicate her. She will see Bellamy down there, and that will implicate him. The other three, who will all guess next day who really killed August Meraulton, will alibi you if necessary by saying that you never left the club. They've got to say this. The whole lot of you have been conspiring to defraud August, and the Meraulton Estates Company, and if anything were to happen to you there wouldn't be a brass farthing for anybody. Bellamy going to Lincoln's Inn Fields doesn't matter a damn, because the fact that he's seen in Lincoln's Inn Fields doesn't prove that he's a murderer.

'So the quartet have got to stick by you just as you've got to stick by them.'

Callaghan tilted his chair back and smiled pleasantly at Willie.

'You made one damn silly mistake,' he said. 'You ought never to have put that copy paper will back into his watch-case. When Cynthis came to me an' I heard of the murder afterwards I was curious to see if the will had gone. When I found it hadn't, an' when I'd read it, I wondered what motive any one of the quartet could have had for killing the old boy and *not* taking that will – a will that dispossessed the lot of them an' gave everything to Cynthis.'

Callaghan got up. Willie sat quite still, looking straight at Callaghan, breathing quietly.

'An' then I got it,' said Callaghan softly. 'I got it. Suddenly I saw that the man who murdered August Meraulton did so *not to take the will out of his watch-case, but to put it back there*.

'I saw something else, too. I realized that if Jeremy, Paul, Percival or Bellamy had killed the old boy they would have destroyed that will, an' I realized that the one person who, if he'd killed August, wouldn't have destroyed it, *would have been you*!

'So I got busy. I got some more money from you the next day. You thought I was just bein' graspin'. You poor sap, you didn't realize that the numbers on the £300 notes you gave me followed on the £500 that Cynthis had given me.

'I got another £200 from Bellamy. I checked up on the numbers. They were in the same group. So I knew that Bellamy had got that £200 from you. I went to see Mayola Ferrival before I went down to see Jeremy not because I really wanted to see her but to give Jeremy time to get some more money to pay me *from you*.'

'Very interesting,' said Willie. 'But even if what you say is right it still doesn't prove who murdered August Meraulton.'

Callaghan smiled.

'Right, Willie,' he said. 'Dead right. It only proves that you were givin' these four money out of the Meraulton Estates and

Trust Company banking account. That's just dishonesty – conspiracy to defraud. As you say, it isn't murder.'

Callaghan leaned over the desk.

'All right, Willie,' he said. 'I've been pretty near it, haven't I? But I agree with you that there's nothing I've said would justify a murder charge against you. If they suspect you they've got to suspect Cynthis and Bellamy and anybody else who had a grouse against August.

'But,' continued Callaghan, 'I've got one in the bag. I said I was the urgent hangman. I'm goin' to be the urgent hangman. I'm the man who can prove that you killed August Meraulton, the only man – an' by God I'm goin' to do it or ...'

'Or what?' said Willie very quietly.

'Or you're goin' to pay me £10,000,' said Callaghan with a grin. 'Well, is it worth it?'

CHAPTER FIFTEEN

To Him Who Waits

Willie got up. He took his hands out of his pockets and stood in front of Callaghan's desk, his face above the beam from the desk light.

Callaghan, his chair tilted on to its back legs, could not see Willie's face distinctly. He saw the suggestion of it.

Willie was still quite relaxed. Callaghan could see that his fingers were loosely curled into the palms of his hands. He thought vaguely that Willie was pretty good, that he didn't frighten easily.

Willie stood there for a moment and then sat down again. There was almost complete silence in the office. Callaghan fancied he could hear his wrist-watch ticking and his own heart beating.

'So you're still a blackmailer,' said Willie quietly. 'But I suppose that one should sometimes take notice of blackmailers – they can be dangerous. However,' he went on casually, '£10,000 is a great deal of money – especially to a bluffer like Mr Slim Callaghan!'

Callaghan shrugged his shoulders.

'I don't see where the bluff comes in,' he said. 'I told you that I had a theory – a *good* theory. I've told you what my theory is, an' after that you can do just what you like about it. I don't give a damn either way.'

'I see,' said Willie slowly. 'I see. So you weren't by any chance making an accusation of murder against me? You were merely letting your imagination wander?'

Callaghan grinned.

'I wouldn't say that, either,' he said quite pleasantly. 'Let's put it another way. If I get £10,000, then so far as I'm concerned it's a theory, an' one that I can forget directly I get my hands on the money. If I don't get the £10,000, then perhaps I can see whether it amounts to something more than a theory. Maybe Gringall would like to try his hand at a nice little jigsaw puzzle like that.'

Willie nodded.

'You've already been to Gringall,' he said. 'You've given him the numbers of certain banknotes. Possibly you've given him some other information as well.'

'Not a damn thing,' said Callaghan. 'I've given him the information about the banknotes because I know damn well that if he hadn't got it one way he would have got it another way; but under certain circumstances his knowing about the money wouldn't matter to you.'

'No?' queried Willie, his eyebrows raised. 'But supposing – merely for the sake of argument, of course – that your story about the money being lent to the four fake companies were correct? Well, wouldn't that implicate me in the conspiracy to defraud charge, leaving the matter of the murder of August Meraulton right out of the question for the moment?'

'Not necessarily,' said Callaghan, still grinning. 'August Meraulton's dead. He can't give evidence. He had placed you in sole charge of his affairs. Supposin' you were to tell the court that August had found out what you were doin' and approved of it? Well, they couldn't prove you a liar, could they? All you'd have to do would be to get someone to support your story – somebody like Cynthis.'

Willie's lips broke into a little smile.

'You're really a very clever fellow, Callaghan,' he said. 'I sometimes think that I've underrated you. But let us return for the moment to this matter of £10,000. I said that was a great deal of money, but I suppose the Meraulton Estate could find that amount easily enough. The question is, however, who is going to get the Meraulton Estate?'

'That's an easy one,' Callaghan answered. 'Cynthis Meraulton is goin' to get it. Remember I saw that will an' I can swear to it.

Even if that will has been destroyed by Jeremy I can still prove that the testator desired his estate to go to Cynthis, an' so could his lawyer, that I'll bet on.'

He paused for a moment and looked straight at Willie.

'Unless,' he went on eventually, 'unless August Meraulton made *another*, will, a *later* will, sayin' something different.'

'Very interesting,' said Willie, 'but I want to get back to this matter of theory. I'm inclined to agree with you that your theory about the Meraulton murder is not at all a bad one. I'm even inclined to believe that if it were put to Gringall he might try to make something out of it; but even so I'm afraid that there's a law in this country that you have to *prove* murder. The accused doesn't have to prove that he *didn't do* the murder; the prosecution has got to prove, beyond all shadow of doubt, that he *did* do it. I really don't see, even with the information which you think is at your disposal and which you have used so excellently in your theory, that Gringall could *prove* that I murdered Meraulton.

'Let me put up the other side of the case. As you have so rightly said, Jeremy, Percival and Paul can all prove that I was with them at my club during the operative times connected with the murder. On the other hand, I doubt if Cynthis could prove just what she was doing at that time. In point of fact, her maid, who was in the kitchen at Cynthis' flat from ten to eleven o'clock, says that she did not hear Cynthis go out, that she might have gone out at any time between a quarter to ten and eleven o'clock.

'It's true that Bellamy saw Cynthis in Lincoln's Inn Fields at eleven o'clock and that the murder had been committed at that time, but that still doesn't clear Cynthis. She might even prove that she did not go to her garage for her car until quite near that time, but that again proves nothing, because she had ample time to have gone to Lincoln's Inn Fields, kill August and then go back to the garage for her car.

'And I'm afraid that there's another point. You will remember that I went to Cynthis' flat and carefully removed a box of bullets which I found there. You remember that one had fallen out of the box and you found it when you called there. I'm afraid that that fact is a very good piece of circumstantial evidence against Cynthis, and I have no doubt that her maid, if put on oath, would tell the truth about it.'

'She wouldn't tell the truth, because she doesn't know the truth,' said Callaghan, still grinning. 'I know the truth. You took that box of bullets to Cynthis' flat. You had it in your pocket. While you were pretending to search through the chest of drawers you deliberately dropped one bullet out of the box, hoping that Gringall would find it. You then showed the box to the maid and pretended to have just found it and to be taking it away, in order to remove yet another suspicious bit of circumstantial evidence against Cynthis. You remember that I rang you up an' told you it was nice work. It *was* nice work, but I didn't mean it in the way you thought I did. I meant it was nice work because that bit of business definitely proved to me that you were the murderer!'

'Possibly,' said Willie. 'Possibly it proved it to you, but the maid won't give evidence on those lines. She thought I'd found the bullets in the drawer, and will say so. I'm afraid in the eyes of the law the point will be rather for me than against me, don't you think?'

Callaghan nodded.

'I do think so, Willie,' he said. 'I'm afraid that I've got to agree with you.'

'You see,' said Willie, 'there doesn't seem to be any *proof*, does there, and £10,000, as I have said, is quite a lot of money. In a minute I shall expect you to reduce the sum to, say, half that amount!'

'All right,' said Callaghan. 'I'll give you another little pointer. When I saw you the day after the murder I asked you who would be the feller most likely to have killed August. You said Bellamy. I then let you know that I was goin' to pull an act on Bellamy with that hat. I asked you questions about August's hats, and you knew damn well what I was goin' to do. I then carefully told you that I was goin' to see Bellamy that afternoon. I went there in a cab an' nobody else knew I was goin' there an' nobody else saw me. But Gringall was able to send a car to pick me up just at the right time an' at the right place. Why? Because somebody had telephoned through to the Yard an' given an anonymous message that Slim Callaghan was goin' to see Bellamy.

'So Gringall jumps to a conclusion. He jumps to the conclusion that Bellamy has had something to do with this murder or that there is some connection between Bellamy and me. He picks me up an' starts askin' me a lot of questions and puttin' me in a position where I've got to say what you wanted me to say. As a result of this Gringall pulls in Bellamy on the drugs charge to make him talk, an' Bellamy talks an' says just what you wanted *him* to say – that he saw Cynthis in Lincoln's Inn Fields at eleven o'clock.

'That fact, combined with the fact that she came on to my office in order – as Gringall would think – to arrange a fake alibi, would make things look pretty bad for her, wouldn't it?'

Willie nodded pleasantly.

'Very good reasoning,' he said. 'But however can you prove that I put that telephone call through? Anybody might have done it. Effie Perkins had already telephoned the Yard about one little matter. Some one else might have known about your proposed visit to Bellamy. I'm afraid that won't wash, Callaghan.'

Willie produced a cigarette-case and took a cigarette. He held the case out to Callaghan, who shook his head. Willie lit his cigarette and drew in a deep breath. He looked almost cheerful.

'No, Callaghan,' he said. 'I'm afraid that your theories are merely theories. There's not one iota of *proof* in anything you say. And I'm certainly not going to even consider a sum of £10,000 for something which might be worth at the most £500 – if that!'

'No?' said Callaghan.

His voice changed. He leaned across the desk. His eyes were glittering, hard, his finger, pointed accusingly at Willie, stuck out into the beam of the desk light like a bayonet.

'Listen, you damn cheap murderer,' he said. 'You're goin' to pay me that £10,000, and you're goin' to like payin' it. I'm goin' to tell you just why you're goin' to pay it to make me keep my mouth shut.

'You've talked, an' you've liked talkin'. In fact you've talked a damn sight too much. There's only one little thing that you've forgotten, an' you've forgotten it because you didn't want to think about it. You've forgotten it because when I talked to you on the telephone earlier tonight you hoped that I was bluffin'. You hoped that I'd put my finger on something by accident, something that I couldn't prove but that I could use as a bluff in order to get some money out of you.'

Willie leaned forward. His face was suddenly drawn, his expression changed. His eyes on Callaghan glittered like a snake's eyes.

'I told you tonight,' Callaghan went on in an intense and relentless monotone, 'that the fact that whoever it was killed August Meraulton murdered him in order to put that gold copy paper will back into his watch-case, proved to me that it was you.'

Callaghan began to grin again, but his grin was mirthless. He tilted his chair back once more and sat looking at Willie easily, but his fingers, tensed and strained, were gripping the edges of his chair.

'You want some proof,' he went on. 'All right, you want proof, an' I'm goin' to give it to you. I'm goin' to smash all the cheap theories that you an' I have put up tonight into smithereens. I'm goin' to make you think that payin' me £10,000 to keep my mouth shut about what I know is cheap.'

Callaghan paused. He ran his tongue over his dry lips. Inside he was praying that now, at the crucial moment, he would not slip up, that he would present the lie – the guess – that he was going to put up in the right way.

'There would only be one reason for you to put that will back in the watch-case,' he said, 'an' that reason would be that you wanted Cynthis to get that money. You wanted Cynthis to get that money because you knew you could marry her any time you liked now that August was dead. Even if she were suspected, convicted, hanged, you would still get the money. You put the will back because you had to marry Cynthis, an' because of the will that August Meraulton made on the afternoon or the evening that you killed him, the will that cancelled any will – including the gold copy paper will – that he had made before.

'When you went round to see August Meraulton at his office, when you went in and faced that poor old man across his desk, he waved that gold copy paper will at you. He told you that he'd made another will. He showed it to you, showed you that he'd written in that will the reason for making it, that he'd told the complete story of your crookedness and the crookedness of the other Meraultons. He said in that will that Cynthis was to have everything, *provided she did not marry you*, and he had the will there in front of him so that he could show it to her when she came round at eleven o'clock, so that he could show her what a cheap double-crossing crook you were.

'You killed him, you took that will and destroyed it, an' you put the gold copy paper will that left everything to Cynthis *without any restriction* back into his watch-case, but like every other damn murderer you were careless, you made the one mistake that is goin' to send you to the gallows. Would you like me to tell you what it was?'

Willie did not answer. He sat staring at Callaghan.

'Unfortunately for you, you hadn't any time to look round the office after you'd shot the old boy,' said Callaghan. 'If you had, if you'd only had the sense to look in the place where he'd put it, you would have seen that August Meraulton had made a duplicate copy of his last will and signed it.

'After I went to the mortuary,' lied Callaghan glibly, 'I went back to the Lincoln's Inn office. The police hadn't arrived. I got in an' searched the place.

'And,' he said triumphantly, 'I've got the duplicate copy of that will. I've got it here, in this office!'

He slumped his chair forward and stood up, then leaned back against the wall in his favourite position.

He pointed with one long forefinger to his desk drawer.

'In that drawer,' he said, 'is August Meraulton's duplicate will – the will that tells the whole story of your trickery; the will that tells that you were comin' round to his office to be confronted with Cynthis. The will that proves that you murdered August Meraulton.

'Well, do I get the £10,000?'

Willie rose slowly to his feet. His lips were twisted into a grin.

'No, you don't,' he said in a peculiar voice. 'You know too much, Callaghan, but that doesn't matter. I'm going to have that will, and I'm going to get it for nothing. I killed August Meraulton, but there's only one person can prove it, and that person is you. I'm not going to take the chance of being blackmailed for life by you, Callaghan. There's only one way out of this.'

Willie put his hand in his pocket.

Callaghan grinned.

'All right, Willie,' he said. 'You've done what I wanted you to. You've confessed. It might interest you to know that there's a dictaphone fixed in this office. The wires run to the outer office. Gringall's been listenin' in ... An' how do you like that? In the meantime maybe you'd like to have a look at August's will?'

Willie brought his hand out of his pocket. At the same moment there was a noise from the outer office. Willie spun round, then turned again to Callaghan, who had opened the desk drawer, had the envelope in his hand.

'You win, Callaghan,' he said. 'I hope it does you a lot of good.'

Callaghan saw the automatic in Willie's hand. He braced himself, tore open the envelope. For one fleeting second his mind went back to the first night of the Meraulton case – the night when Cynthis had sat in the chair in front of his desk.

As Gringall flung the door open Willie fired. Callaghan swayed for a moment, then slumped across the desk, a thin stream of blood running from one side of his mouth.

Gringall's fist crashed into Willie's face, sent him sprawling to the floor. Gringall kicked the pistol into the corner, snapped a pair of handcuffs on to Willie.

'Telephone for an ambulance, Fields,' he snapped.

Callaghan lay across the desk. His fingers were fumbling with the envelope. As Gringall came towards him he managed to pull out the two sheets of newspaper.

Willie, pallid-faced, saw them as Callaghan, slithering towards the floor, managed a final grin.

Callaghan opened his eyes and allowed them to wander round the room. A touch of winter sunshine came through the window. Somewhere in the neighbourhood he could hear a street organ playing.

The charge-sister came in.

'There are two letters for you, Mr Callaghan,' she said. 'But you're to read them quietly. Another thing, I hear you've been asking for cigarettes. The surgeon said that you weren't to smoke for at least two months. You've got a smoker's throat anyhow, besides which you're a lung case. Lung cases don't smoke in this hospital, in any event.'

'Too bad,' said Callaghan.

He lay back against the supporting frame behind him and fumbled with the letters, concentrating on the difficult task of opening them. The charge-sister, with a cheerful smile, disappeared.

Callaghan opened the first letter. It was from New Scotland Yard. It was addressed to: *Slim Callaghan Esq., Callaghan Investigations, Samaritan Hospital, W.C.*, and said:

Dear Sir,

I am instructed by the Commissioner of Police for the Metropolis to convey to you his thanks for your co-operation and assistance in the Meraulton Murder Case.

The Commissioner realizes that from the first your intentions were to assist the authorities by every means in your power, and that any irregularity of procedure on your part is more than excused by results.

The Commissioner instructs me to say that he hopes most sincerely that you are now well on the way to recovery from your wound.

I am, faithfully yours
W. J. R. Gringall,
Detective-Inspector

There was another note enclosed. It was from Gringall:

Dear Slim,

I enclose a formal letter of thanks from the Commissioner. I'm glad to hear that you are out of danger, and one day I'll look in and have a talk with you. Perhaps I can still learn something!

Good luck,
Jigger

Callaghan grinned. Life was funny, he thought. When police officers began to write letters of thanks to Callaghan Investigations – well, anything might happen.

He opened the other letter. This read:

Dear Sir,

As Joint Executor with Miss Cynthis Meraulton of the Estate of the late August Meraulton, I am at the moment engaged in probating a Will which was stolen by William Meraulton, made on the day of his death by the late Testator. A duplicate copy of this Will has been found in the Lincoln's Inn office. I am also generally investigating into the current position of the Meraulton Estates and Trust Company, Ltd., and allied organizations.

Having regard to defalcations on the part of William Meraulton (who was, as you may have heard, yesterday found guilty of the murder of August Meraulton and the attempted murder of yourself and sentenced to death), and other irregularities in the conduct of the Company, it is considered necessary by both Miss Meraulton and myself that there should be a full and complete investigation into the position which will entail examination of Jeremy, Paul and Bellamy Meraulton, and such other persons as may be involved. These gentlemen, now in prison, have consented to give full information, but it will be necessary to investigate the operations of the four companies formed by Paul Meraulton over a period.

Therefore, on the recommendation of Detective-Inspector Gringall, I would like to appoint Messrs. Callaghan Investigations, when you are fully recovered, to take over this business, and hope in the course of a few weeks to make a personal contact with you hereon.

I am, faithfully yours,
H. A. F. Gazeling,
Joint Executor

Callaghan dropped the letter on to the bed. His eyes, looking up, encountered those of Cynthis Meraulton.

She stood at the foot of the bed looking at him. She was dressed in black, and the splash of colour formed by the flowers she carried caught the sunlight.

Callaghan grinned.

'This looks like bein' a rather nice day,' he said. 'Won't you sit down? Callaghan Investigations always gives its clients a chair, even if it doesn't give 'em anything else.'

She moved to the side of the bed, put the flowers on a table.

'You don't improve, Mr Callaghan,' she said. 'Even a bullet through the chest doesn't seem to affect your sense of humour.'

She sat down. Callaghan hoped that she would cross her legs, so that he could get a better view of her feet. He'd remembered them whilst he had been going under the anaesthetic.

'It isn't much good my saying anything, is it?' she asked. 'I can only say that I didn't know what you were doing at any time, that I didn't know what was in your mind, that I couldn't possibly know that you were really a rather splendid person playing at being beastly.'

Callaghan raised his eyebrows.

'I think you've got me wrong,' he said. 'I just played the Merauton case the way it came. It was just one of those things . . .'

She nodded.

'It was just one of those things, was it?' she said with a smile. 'Mr Gringall tells me that you *knew* Willie would try to kill you. He tells me that you told him that in the letter you wrote to him at the Yard, but that even he didn't believe it could be true. Well, it was true. Why were you prepared to take that chance? There wasn't any money in that, was there?'

Callaghan grinned.

'Every man has a weakness,' he said. 'My weakness is nice ankles. It must have been your ankles.'

She looked out of the window.

'Mr Gazeling said he was going to ask you to do the Estate investigation,' she said. 'Are you going to do it? Or are you going to be stupid and proud and go back to smoking too many cigarettes and climbing up four flights of stairs to that very dusty office every day?'

'Not on your life,' said Callaghan. 'I'm goin' to do the investigation. When that's done I'm goin' to get out of here. I've been reading the steamship companies' folders. I feel some strange country or other callin' me!'

She got up.

'I've got to go now,' she said. 'They told me I was only to stay for a minute or two. I'm sorry you feel like that about going away.'

She leaned over the bed and kissed him on the mouth.

Callaghan looked adequately shocked.

'If I'd known about that I wouldn't have charged a sou,' he said. 'Not even expenses!'

'*Au revoir*, Slim,' said Cynthis. 'I know all about *you* and all about *it*. And you won't go abroad.'

Callaghan raised his eyebrows.

'No?' he queried. 'An' how do you know that?'

She walked towards the door.

'You said you liked my ankles,' she said. 'And you once told me that Callaghan Investigations never lets its clients down!'

The door closed behind her.

Callaghan, looking out of the window, saw the sunshine break through a winter cloud.